Everyman, I will go with thee,
and be thy guide

Thomas Hardy

SELECTED SHORT STORIES AND POEMS

Edited by
JAMES GIBSON

EVERYMAN
J. M. DENT · LONDON
CHARLES E. TUTTLE
VERMONT

Selection and introduction © James Gibson 1992
First published in Everyman's Library 1992
Reissued 1993

Photoset by Deltatype Ltd, Ellesmere Port, Cheshire
Printed in Great Britain by
The Guernsey Press Company Ltd, Guernsey, C.I.
for J. M. Dent
Orion Publishing Group
Orion House
5 Upper St Martin's Lane, London WC2H 9EA
and
Charles E. Tuttle Co. Inc.
28 South Main Street
Rutland, Vermont 05701, USA

British Library Cataloguing-in-Publication Data for this title is
available upon request.

ISBN 0 460 87386 5

CONTENTS

Note on the Editor   ix
Chronology of Hardy's Life and Times   x
Introduction   xxi
Suggestions for Further Reading   xxxix

THE SHORT STORIES

The Three Strangers   3
The Withered Arm   26
The Melancholy Hussar of the German Legion   56
Dame the Third: Marchioness of Stonehenge   75
A Few Crusted Characters *from* Life's Little Ironies   90
Andrey Satchel and the Parson and Clerk   94
Old Andrey's Experience as a Musician   103
Absent-Mindedness in a Parish Choir   105
Netty Sargent's Copyhold   108
An Imaginative Woman   116

THE POEMS

Home and Family
Domicilium   143
A Church Romance   144
Afternoon Service at Mellstock   144
One We Knew   145
The Self-Unseeing   146
On One Who Lived and Died Where He Was Born   147

Love
When I Set Out for Lyonnesse   149
The Going   149

The Haunter   151
The Voice   152
After a Journey   152
Beeny Cliff   154
At Castle Boterel   155
During Wind and Rain   156
To Meet, or Otherwise   157
A Broken Appointment   158
Neutral Tones   158
Beyond the Last Lamp   159
To Lizbie Browne   160
The Ruined Maid   162
One Ralph Blossom Soliloquizes   163

Faith and Doubt
The Impercipient   164
The Darkling Thrush   165
The Oxen   166
In the Servants' Quarters   167

Lyrics and Meditations
Great Things   169
Going and Staying   170
Shut Out That Moon   170
The Pine Planters   171
On the Esplanade   173
After a Romantic Day   174
The Five Students   175
Heredity   176
The Superseded   176
I Look Into My Glass   177
Afterwards   177

Nature: Flowers, Birds and Animals
Weathers   179
The Yellow-Hammer   179
Before and After Summer   180
Last Week in October   181
The Blinded Bird   181

Birds at Winter Nightfall   182
The Selfsame Song   182
The Robin   183
The Last Chrysanthemum   183
To Flowers from Italy in Winter   184
A Sheep Fair   185
Last Words to a Dumb Friend   186
Shortening Days at the Homestead   187
Snow in the Suburbs   188

War
The Eve of Waterloo (from *The Dynasts*)   189
Drummer Hodge   190
The Man He Killed   191
Channel Firing   192
A Jingle on the Times   193

Narrative
The Bride-Night Fire   196
A Trampwoman's Tragedy   200
The Sacrilege   204

Occasional
The Last Signal   209
The Convergence of the Twain   210
To Shakespeare   211
At Lulworth Cove a Century Back   212

NOTE ON THE EDITOR

Dr James Gibson was educated at King's College School, Wimbledon, and Queens' College, Cambridge, and worked for a PhD at Birkbeck College. His appointments have included Head of English at Dulwich College and Principal Lecturer at Christ Church College, Canterbury. He has edited many of the works of Thomas Hardy including *The Complete Poems* and the Variorum Edition of that work. He was founder and first Editor of *The Thomas Hardy Journal* and is an Honorary Vice President of the Thomas Hardy Society.

CHRONOLOGY OF HARDY'S LIFE

Year	Age	Life
1840		Hardy born 2 June at Higher Bockhampton in the cottage built by his grandfather.
1841		His sister, Mary, born
1842		
1846		
1847		
1848	8	Attended village school
1849–56		Attended school in Dorchester
1850		
1851		
1853		
1853–6		
1855		
1856	16	Articled to John Hicks, a Dorchester architect
1858	18	About now wrote his first surviving poem, 'Domicilium'
1859		
1860		
1861		

CHRONOLOGY OF HIS TIMES

Year	Literary Context	Historical Events
1840		Great Irish famine. Penny post introduced
1841		
1842		Chartist riots
1846		Repeal of Corn Laws
1847	C. Brontë, *Jane Eyre*	Railway reached Dorchester
1848	Dickens, *Dombey & Son* Thackeray, *Vanity Fair* Pre-Raphaelite Brotherhood active	
1849	Ruskin, *Seven Lamps of Architecture*	
1850	Wordsworth died: Tennyson became Poet Laureate.	
1851		The Great Exhibition
1853	Arnold, *Poems*	
1853–6		The Crimean War
1855	Browning, *Men and Women* Mrs Gaskell, *North and South*	
1856		
1858	George Eliot, *Scenes of Clerical Life*;	
1859	Darwin, *Origin of Species*;	
1860	Wilkie Collins, *Woman in White*	
1861	Palgrave's anthology, *The Golden Treasury* *Hymns Ancient and Modern*	American Civil War

Year	Age	Life
1862–7	22	Lived in London, working as an architect; wrote poetry but failed to get it published.
1860s		Throughout this decade Hardy steadily lost his religious faith
1864		
1865	25	A short fictional piece called 'How I Built Myself a House' published
1866		
1867	27	Returned to Dorset, began his first novel, *The Poor Man and the Lady*
1868	28	Romantic affair with his cousin, Tryphena Sparks. *The Poor Man and The Lady* rejected by publishers
1869	29	Worked in Weymouth for an architect
1870	30	Met and fell in love with Emma Lavinia Gifford while at St Juliot in Cornwall planning the restoration of the church
1871	31	*Desperate Remedies*, published anonymously was a commercial failure
1872	32	Has minor success with *Under the Greenwood Tree*
1873	33	*A Pair of Blue Eyes*, Hardy's first novel to appear as a serial. Becomes a full-time novelist
1874	34	*Far from the Madding Crowd*, his first real success. Marries Emma Gifford. For next nine years they moved from one lodging to another
1876		
1878	38	*The Return of the Native*. Became member of London's Savile Club
1879	39	His short story 'The Distracted Preacher' published
1880	40	*The Trumpet-Major*. Is taken ill for several months
1881	41	*A Laodicean*

Year	Literary Context	Historical Events
1862–7		
1863	Thackeray died Mill, *Utilitarianism*	
1864	Newman, *Apologia pro Vita Sua*	
1865	Mrs Gaskell died	
1866	Swinburne, *Poems and Ballads*	
1867	Ibsen, *Peer Gynt*	Second Reform Bill
1868		Gladstone became Prime Minister
1869	Mill, *Subjection of Women*	
1870	Dickens died	Franco-Prussian War Education Act brought education for all
1871	*The Descent of Man*	Trade Unions legalised
1872		
1873		
1874		The modern bicycle arrived Disraeli became Prime Minister
1876	Henry James's novels began to be published	
1878		Edison invented the incandescent electric lamp
1879	James Murray became editor of what was later to become *The Oxford English Dictionary* Ibsen, *A Doll's House*	
1880	George Eliot died Zola, *Nana*	
1881	Revised Version of New Testament	Married Woman's Property Act

Year	Age	Life
1882	42	*Two on a Tower*. Visits Paris
1885	45	Moved into Max Gate, house on outskirts of Dorchester. Lived there for the rest of his life.
1886	46	*The Mayor of Casterbridge*
1887	47	*The Woodlanders*. Visits France and Italy
1888	48	*Wessex Tales*, his first collection of short stories, and an essay on 'The Profitable Reading of Fiction'
1889		
1890	50	An essay, 'Candour in English Fiction'
1891	51	*Tess of the d'Urbervilles* *A Group of Noble Dames* (short stories)
1892	52	Hardy's father died
1893	53	On visit to Ireland met Florence Henniker, for whom he developed a great affection
1894	54	*Life's Little Ironies* (short stories)
1895	55	*Jude the Obscure*
1895–6		First collected edition of novels, entitled 'Wessex Novels'
1896	56	Ceased novel-writing and returned to poetry
1897	57	*The Well-Beloved*, much revised after publication as a serial in 1892
1898	58	*Wessex Poems* (51 poems): Hardy's first book of verse, including Hardy's own illustrations
1899		
1900		

Year	Literary Context	Historical Events
1882	Darwin, D. G. Rossetti and Trollope died	Daimler's petrol engine
1885	D. H. Lawrence born	Salisbury became Prime Minister
1886	William Barnes, friend of Hardy, poet, philologist, polymath, died	
1887	Strindberg, *The Father*	
1888	Matthew Arnold died; T. S. Eliot born About now the work of Kipling and Yeats began to be published.	
1889	Browning, G. M. Hopkins, and Wilkie Collins died	
1890	Newman died	First underground railway in London
1891	Shaw, *Quintessence of Ibsenism*	
1892	Tennyson died	Gladstone Prime Minister
1893	Pinero, *The Second Mrs Tanqueray*	Independent Labour Party set up
1894	R. L. Stevenson and Pater died	Rosebery became Prime Minister
1895	Conrad's first novel, *Almayer's Folly* published Wilde, *The Importance of Being Earnest*	Salisbury became Prime Minister; Freud's first work on psycho-analysis Marconi's 'wireless' telegraphy
1895–6		
1896	Housman, *A Shropshire Lad*	
1897		
1898	Wells, *War of the Worlds*	The Curies discovered radium
1899		The Boer War began
1900	Ruskin and Wilde died	

Year	Age	Life
1901	61	*Poems of the Past and the Present* (99 poems)
1902	62	Macmillan became his main publishers
1903		
1904	64	*The Dynasts*, Part I
		His mother, Jemima, died
1905	65	Received honorary doctorate from Aberdeen University, the first of several
1906	66	*The Dynasts*, Part II
		About now meets Florence Dugdale
1907		
1908	68	*The Dynasts*. Part III
		Edited a selection of Barnes's verse
1909	69	*Time's Laughingstocks* (94 poems)
1910	70	Awarded the Order of Merit
1911	71	Ceased spending 'the season' in London
1912	72	His wife, Emma, died
		The definitive Wessex Edition of his works published by Macmillan.
1913	73	*A Changed Man and Other Tales*
		Revisited Cornwall and the scenes of his courtship of Emma
1914	74	*Satires of Circumstance* (107 poems)
		Married Florence Dugdale
1915	75	His sister, Mary, died
1916	76	*Selected Poems of Thomas Hardy* edited by Hardy himself

Year	Literary Context	Historical Events
1901		Queen Victoria died; succeeded by Edward VII
1902	Zola died; Hardy lamented his death	Balfour became Prime Minister
1903	Wright brothers made first flight in aeroplane with engine	
1904	Chekov, *The Cherry Orchard*	
1905		
1906		Liberals win election
1907	Kipling awarded Nobel Prize	
1908		Asquith became Prime Minister
1909	Swinburne and Meredith died	
1910		Edward VII died; succeeded by George V
1911	Bennett, *Clayhanger* Rupert Brooke, Poems	
1912		Sinking of *Titanic*
1913	D. H. Lawrence, *Sons and Lovers*	First Morris Oxford car
1914	Ezra Pound edited the first anthology of imagist poetry Robert Frost, *North of Boston*	The first World War began
1915	V. Woolf, *The Voyage Out*	
1916	Henry James died D. H. Lawrence's *The Rainbow* seized by police	Lloyd George became Prime Minister The Russian Revolution

Year	Age	Life
1917	77	*Moments of Vision* (159 poems) Began to write his autobiography with intention that Florence should publish it under her own name after his death
1918		
1919–20	79	A de-luxe edition of his work, the Mellstock Edition, published
1920 onwards	80	Max Gate became a place of pilgrimage for hundreds of admirers
1922	82	*Late Lyrics and Earlier* (151 poems)
1923	82	*The Queen of Cornwall* (a poetic play)
1924	84	Hardy's adaptation of *Tess* performed in Dorchester.
1925		*Human Shows* (152 poems)
1926		
1927		
1928	87	Hardy died on 11 January; part buried in Westminster Abbey, part at the family church at Stinsford *Winter Words* (105 poems) published posthumously *The Early Life of Thomas Hardy*, his disguised autobiography, published
1930		*The Later Years of Thomas Hardy*, the second volume of the autobiography published *Collected Poems* (918 poems) followed by *Complete Poems* (947 poems) in 1976
1937		Death of Hardy's second wife, Florence

Year	Literary Context	Historical Events
1917		
1918	Siegfried Sassoon, *Counter-Attack* G. M. Hopkins, *Poems*	The war ended Women over 30 given the vote
1919		Treaty of Versailles First Woman MP
1920	Edward Thomas, *Collected Poems* Wilfred Owen, *Poems*	First meeting of League of Nations
1922	T. S. Eliot, *The Waste Land* James Joyce, *Ulysses*	Mussolini came to power Women given equality in divorce proceedings
1923		
1924	E. M. Forster, *A Passage to India*	Ramsay MacDonald forms first Labour Government. Stalin becomes Soviet Dictator
1925		
1926	T. E. Lawrence, *Seven Pillars of Wisdom*	The General Strike
1927		Lindbergh makes first crossing by air of the Atlantic
1928	D. H. Lawrence's *Lady Chatterley's Lover* privately printed in Florence	
1930		
1937		

INTRODUCTION

Hardy's Life

Hardy was fascinated by the relationship of time and place, and part of his greatness as a writer results from his strong sense of the transience of time and the permanence of place. When he was born in the village of Bockhampton on 2 June 1840 there were many alive who could well remember the Napoleonic Wars. When he died on 11 January 1928 those early Victorian years of his youth must have seemed several lifetimes away. Bockhampton in 1840 was a remote hamlet, three miles out of the small country town of Dorchester. Hardy's father had an old-established building business, but the great love of his life was music, and his son grew up in a rural setting to the accompaniment of music both in the parish church of Stinsford and at local festivities. These early years of his life, the Wessex people and the Wessex countryside, were to be immortalized in the finest of his novels and in some of his greatest poems.

It is wrong to regard Hardy as an uneducated countryman and a clumsy literary craftsman. He went to the village school, and at nine moved on to a day-school in Dorchester. Here he stayed until he was sixteen, when he was apprenticed to a local architect. He himself describes how, for the next six years, he lived:

> a triple existence unusual for a young man . . . a life twisted of three strands – the professional life, the scholar's life, and the rustic life, combined in the twenty-four hours of one day . . . . He would be reading the *Iliad*, the *Aeneid*, or the Greek Testament from six to eight in the morning, would work at Gothic architecture all day, and then in the evening rush off with his fiddle . . . to play country dances.

He read widely and deeply at a time when Christian beliefs

were under severe attack from the new scientific and philosophic knowledge, and he became painfully aware of the dynamic new forces which were to destroy the Wessex of that time. He lost his own belief in the simple Faith of his people, became an unwilling agnostic, and was deeply disturbed by his consciousness of the tensions that existed between the old way of life and the new.

In 1862 he left Dorchester for London and spent five important years there, not only practising as an architect but furthering his education by partaking of the cultural activities of the capital. He saw Shakespeare being acted, visited the opera, heard Dickens reading, and studied art at the National Gallery. But the pull of Wessex was strong and, tiring of London, he returned in 1867 to his former employer in Dorchester. It was now that he began to think seriously of being a writer. In London he had written poetry but had failed to get it published. In 1868 he sent his first novel to Macmillan's, who rejected it while recognizing that it showed promise. Hardy tried again and his next novel, *Desperate Remedies*, was published by Tinsley's in 1871. It had a mixed reception and he tried yet again. *Under the Greenwood Tree* was published in 1872 and did rather better. *A Pair of Blue Eyes* followed in 1873, but it was not until 1874 that he achieved a solid success with *Far from the Madding Crowd* and was able to regard himself as a writer rather than an architect. In the next twenty-two years he was to write a further ten novels, including *The Return of the Native* (1878), *The Mayor of Casterbridge* (1886) and *The Woodlanders* (1887), and more than fifty short stories, and to establish himself as one of England's great masters of fiction. The best of his novels are deeply rooted in his native Wessex and in his own life, for he was an intensely personal writer. Memories of his youth, his love for the old rural way of life, his interest in architecture and music, his knowledge of Shakespeare and of the great writers of the world, his religious and philosophical doubts – all these appear again and again in his stories. And there was another major influence.

Hardy was a passionate and emotional person with a deep need for a happy relationship with a woman. But this was not to be. In the late 1860s he had an unhappy affair with his cousin, Tryphena Sparks. Not long after this he met the most

powerful influence in his life, Emma Gifford, at St Juliot in
Cornwall, on a day he was never to forget – 7 March 1870. He
had journeyed to Cornwall to restore St Juliot church, and his
meeting with Emma, the rector's sister-in-law, was the
beginning of an idyllic courtship which led to their marriage in
1874. It should have been a marriage of great happiness, but it
turned out to be as much of a failure as his career was a
success. It was childless, and it became loveless, but it did
provide the material and emotional pressure which resulted in
some of his finest stories. His constant preoccupation with the
marriage relationship came straight out of his own experience.

Tess of the d'Urbervilles (1891) and *Jude the Obscure*
(1895) are his last great novels. Both were well received, but
there was some strident criticism by the more puritanical
reviewers, who accused Hardy of corrupting morals by
attacking the institution of marriage. Hardy, always a very
sensitive man, was distressed by the fury of some of the attacks
on him and announced that he would never write another
novel. He would return to his first love, poetry, and so, in
1898, when almost sixty, he published *Wessex Poems*, his first
book of verse. In the next thirty years he was to publish a
further seven books of verse, the last, *Winter Words*, appearing
shortly after his death in 1928. Altogether he published over
nine hundred poems in those thirty years, a remarkable
achievement for someone of his age.

In 1912 Emma died and her death provided him with yet
another source of inspiration. Shortly before her death she had
written an account of her childhood and of her romantic
meeting with Hardy in Cornwall. She called these remi-
niscences *Some Recollections*. Immediately after her death
Hardy found the exercise-book containing these memories and
it helped to increase his sense of loss and his realization of the
tragedy of his married life and of its lost opportunities. He
poured out his feeling of remorse and his still vivid memories of
the happy early days in Cornwall in the 'Vestigia' poems which
are to be found in *Satires of Circumstance* (1914); six are here
printed. These have been judged to be the peak of his poetic
achievement. Although he married Florence Dugdale in 1914
and she looked after him devotedly for the rest of his life, he
never forgot Emma, and poems about her appeared in volume
after volume of the verse which with such remarkable energy

he continued to produce in his seventies and eighties.

During these years he lived at his house, Max Gate, on the outskirts of Dorchester, the Grand Old Man of English Literature, visited by other great writers, respected by the famous, and yet still very much that young boy who had grown up in the Bockhampton cottage so many lifetimes ago, still sensitively aware of the sadnesses and injustices of the world, the greatness of man's spirit, and of the ironies of man's existence. Ironically enough, even his wish that he should be buried in Stinsford churchyard, the heart of his Wessex and the burial place of his family, was partly ignored. A proud nation demanded that this humble man should be buried with the great in Westminster Abbey, and a typical English compromise was agreed over his dead body. His heart was buried at Stinsford – the rest of him was cremated and the ashes buried in the Abbey, shrine of a religion in which he could not believe. 'What a subject for a poem!' his spirit must have thought!

The Short Stories

Hardy's fame rests primarily on his great Wessex novels, from *Far from the Madding Crowd* in 1874 to *Jude the Obscure* in 1895, and secondarily on his great outpouring of poetry published between 1898 and his death in 1928. That he is also a short-story writer of a very remarkable kind is not nearly as well known. Yet between 1874 and his farewell to prose fiction in the late 1890s, he wrote and published more than fifty short stories, and among them are at least a dozen which deserve to rank among the very best in our language.

The short story did not become a significant literary genre until the last thirty years of the nineteenth century, and its emergence coincided almost exactly with Hardy's development as a significant novelist. Writers and publishers are necessarily controlled to some extent by the need to make a living, and that living will depend upon supply and demand. The nineteenth century witnessed scientific and educational revolutions: the first of these resulted in the invention of hot-metal composing machines and the ability to produce paper much more cheaply than had previously been possible. The second, marked most importantly by the Forster Education Act of 1870 which introduced schooling for all, meant a rapid increase in literacy and a huge demand from a rapidly growing population for reading matter of every kind. The figures are impressive. In the 1830s about 42 per cent of the population was illiterate, but by 1893 this had been reduced to about 6 per cent, whereas the population had more than doubled in these sixty years. To meet an insatiable demand, publishers rushed to bring out novels and journals. In 1859 115 new periodicals were launched in London alone, and such was the interest that in 1860 the *Cornhill* sold 120,000 copies of its first number. Cashing in on the success of Dickens's publishers in selling his novels in parts, and his own success in publishing some of his later novels as serials in his *Household Words* and *All the Year Round*, later publishers rushed to commission serials for their journals. These were the television soap operas of that time, with readers anxiously awaiting each new instalment of the story and writers glad to earn the very large sums of money which were available to the successful serial writer. Twelve of Hardy's fourteen published novels appeared as serials and they provided a substantial part of his income.

Before long the journal editors saw the attraction to their readers of the short story. The more serious journals tended to prefer the serialized novel, but the hundreds of lighter, general-interest magazines which first appeared in the 1880s and 1890s were great consumers of short stories, and Hardy did not hesitate to take advantage of the requests for them which reached him from editors at home and abroad. Looking back now we can see that he regarded the short story as an important literary form and that it played a significant part in his career. His very first publication of any length, entitled 'How I Built Myself a House', was of the nature of a short story and appeared in *Chamber's Journal* in 1865. He was to continue writing short stories for almost another thirty-five years with the period of greatest activity being the 1880s. By the mid-eighties he had written enough to be able to consider collecting some of them into a book, and in 1888 he published *Wessex Tales*, in 1891 *A Group of Noble Dames* and in 1894 *Life's Little Ironies*. Nearly twenty years later, in 1913, he was prevailed upon to collect together a further twelve stories which had been published between 1881 and 1890. He called the volume *A Changed Man* and excused himself for their publication by saying that they 'would probably have never been collected by me at this time of day if frequent reprints of some of them in America and elsewhere had not set many readers inquiring for them in a volume'. It is, indeed, a mixed bag but includes two or three of his best stories, including 'The Waiting Supper' and 'A Changed Man'.

Hardy became the 'Chronicler of Wessex' after the publication of *Far from the Madding Crowd*, and it is not surprising that he called his first collection of short stories *Wessex Tales*. Wessex, described by him as 'a part real, part dream country', was his name for Dorset and its neighbouring counties, once the home of the West Saxons. His best short stories, like his best novels, are deeply rooted in that part of rural England in which he was born, lived for most of his life, and died, and *Wessex Tales* is regarded by many as his finest collection. Every one of the stories is firmly based on Dorset life and folklore. They grow from Hardy's vast knowledge of written and oral sources about a way of life that, even when he was a boy, was rapidly disappearing. Three of the short stories in this book – 'The Three Strangers', 'The Withered Arm' and 'The Melancholy Hussar' – come from *Wessex Tales*. They are all set in the heart of the Wessex countryside, close to Hardy's home at Bockhampton, near Dorchester. 'The Three Strangers' takes place in a lonely shepherd's cottage about three miles from Casterbridge (Dorchester); 'The Withered Arm' in the country between Anglebury (Wareham) and Casterbridge where the final tragic incidents occur, and 'The Melancholy Hussar' at Bincombe about three miles south of Casterbridge, near to the Weymouth road.

Hardy knew this part of Dorset intimately and had listened as a child to his mother and grandmother talking of the past. In his poem 'One We Knew' (see p. 145), he describes his grandmother recalling her memories of dancing around the maypole, of the French Revolution and the Napoleonic Wars, and of the gibbet with its grim contents swaying 'in the lightning flash', and a child being whipped 'At the cart-tail'. 'The Melancholy Hussar', he tells us had

'a hold upon myself for the technically inadmissible reasons that the old people who gave me their recollections of its incidents did so in circumstances that linger pathetically in the memory; that she who, at the age of ninety, pointed out the unmarked resting-place of the two soldiers of the tale, was probably the last remaining eye-witness of their death and interment; that the extract from the register of burials is literal, to be read any day in the original by the curious who recognize the village.'

Hardy imparts a strong sense of authenticity to his stories by such means as this. Two soldiers were, in fact, shot for desertion near to Bincombe in 1801, and no doubt prisoners did escape from Dorchester gaol, although it required a remarkable imagination to conceive of an escaped prisoner accidentally meeting his own executioner.

Hardy more than once said that 'A story must be exceptional enough to justify its telling', and on this basis 'The Withered Arm' more than justifies its place in the book. It is a story which makes substantial use of superstition, of witchcraft, of the oppression of an incubus and of such primitive beliefs as that the hangman had the ability to produce 'the ultimate turning of blood'. Hardy makes no attempt to explain or discredit such credulity, but allows his narrator to present the story with a studied objectivity. The result is a moving and powerful account of events in the 1820s, which still holds us today, when it is customary, if not always convincing, to believe that we are no longer superstitious.

A Group of Noble Dames which provides the fourth story in this collection, 'The Marchioness of Stonehenge', consists mainly of a group of stories about aristocratic ladies, first published in *The Graphic* at the end of 1890. Like *Wessex Tales* it is a collection of stories drawn from Wessex history, but a more distant history. The *Wessex Tales* stories were of a fairly recent past, the early nineteenth century, but for his new collection Hardy went back to the seventeenth and eighteenth centuries, with the result that these stories lack the realism, the immediacy, the living quality of *Wessex Tales*. In *Wessex Tales* Hardy had depended for much of his material on people he knew who had personal experience of the events described. For *A Group of Noble Dames* his main source was a book – John Hutchins's *History and Antiquities of the County of Dorset* – and these later stories may seem thin by comparison. However, they have much to recommend them, not least the fact that the ten stories exhibit a fascinating set of variations on two themes which dominated the whole of Hardy's writing life – the position of women in love and marriage, and class distinction.

This gives the book its unity, but there is a considerable diversity within this unity created by Hardy's use of a device employed by many great story-tellers. He imagines the stories being told by individual members of the Wessex Field and Antiquarian Club (a historian, an old surgeon, a rural dean, a sentimental member, a churchwarden, etc.), who are unable to go on an excursion because of bad weather and sit in the museum telling their stories of the past. This framework enables Hardy to add subtlety to his stories by telling them through characters who add their own individual interpretation.

It is a world of arranged marriages in which the wishes of the woman are seldom paramount, of passionate love transcending class distinctions, of rival suitors, of hatred, jealousy and even sadistic cruelty. Hardy's sympathies are with the oppressed, as always, and the reader cannot miss his overriding compassion for the women who were so often the innocent victims. It is no coincidence that he was working on *Tess of the d'Urbervilles* at the time of writing *A Group of Noble Dames*. Lady Caroline behaves badly but she is caught in a web of deceit because of the difference in class between her and the 'young man of humble birth' with whom she falls in love. Subject to the prejudices and snobberies of the time, she moves from one mistaken action to another, and the *dénouement* comes when she realizes that she has forfeited the love of her own son. The final comment by the rural dean who tells the story that, 'There is no pathos like the pathos of childhood, when a child found itself in a world where it was not wanted, and could not understand the reason why', gives the story a universality which strikes home as much today as it did one hundred years ago. Here Hardy is questioning whether a natural mother's love is always stronger and purer than that of a foster mother, and we learn something about selfless and selfish love.

Four years after *A Group of Noble Dames*, Hardy published *Life's Little Ironies*. It came almost midway between *Tess* and *Jude* and the lasting impression it gives the reader is of a writer increasingly aware of the tragic ironies which so often mar human happiness. From the rural stories of *Wessex Tales* and the historical tales of *A Group of Noble Dames*, Hardy moved on to write stories mainly about the middle class, and the reader is aware of Hardy's growing condemnation of the rigid, intolerant and merciless social and economic conventions of the time. In an article in *The New Review* in 1894 he actually questioned 'whether marriage, as we at present understand it, is such a desirable goal for all women as it is assumed to be.' This is to be an important issue in *Jude*. Hardy was also challenging the conventional Victorian happy ending and there are no happy endings in *Life's Little Ironies*, except for those which occur in the group of very short stories called 'A Few Crusted Characters'.

Until Hardy there were few Victorian writers who were willing to portray women as having strong sexual desires. Dickens' heroines, for example, seem almost completely sexless, while George Eliot's lack any strong sexuality. Ella Marchmill in 'An Imaginative Woman' is a frustrated wife married to an armaments manufacturer, who thinks of her – when he thinks of her at all – as a piece of sexual property. Impassioned and romantic, she is portrayed as having powerful sexual impulses and her falling in love with a poet, Robert Trewe, who longs for a woman's love as much as she longs for his, is wholly convincing, possibly because Hardy himself was at that time a frustrated poet longing for someone to love. The scene in which she gets into bed with a book of her poet's verse and his photograph is full of sexual nuances conveyed with a subtlety at which Hardy had become adept. Poor bored Ella, caught in a marriage brought about by 'the necessity of getting life-leased at all cost', she can live only in a fantasy world. Both she and Trewe are seeking an ideal love which the cruelty of fate and the ironies of chance deny them. It is a short story well in advance of its time which can still move us by its universal qualities of thwarted love and hopeless longing, and its exposure of the psychological damage wrought on those caught in the Victorian social and sexual strait-jacket. What is particularly impressive about the achievement of Hardy as a short-story writer is the range of tone and mood he controls.

The remaining stories in this selection all come from the group of stories which ends *Life's Little Ironies*. It is called 'A Few Crusted Characters' and strikes a note of humour which might surprise those who are not familiar with the dry, occasionally grim, comedy which sometimes appears in Hardy's most sombre narratives. *Tess*, for example, begins with a chapter which might lead the reader to expect that this will be a comic novel. For 'A Few Crusted Characters' Hardy again uses the device of stories told by a group of people brought together by a common activity. We see his characters boarding a large carrier's van in the High Street in Casterbridge. The carrier's van, the omnibus of that time, will take them to Longpuddle and we are introduced to the storytellers who are prompted to reminisce by the presence among them of a Mr Lackland, who is returning to his old home at Longpuddle after thirty-five years abroad. They tell him anecdotes from the past which have clearly become part of an oral tradition. There is a rich subtlety here in the way in which, as readers, we are not listening to Hardy but to Hardy's narrators. They tell their stories not for us, but for the special benefit of the returned Mr Lackland who, at the end of his visit to the place of his birth, has to face the truth that 'Time had not condescended to wait his pleasure, nor local life his greeting.' His roots with his past have been broken by his long absence and he is no longer a member of the community which gave his birthplace a meaning for him.

'Absent-Mindedness in a Parish Choir' is recognized as a small masterpiece of humour. Its near farcical story is made realistic by circumstantial detail and the masterly use of dialect, making the reader vividly aware of the two worlds inhabited by the choir members, which at that time included instrumentalists as well as singers: the secular world of playing jigs and reels at 'one rattling randy after another', and the religious world of playing hymns and chants in the gallery of the village church. The clash of the two worlds, when the choir in its drunken stupor plays a very bawdy folk tune in the church, is both uproariously funny, and sadly serious, because the choir, so important a part of community life, is banished from the church and replaced by a characterless barrel-organ.

In all three of these humorous stories, 'Andrey Satchel and the Parson and Clerk', 'Old Andrey's Experience as a Musician' and 'Absent-Mindedness in a Parish Choir', we are aware, even while we are laughing, of the gap between the work-folk and the squire and parson, and once again Hardy shows his sensitivity about class. His work-folk may drink too much and have to get married as a baby is imminent, but there is an integrity about them which is plainly missing from the parson whose main worship is hunting, and from the squire, wittily described as 'a wickedish man . . . though now for once he happened to be on the Lord's side,' who reveals his priorities with his 'not if the Angels of Heaven come down . . . shall one of you villainous players ever sound a note in this church again; for the insult to me, and my family, and my visitor, and the pa'son, and God Almighty . . .' Here, as in the stories which began this selection, we are back in the real Wessex of Thomas Hardy, for he himself had heard from his father about the way in which the instrumental choirs of the local churches had been abolished when the barrel-organ was invented. It was a sad end to a great community tradition, and it says something for Hardy's ambivalent attitude towards life that he could see that the humorous and the serious, comedy and tragedy, are closely related.

The nine short stories chosen for this selection show a remarkable variety of tone and mood and a wide range of characters and locations. Above all, however, we are aware of Hardy's powerful creative imagination and his sympathy for others, in particular nineteenth-century women whose disadvantages are so clearly demonstrated. His short stories are still relevant and remain well worth reading, both for the entertainment they provide and for their compassionate and sensitive exploration of human relationships.

The Poems

As a young man Hardy expressed the view that in poetry was concentrated the essence of all imaginative and emotional literature. In the 1850s and 1860s he might well have thought so. The novel had not yet established its complete ascendancy, and many educated readers looked back to the poets of the Romantic period – Wordsworth, Coleridge, Keats and Shelley in particular – with a respect verging on worship. It was these poets who had claimed an almost religious quality for poetry. Poets were 'the unacknowledged legislators of the world', wrote Shelley, and for Wordsworth poetry was 'the breath and finer spirit of all knowledge'. In 1922, in an 'Apology' to his book of verse, *Late Lyrics and Earlier*, Hardy wrote, 'poetry and religion touch each other, or rather modulate into each other'. By this he meant that both religion and poetry at its greatest are concerned with universal truths, with what Keats so succinctly termed 'the holiness of the heart's affection and the truth of imagination'.

It was not surprising, then, that Hardy's first literary ambition was to be a poet. He was writing poetry in his teens while living in the family cottage at Bockhampton, and the first poem in this selection, 'Domicilium' (p. 143), was written when he was about eighteen. It describes the cottage in the 1850s and his grandmother recalling her memories of living there fifty years before. The blank verse used is exceptionally competent for someone so young and there are echoes of Wordsworth in the vocabulary and style. In the *Life* he admits that he wrote a good deal of poetry in the 1860s, while in London practising as an architect, but failed to get it published. Many of these unpublished poems were buried by him in what must have been a very capacious bottom-drawer, and then exhumed, revised, and published many years later. They reveal a young poet actively developing his skills in a variety of forms, while consciously imitating his predecessors: for example, the great Elizabethan sonneteers. During this period he assiduously read his way through almost the whole of English poetry from Chaucer onwards, and he invested in copies of Nuttall's *Standard Pronouncing Dictionary* and Walker's *Rhyming Dictionary*. He kept a notebook entitled 'Studies, Specimens, & c' which contained quotations and word lists: he was obviously preparing himself with a Victorian thoroughness to be a poet.

But it was not to be. Very few poets have ever earned a living from their poetry and probably only Tennyson, the Poet Laureate, could have lived at that time on his income from writing verse. Hardy turned to novel-writing as the only alternative. He did so regretfully, but he was a 'poor man' and needed an income. Over a period of almost thirty years, from about 1868 to 1897, he wrote hardly any poetry at all, but the novels he wrote during this period were a further preparation for his career as a poet because they taught him the power of words and imagery. As a novelist he is at his best when he is poetic. We all have our favourite passages in the novels and these are nearly always nearer to verse than to prose.

Hardy's opportunity to take up poetry again occurred in the mid-1890s when, disgusted with the vicious attacks on him by critics of *Tess* and *Jude*, who regarded both books as morally corrupting and obscene, he decided to give up novel-writing. Ironically, both these novels had enjoyed a *succès de scandale* and he was now a wealthy man with an assured income. He had always resented the restrictions imposed on novelists by the powerful circulating libraries and the Mrs Grundys of the Victorian Establishment, and felt sure that he would be able to say things in verse that would cause an outcry if expressed in a novel. As he stated in his note of 1896, 'If Galileo had said in verse that the world moved, the Inquisition might have let him alone.' That there was some truth in this is evidenced by his publication in 1901 in *Poems of the Past and the Present* of the poem 'The Ruined Maid' (p. 162) and in 1909 in *Time's Laughingstocks* of 'One Ralph Blossom Soliloquizes' (p. 163). These two books of verse also contained a number of poems totally explicit in their querying of certain religious beliefs, including one, 'Panthera', which questions Christ's divinity. Yet such outspoken criticism of Establishment beliefs caused hardly a stir.

It is one of the wonders of literature that Hardy did not publish his first book of verse, *Wessex Poems*, until 1898 when he was nearly sixty. During the next thirty years a further seven volumes of verse were published and in his *Complete Poems*, there are nearly a thousand poems. His fame as a poet grew slowly and *Wessex Poems* sold fewer than five hundred copies in its first two years. Reviewers exhorted Hardy to return to the novel, but he continued to write poetry and gradually won approval. It was *The Dynasts*, his great epic on the Napoleonic wars published between 1904 and 1908, which did most to establish him as a poet, although today few critics hold it in high esteem and it is very little read. Eventually his poetry sold well and Hardy was under constant pressure from newspaper and journal editors to provide them with a poem. When he died in 1928, he was hailed both as a great novelist and poet, and he has continued to be read ever since. His *Collected Poems* was first published in 1919 and was continuously in print until it was superseded by *Complete Poems* in 1976. This edition of his work sold more than seven thousand copies in its first year and has been reprinted many times.

Why? Perhaps what Philip Larkin wrote about *Collected Poems* in 1968 will provide a partial explanation:

Curiously enough . . . I like him because he wrote so much. I love
the great Collected Hardy which runs for something like 800 pages.
One can read him for years and years and still be surprised, and I
think that's a marvellous thing to find in any poet . . . In almost
every Hardy poem . . . there is a little spinal cord of thought and
each has a little tune of its own, and that is something you can say
of very few poets. Immediately you begin a Hardy poem your own
inner response begins to rock in time with the poem's rhythm and I
think that this is quite inimitable.

This ability to surprise is something that all admirers of
Hardy's poems experience. Part of his appeal is that almost all
of his poems are accessible: Hardy was a man of humble origin
who wrote for ordinary people and, although he may
occasionally use archaic or unusual words, it is not necessary
to do a university course to understand him. However, as he
pointed out, his is an art that conceals art, and with greater
knowledge the reader realizes that most of his poems are full of
subtleties of meaning and technique, so that the simplicity
eventually surprises one by revealing a remarkable profundity.
In 'The Oxen' (p. 166) which is immediately understandable
at a simple level, further readings reveal that Hardy's careful
structuring establishes a tension between the first two stanzas
(the past) and the last two (the present); the running of the
third stanza into the fourth conveys the excitement that it
'might be so'; the companionable use in the first two stanzas of
'we' and 'us' contrasts with the lonely 'I' of the remainder of
the poem; also revealed are the clever use of Biblical language
in the first stanza; the importance of the archetypal image of
sitting round the fire as a community, and the double meaning
of 'gloom'; and so much more.
Larkin also comments on the rhythmic power of Hardy's
poetry, and reveals his awareness of Hardy's astonishing grasp
of poetic techniques. Hardy is a traditional poet, in that he uses
the system of accentual-syllabics used by virtually all the great
English poets from Chaucer onwards. Sadly, many poets of this
century have abandoned it, a process Robert Frost described as
being like playing tennis without a net, and Hardy always had
a net! He loved the challenge of rhyme and rhythm and was a
traditionalist who was always experimenting. No other poet
has produced such a variety of stanza lengths, line lengths and

rhyming schemes. He must have particularly enjoyed the appropriately shapeless shape on the page of 'Snow in the Suburbs' (p. 188), or the way in which the stanzas of 'The Convergence of the Twain' (p. 210) make the shape of a ship.

But our final impressions of his poetry must be of its near-Shakespearean range of emotions and subject-matter. For Hardy poetry was 'emotion put into metre' and to live with his poetry is to live with him. In one of the many notebooks, methodically kept throughout most of his life, he wrote down with obvious approval these words of Leslie Stephen: 'The ultimate aim of the poet should be to touch our hearts by showing his own.' In the great poems he wrote after the death of Emma, his first wife (pp. 149–58), we feel his grief and share it. There is a danger here of sentimentality and of egocentricity, but this is avoided by the universality of Hardy's expressions of feeling. This quality caused the writer, Irving Howe, to comment that 'What begins as an obscure private hurt ends with the common wound of experience.' His ability to universalize experience results from a cosmic compassion, an ability to empathize with others, which is possessed by only a few of the greatest writers. Shakespeare, Chekov and Hardy all had it.

In 'Beyond the Last Lamp' (p. 159), Hardy makes a memorable poem out of so slight an incident as a pair of unhappy lovers standing under the lamplight in the rain. We don't know who they are or why they are so distressed (Hardy does not know and leaves it to our imagination), but through his skill as a poet he makes us share their sorrow and feel pity for them. It is part of his greatness that the situations he describes in his poems always have the stamp of truth about them. It is difficult to doubt that this experience really happened. It is, after all, the kind of incident we might well have experienced ourselves and Hardy provides just enough circumstantial evidence to make it seem genuine. He tells the reader that it happened near Tooting Common, where he was living in 1880, that it is a wet night and somehow the lovers become a symbol of all unhappy couples everywhere. Then, the poem is given even greater meaning by the discovery in stanza four that the incident, described as if it had just happened, took place thirty years before. Hardy repeatedly uses this kind of double vision by which he sees the past as if it were the present, and then distances it as if he were taking away a telescope from his eye (he uses the same technique in 'Beeny Cliff' p. 154). Thus he puts our lives against a threatening background of passing time, the enemy of all.

It is not easy to divide Hardy's poems into categories. He thought that poetry ought to be available to everyone and that it could be about almost anything, with the result that a poem can be simultaneously about place, time, death and people and be lyrical, meditative and even narrative. However, the poems in this selection have been divided roughly into eight groups. In the first group, entitled *Home and Family*, the reader needs to know that 'Mellstock' is Hardy's name for Stinsford, the parish in which the family cottage is located, and that 'A Church Romance' is his description of the falling in love of his mother and father. In 'The Self-Unseeing' Hardy returns in later years to the family cottage, and 'On One Who Lived and Died Where He Was Born' was written about the death of his father in 1892.

The first eight poems of the second group, *Love*, are all about Emma, his first wife, with the final poem 'During Wind and Rain' based upon Emma's description of her childhood in Plymouth. Hardy was greatly moved when — after her death — he came upon the memoir she had written about her childhood and her meeting with him in Cornwall in the 1870s. 'Neutral Tones' may be about the affair he had with his cousin, Tryphena Sparks, but no one is sure. However, we do know that the person who failed to turn up in 'A Broken Appointment' was the beautiful and aristocratic Mrs Henniker with whom, in the early 1890s, Hardy would have liked to have had an affair, but she did not love him. It would be difficult to find a tighter and yet more emotional poem about being 'stood up'. 'To Meet, or Otherwise' is one of the only two poems about Hardy's second wife, Florence. She, quite naturally, resented the fact that Hardy had written far more poems about Emma, but she had married a man in his seventies who was forty years older than herself. Of the remaining groups – *Faith and Doubt, Lyrics and Meditations, Nature: Flowers, Birds and Animals, War, Narrative* and *Occasional* no more need be said than that here is 'God's plenty'. Hardy's ability as a writer of occasional verse meant that England lost an outstanding Poet Laureate when it was decided by the Establishment that he was not

morally acceptable – an error of judgment modern readers find
hard to believe.

SUGGESTIONS FOR FURTHER READING

Readers who wish to know more about Hardy's life and times should read Hardy's autobiography, *The Life and Work of Thomas Hardy by Thomas Hardy* edited by Michael Millgate (Macmillan 1984). The best modern biography is *Thomas Hardy: A Biography* by Michael Millgate (Oxford 1982).

Critical works which contain useful discussion of Hardy's short stories and poems include the following:

The Short Stories of Thomas Hardy by Kristin Brady (Macmillan 1982)

A Casebook: Thomas Hardy: The Poems, edited by James Gibson and Trevor Johnson (Macmillan 1979).

A Critical Introduction to the Poems of Thomas Hardy by Trevor Johnson (Macmillan 1991).

For a wider reading of Hardy's short stories and poems the following are recommended:

Thomas Hardy: Collected Short Stories, edited by Desmond Hawkins (Macmillan 1988).

Thomas Hardy: The Complete Poems, edited by James Gibson (Macmillan 1976).

Articles on Hardy's short stories and novels by leading scholars of today are published in *The Thomas Hardy Journal* (The Hardy Society, P.O. Box 1438, Dorchester, Dorset DT1 1YH).

THE SHORT STORIES

The Three Strangers

Among the few features of agricultural England which retain an appearance but little modified by the lapse of centuries, may be reckoned the long, grassy and furzy downs, coombs, or ewe-leases, as they are called according to their kind, that fill a large area of certain counties in the south and south-west. If any mark of human occupation is met with hereon, it usually takes the form of the solitary cottage of some shepherd.

Fifty years ago such a lonely cottage stood on such a down, and may possibly be standing there now. In spite of its loneliness, however, the spot, by actual measurement, was not three miles from a county-town. Yet that affected it little. Three miles of irregular upland, during the long inimical seasons, with their sleets, snows, rains, and mists, afford withdrawing space enough to isolate a Timon or a Nebuchadnezzar; much less, in fair weather, to please that less repellent tribe, the poets, philosophers, artists, and others who 'conceive and meditate of pleasant things'.

Some old earthen camp or barrow, some clump of trees, at least some starved fragment of ancient hedge is usually taken advantage of in the erection of these forlorn dwellings. But, in the present case, such a kind of shelter had been disregarded. Higher Crowstairs, as the house was called, stood quite detached and undefended. The only reason for its precise situation seemed to be the crossing of two footpaths at right angles hard by, which may have crossed there and thus for a good five hundred years. Hence the house was exposed to the elements on all sides. But, though the wind up here blew unmistakably when it did blow, and the rain hit hard whenever it fell, the various weathers of the winter season were not quite so formidable on the down as they were imagined to be by dwellers on low ground. The raw rimes were not so pernicious as in the hollows, and the frosts were scarcely so severe. When the shepherd and his family who tenanted the house were pitied for their sufferings from the exposure, they said that upon the whole they were less inconvenienced by 'wuzzes and flames' (hoarses and phlegms) than when they had lived by the stream of a snug neighbouring valley.

The night of 28 March 182–, was precisely one of the nights that were wont to call forth these expressions of commiseration. The level rainstorm smote walls, slopes, and hedges like the clothyard shafts of Senlac and Crecy. Such sheep and outdoor animals as had no shelter stood with their buttocks to the winds; while the tails of little birds trying to roost on some scraggy thorn were blown inside-out like umbrellas. The gable-end of the cottage was stained with wet, and the eavesdroppings flapped against the wall. Yet never was commiseration for the shepherd more misplaced. For that cheerful rustic was entertaining a large party in glorification of the christening of his second girl.

The guests had arrived before the rain began to fall, and they were all now assembled in the chief or living-room of the dwelling. A glance into the apartment at eight o'clock on this eventful evening would have resulted in the opinion that it was as cosy and comfortable a nook as could be wished for in boisterous weather. The calling of its inhabitant was proclaimed by a number of highly-polished sheep-crooks without stems that were hung ornamentally over the fireplace, the curl of each shining crook varying from the antiquated type engraved in the patriarchal pictures of old family Bibles to the most approved fashion of the last local sheep-fair. The room was lighted by half-a-dozen candles, having wicks only a trifle smaller than the grease which enveloped them, in candlesticks that were never used but at high-days, holy-days, and family feasts. The lights were scattered about the room, two of them standing on the chimney-piece. This position of candles was in itself significant. Candles on the chimney-piece always meant a party.

On the hearth, in front of a back-brand to give substance,

blazed a fire of thorns, that crackled 'like the laughter of the fool'.

Nineteen persons were gathered here. Of these, five women, wearing gowns of various bright hues, sat in chairs along the wall; girls shy and not shy filled the window-bench; four men, including Charley Jake the hedge-carpenter, Elijah New the parish-clerk, and John Pitcher, a neighbouring dairyman, the shepherd's father-in-law, lolled in the settle; a young man and maid, who were blushing over tentative *pourparlers* on a life-companionship, sat beneath the corner-cupboard; and an elderly engaged man of fifty or upward moved restlessly about from spots where his betrothed was not to the spot where she was. Enjoyment was pretty general, and so much the more prevailed in being unhampered by conventional restrictions. Absolute confidence in each other's good opinion begat perfect ease, while the finishing stroke of manner, amounting to a truly princely serenity, was lent to the majority by the absence of any expression or trait denoting that they wished to get on in the world, enlarge their minds, or do any eclipsing thing whatever – which nowadays so generally nips the bloom and *bonhomie* of all except the two extremes of the social scale.

Shepherd Fennel had married well, his wife being a dairyman's daughter from a vale at a distance, who brought fifty guineas in her pocket – and kept them there, till they should be required for ministering to the needs of a coming family. This frugal woman had been somewhat exercised as to the character that should be given to the gathering. A sit-still party had its advantages; but an undisturbed position of ease in chairs and settles was apt to lead on the men to such an unconscionable deal of toping that they would sometimes fairly drink the house dry. A dancing-party was the alternative; but this, while avoiding the foregoing objection on the score of good drink, had a counterbalancing disadvantage in the matter of good victuals, the ravenous appetites engendered by the exercise causing immense havoc in the buttery. Shepherdess Fennel fell back upon the intermediate plan of mingling short dances with short periods of talk and singing, so as to hinder any ungovernable rage in either. But this scheme was entirely confined to her own gentle mind: the shepherd himself was in the mood to exhibit the most reckless phases of hospitality.

The fiddler was a boy of those parts, about twelve years of age, who had a wonderful dexterity in jigs and reels, though his fingers were so small and short as to necessitate a constant shifting for the high notes, from which he scrambled back to the first position with sounds not of unmixed purity of tone. At seven the shrill tweedle-dee of this youngster had begun, accompanied by a booming ground-bass from Elijah New, the parish-clerk, who had thoughtfully brought with him his favourite musical instrument, the serpent. Dancing was instantaneous, Mrs Fennel privately enjoining the players on no account to let the dance exceed the length of a quarter of an hour.

But Elijah and the boy in the excitement of their position quite forgot the injunction. Moreover, Oliver Giles, a man of seventeen, one of the dancers, who was enamoured by his partner, a fair girl of thirty-three rolling years, had recklessly handed a new crown-piece to the musicians, as a bribe to keep going as long as they had muscle and wind. Mrs Fennel, seeing the steam begin to generate on the countenances of her guests, crossed over and touched the fiddler's elbow and put her hand on the serpent's mouth. But they took no notice, and fearing she might lose her character of genial hostess if she were to interfere too markedly, she retired and sat down helpless. And so the dance whizzed on with cumulative fury, the performers moving in their planet-like courses, direct and retrograde, from apogee to perigee, till the hand of the well-kicked clock at the bottom of the room had travelled over the circumference of an hour.

While these cheerful events were in course of enactment within Fennel's pastoral dwelling an incident having considerable bearing on the party had occurred in the gloomy night without. Mrs Fennel's concern about the growing fierceness of the dance corresponded in point of time with the ascent of a human figure to the solitary hill of Higher Crowstairs from the direction of the distant town. This personage strode on through the rain without a pause, following the little-worn path which, further on in its course, skirted the shepherd's cottage.

It was nearly the time of full moon, and on this account, though the sky was lined with a uniform sheet of dripping cloud, ordinary objects out of doors were readily visible. The sad wan light revealed the lonely pedestrian to be a man of supple frame; his gait suggested that he had somewhat passed the period of perfect and instinctive agility, though not so far as to be otherwise than rapid of motion when occasion required. At a rough guess, he might have been about forty years of age. He appeared tall, but a recruiting sergeant, or other person accustomed to the judging of men's height by the eye, would have discerned that this was chiefly owing to his gauntness, and that he was not more than five-feet-eight or nine.

Notwithstanding the regularity of his tread there was caution in it, as in that of one who mentally feels his way; and despite the fact that it was not a black coat nor a dark garment of any sort that he wore, there was something about him which suggested that he naturally belonged to the black-coated tribes of men. His clothes were of fustian, and his boots hobnailed, yet in his progress he showed not the mud-accustomed bearing of hobnailed and fustianed peasantry.

By the time that he had arrived abreast of the shepherd's premises the rain came down, or rather came along, with yet more determined violence. The outskirts of the little settlement partially broke the force of wind and rain, and this induced him to stand still. The most salient of the shepherd's domestic erections was an empty sty at the forward corner of his hedgeless garden, for in these latitudes the principle of masking the homelier features of your establishment by a conventional frontage was unknown. The traveller's eye was attracted to this small building by the pallid shine of the wet slates that covered it. He turned aside, and, finding it empty, stood under the pent-roof for shelter.

While he stood, the boom of the serpent within the adjacent house, and the lesser strains of the fiddler, reached the spot as an accompaniment to the surging hiss of the flying rain on the sod, its louder beating on the cabbage-leaves of the garden, on the straw hackles of eight or ten beehives just discernible by the path, and its dripping from the eaves into a row of buckets and pans that had been placed under the walls of the cottage. For at Higher Crowstairs, as at all such elevated domiciles, the grand difficulty of housekeeping was an unsufficiency of water; and a casual rainfall was utilized by turning out, as catchers, every utensil that the house contained. Some queer stories might be told of the contrivances for economy in suds and dish-waters that are absolutely necessitated in upland habitations during the droughts of summer. But at this season there were no such exigencies; a mere acceptance of what the skies bestowed was sufficient for an abundant store.

At last the notes of the serpent ceased and the house was silent. This cessation of activity aroused the solitary pedestrian from the reverie into which he had lapsed, and, emerging from the shed, with an apparently new intention, he walked up the path to the house-door. Arrived here, his first act was to kneel down on a large stone beside the row of vessels, and to drink a copious draught from one of them. Having quenched his thirst he rose and lifted his hand to knock, but paused with his eye upon the panel. Since the dark surface of the wood revealed absolutely nothing, it was evident that he must be mentally looking through the door, as if he wished to measure thereby all the possibilities that a house of this sort might include, and how they might bear upon the question of his entry.

In his indecision he turned and surveyed the scene around. Not a soul was anywhere visible. The garden-path stretched downward from his feet, gleaming like the track of a snail; the roof of the little well (mostly dry), the well-cover, the top rail of the garden-gate, were varnished with the same dull liquid glaze; while, far away in the vale, a faint whiteness of more than usual extent showed that the rivers were high in the meads. Beyond all this winked a few bleared lamplights through the beating drops – lights that denoted the situation of the county-town from which he had appeared to come. The absence of all notes of life in that direction seemed to clinch his intentions, and he knocked at the door.

Within, a desultory chat had taken the place of movement and musical sound. The hedge-carpenter was suggesting a song to the company, which nobody just then was inclined to undertake, so that the knock afforded a not unwelcome diversion.

'Walk in!' said the shepherd promptly.

The latch clicked upward, and out of the night our pedestrian appeared upon the door-mat. The shepherd arose, snuffed two of the nearest candles, and turned to look at him.

Their light disclosed that the stranger was dark in complexion and not unprepossessing as to feature. His hat, which for a moment he did not remove, hung low over his eyes, without concealing that they were large, open, and determined, moving with a flash rather than a glance round the room. He seemed pleased with his survey, and, baring his shaggy head, said, in a rich deep voice, 'The rain is so heavy, friends, that I ask leave to come in and rest awhile.'

'To be sure, stranger,' said the shepherd. 'And faith, you've been lucky in choosing your time, for we are having a bit of a fling for a glad cause – though, to be sure, a man could hardly wish that glad cause to happen more than once a year.'

'Nor less,' spoke up a woman. 'For 'tis best to get your family over and done with, as soon as you can, so as to be all the earlier out of the fag o't.'

'And what may be this glad cause?' asked the stranger.

'A birth and christening,' said the shepherd.

The stranger hoped his host might not be made unhappy either by too many or too few of such episodes, and being invited by a gesture to a pull at the mug, he readily acquiesced. His manner, which, before entering, had been so dubious, was now altogether that of a careless and candid man.

'Late to be traipsing athwart this coomb – hey?' said the engaged man of fifty.

'Late it is, master, as you say. – I'll take a seat in the chimney-corner, if you have nothing to urge against it, ma'am; for I am a little moist on the side that was next the rain.'

Mrs Shepherd Fennel assented, and made room for the self-invited comer, who, having got completely inside the chimney-corner, stretched out his legs and arms with the expansiveness of a person quite at home.

'Yes, I am rather cracked in the vamp,' he said freely, seeing that the eyes of the shepherd's wife fell upon his boots, 'and I am not well fitted either. I have had some rough times lately, and have been forced to pick up what I can get in the way of wearing, but I must find a suit better fit for working-days when I reach home.'

'One of hereabouts?' she inquired.

'Not quite that – further up the country.'

'I thought so. And so be I; and by your tongue you come from my neighbourhood.'

'But you would hardly have heard of me,' he said quickly. 'My time would be long before yours, ma'am, you see.'

This testimony to the youthfulness of his hostess had the effect of stopping her cross-examination.

'There is only one thing more wanted to make me happy,' continued the new-comer. 'And that is a little baccy, which I am sorry to say I am out of.'

'I'll fill your pipe,' said the shepherd.

'I must ask you to lend me a pipe likewise.'

'A smoker, and no pipe about 'ee?'

'I have dropped it somewhere on the road.'

The shepherd filled and handed him a new clay pipe, saying, as he did so, 'Hand me your baccy-box – I'll fill that too, now I am about it.'

The man went through the movement of searching his pockets.

'Lost that too?' said his entertainer, with some surprise.

'I am afraid so,' said the man with some confusion. 'Give it to me in a screw of paper.' Lighting his pipe at the candle with a suction that drew the whole flame into the bowl, he resettled himself in the corner and bent his looks upon the faint steam from his damp legs, as if he wished to say no more.

Meanwhile the general body of guests had been taking little notice of this visitor by reason of an absorbing discussion in which they were engaged with the band about a tune for the next dance. The matter being settled, they were about to stand up when an interruption came in the shape of another knock at the door.

At sound of the same the man in the chimney-corner took up the poker and began stirring the brands as if doing it thoroughly were the one aim of his existence; and a second time the shepherd said, 'Walk in!' In a moment another man stood upon the straw-woven door-mat. He too was a stranger.

This individual was one of a type radically different from the first. There was more of the commonplace in his manner, and a certain jovial cosmopolitanism sat upon his features. He was several years older than the first arrival, his hair being slightly frosted, his eyebrows bristly, and his whiskers cut back from his cheeks. His face was rather full and flabby, and yet it was not altogether a face without power. A few grogblossoms marked the neighbourhood of his nose. He flung back his long drab greatcoat, revealing that beneath it he wore a suit of cinder-grey shade throughout, large heavy seals, of some metal or other that would take a polish, dangling from his fob as his only personal ornament. Shaking the water-drops from his low-crowned glazed hat, he said, 'I must ask for a few minutes' shelter, comrades, or I shall be wetted to my skin before I get to Casterbridge.'

'Make yourself at home, master,' said the shepherd, perhaps a trifle less heartily than on the first occasion. Not that Fennel had the least tinge of niggardliness in his composition; but the room was far from large, spare chairs were not numerous, and damp companions were not altogether desirable at close quarters for the women and girls in their bright-coloured gowns.

However, the second comer, after taking off his greatcoat, and hanging his hat on a nail in one of the ceiling-beams as if he had been specially invited to put it there, advanced and sat down at the table. This had been pushed so closely into the chimney-corner, to give all available room to the dancers, that its inner edge grazed the elbow of the man who had ensconced himself by the fire; and thus the two strangers were brought into close companionship. They nodded to each other by way of breaking the ice of unacquaintance, and the first stranger handed his neighbour the family mug – a huge vessel of brown ware, having its upper edge worn away like a threshold by the rub of whole generations of thirsty lips that had gone the way of all flesh, and bearing the following inscription burnt upon its rotund side in yellow letters: –

THERE IS NO FUN

UNTILL i CUM

The other man, nothing loth, raised the mug to his lips, and drank on, and on, and on – till a curious blueness overspread the countenance of the shepherd's wife, who had regarded with no little surprise the first stranger's free offer to the second of what did not belong to him to dispense.

'I knew it!' said the toper to the shepherd with much satisfaction. 'When I walked up your garden before coming in, and saw the hives all of a row, I said to myself, "Where there's bees there's honey, and where there's honey there's mead." But mead of such a truly comfortable sort as this I really didn't expect to meet in my older days.' He took yet another pull at the mug, till it assumed an ominous elevation.

'Glad you enjoy it!' said the shepherd warmly.

'It is goodish mead,' assented Mrs Fennel, with an absence of enthusiasm which seemed to say that it was possible to buy praise for one's cellar at too heavy a price. 'It is trouble enough to make – and really I hardly think we shall make any more. For honey sells well, and we ourselves can make shift with a drop o' small mead and metheglin for common use from the comb-washings.'

'O, but you'll never have the heart!' reproachfully cried the stranger in cinder-grey, after taking up the mug a third time and setting it down empty. 'I love mead, when 'tis old like this, as I love to go to church o' Sundays or to relieve the needy any day of the week.'

'Ha, ha, ha!' said the man in the chimney-corner, who, in spite of the taciturnity induced by the pipe of tobacco, could not or would not refrain from this slight testimony to his comrade's humour.

Now the old mead of those days, brewed of the purest first-year or maiden honey, four pounds to the gallon – with its due complement of white of eggs, cinnamon, ginger, cloves, mace, rosemary, yeast, and processes of working, bottling, and cellaring – tasted remarkably strong; but it did not taste so strong as it actually was. Hence, presently, the stranger in cinder-grey at the table, moved by its creeping influence, unbuttoned his waistcoat, threw himself back in his chair, spread his legs, and made his presence felt in various ways.

'Well, well, as I say,' he resumed, 'I am going to Casterbridge, and to Casterbridge I must go. I should have been almost there by this time; but the rain drove me into your dwelling, and I'm not sorry for it.'

'You don't live in Casterbridge?' said the shepherd.

'Not as yet; though I shortly mean to move there.'

'Going to set up in trade perhaps?'

'No, no,' said the shepherd's wife. 'It is easy to see that the gentleman is rich, and don't want to work at anything.'

The cinder-grey stranger paused, as if to consider whether he would accept that definition of himself. He presently rejected it by answering, 'Rich is not quite the word for me, dame. I do work, and I must work. And even if I only get to Casterbridge by midnight I must begin work there at eight tomorrow morning. Yes, het or wet, blow or snow, famine or sword, my day's work tomorrow must be done.'

'Poor man! Then, in spite o' seeming, you be worse off than we?' replied the shepherd's wife.

''Tis the nature of my trade, men and maidens. 'Tis the nature of my trade more than my poverty. . . . But really and truly I must up and off, or I shan't get a lodging in the town.' However, the speaker did not move, and directly added, 'There's time for one more draught of friendship before I go; and I'd perform it at once if the mug were not dry.'

'Here's a mug o' small,' said Mrs Fennel. 'Small, we call it, though to be sure 'tis only the first wash o' the combs.'

'No,' said the stranger disdainfully. 'I won't spoil your first kindness by partaking o' your second.'

'Certainly not,' broke in Fennel. 'We don't increase and multiply every day, and I'll fill the mug again.' He went away to the dark place under the stairs where the barrel stood. The shepherdess followed him.

'Why should you do this?' she said reproachfully, as soon as they were alone. 'He's emptied it once, though it held enough for ten people; and now he's not contented wi' the small, but must needs call for more o' the strong! And a stranger unbeknown to any of us. For my part, I don't like the look o' the man at all.'

'But he's in the house, my honey; and 'tis a wet night, and a christening. Daze it, what's a cup of mead more or less? There'll be plenty more next bee-burning.'

'Very well – this time, then,' she answered, looking wistfully at the barrel. 'But what is the man's calling, and where is he one of, that he should come in and join us like this?'

'I don't know. I'll ask him again.'

The catastrophe of having the mug drained dry at one pull by the stranger in cinder-grey was effectually guarded against this time by Mrs Fennel. She poured out his allowance in a small cup, keeping the large one at a discreet distance from him. When he had tossed off his portion the shepherd renewed his inquiry about the stranger's occupation.

The latter did not immediately reply, and the man in the chimney-corner, with sudden demonstrativeness, said, 'Anybody may know my trade – I'm a wheelwright.'

'A very good trade for these parts,' said the shepherd.

'And anybody may know mine – if they've the sense to find it out,' said the stranger in cinder-grey.

'You may generally tell what a man is by his claws,' observed the hedge-carpenter, looking at his own hands. 'My fingers be as full of thorns as an old pin-cushion is of pins.'

The hands of the man in the chimney-corner instinctively sought the shade, and he gazed into the fire as he resumed his pipe. The man at the table took up the hedge-carpenter's remark, and added smartly, 'True; but the oddity of my trade is that, instead of setting a mark upon me, it sets a mark upon my customers.'

No observation being offered by anybody in elucidation of this enigma the shepherd's wife once more called for a song.

The same obstacles presented themselves as at the former time – one had no voice, another had forgotten the first verse. The stranger at the table, whose soul had now risen to a good working temperature, relieved the difficulty by exclaiming that, to start the company, he would sing himself. Thrusting one thumb into the arm-hold of his waistcoat, he waved the other hand in the air, and, with an extemporizing gaze at the shining sheep-crooks above the mantelpiece, began: –

> 'O my trade is the rarest one,
>   Simple shepherds all –
>   My trade is a sight to see;
> For my customers I tie, and take them up on high,
>   And waft 'em to a far countree!'

The room was silent when he had finished the verse – with one exception, that of the man in the chimney-corner, who, at the singer's word, 'Chorus!' joined him in a deep bass voice of musical relish –

> 'And waft 'em to a far countree!'

Oliver Giles, John Pitcher the dairyman, the parish-clerk, the engaged man of fifty, the row of young women against the wall, seemed lost in thought not of the gayest kind. The shepherd looked meditatively on the ground, the shepherdess gazed keenly at the singer, and with some suspicion; she was doubting whether this stranger were merely singing an old song from recollection, or was composing one there and then for the occasion. All were as perplexed at the obscure revelation as the guests at Belshazzar's Feast, except the man in the chimney-corner, who quietly said, 'Second verse, stranger,' and smoked on.

The singer thoroughly moistened himself from his lips inwards, and went on with the next stanza as requested: –

> 'My tools are but common ones,
>   Simple shepherds all –
>   My tools are no sight to see:
> A little hempen string, and a post whereon to swing,
>   Are implements enough for me!'

Shepherd Fennel glanced round. There was no longer any doubt that the stranger was answering his question rhythmically. The guests one and all started back with suppressed exclamations. The young woman engaged to the man of fifty fainted half-way, and would have proceeded, but finding him wanting in alacrity for catching her she sat down trembling.

'O, he's the ——!' whispered the people in the background, mentioning the name of an ominous public officer. 'He's come to do it! 'Tis to be at Casterbridge jail tomorrow – the man for sheep-stealing – the poor clockmaker we heard of, who used to live away at Shottsford and had no work to do – Timothy Summers, whose family were a-starving, and so he went out of Shottsford by the high-road, and took a sheep in open daylight, defying the farmer and the farmer's wife and the farmer's lad, and every man jack among 'em. He' (and they nodded towards the stranger of the deadly trade) 'is come from up the country to do it because there's not enough to do in his own county-town, and he's got the place here now our own county man's dead; he's going to live in the same cottage under the prison wall.'

The stranger in cinder-grey took no notice of this whispered string of observations, but again wetted his lips. Seeing that his friend in the chimney-corner was the only one who reciprocated his joviality in any way, he held out his cup towards that appreciative comrade, who also held out his own. They clinked together, the eyes of the rest of the room hanging upon the singer's actions. He parted his lips for the third verse; but at that moment another knock was audible upon the door. This time the knock was faint and hesitating.

The company seemed scared; the shepherd looked with consternation towards the entrance, and it was with some effort that he resisted his alarmed wife's deprecatory glance, and uttered for the third time the welcoming words, 'Walk in!'

The door was gently opened, and another man stood upon the mat. He, like those who had preceded him, was a stranger. This time it was a short, small personage, of fair complexion, and dressed in a decent suit of dark clothes.

'Can you tell me the way to –?' he began: when, gazing

round the room to observe the nature of the company amongst whom he had fallen, his eyes lighted on the stranger in cinder-grey. It was just at the instant when the latter, who had thrown his mind into his song with such a will that he scarcely heeded the interruption, silenced all whispers and inquiries by burst-ing into his third verse: –

> 'Tomorrow is my working day,
>   Simple shepherds all –
>   Tomorrow is a working day for me:
> For the farmer's sheep is slain, and the lad who did it ta'en,
>   And on his soul may God ha' merc-y!'

The stranger in the chimney-corner, waving cups with the singer so heartily that his mead splashed over on the hearth, repeated in his bass voice as before: –

> 'And on his soul may God ha' merc-y!'

All this time the third stranger had been standing in the doorway. Finding now that he did not come forward or go on speaking, the guests particularly regarded him. They noticed to their surprise that he stood before them the picture of abject terror – his knees trembling, his hand shaking so violently that the door-latch by which he supported himself rattled audibly: his white lips were parted, and his eyes fixed on the merry officer of justice in the middle of the room. A moment more and he had turned, closed the door, and fled.

'What a man can it be?' said the shepherd.

The rest, between the awfulness of their late discovery and the odd conduct of this third visitor, looked as if they knew not what to think, and said nothing. Instinctively they withdrew further and further from the grim gentleman in their midst, whom some of them seemed to take for the Prince of Darkness himself, till they formed a remote circle, an empty space of floor being left between them and him –

> '. . . circulus, cujus centrum diabolus'.

The room was so silent – though there were more than twenty people in it – that nothing could be heard but the patter of the rain against the window-shutters, accompanied by the occasional hiss of a stray drop that fell down the chimney into the fire, and the steady puffing of the man in the corner, who had now resumed his pipe of long clay.

The stillness was unexpectedly broken. The distant sound of a gun reverberated through the air – apparently from the direction of the county-town.

'Be jiggered!' cried the stranger who had sung the song, jumping up.

'What does that mean?' asked several.

'A prisoner escaped from the jail – that's what it means.'

All listened. The sound was repeated, and none of them spoke but the man in the chimney-corner, who said quietly, 'I've often been told that in this county they fire a gun at such times; but I never heard it till now.'

'I wonder if it is *my* man?' murmured the personage in cinder-grey.

'Surely it is!' said the shepherd involuntarily. 'And surely we've zeed him! That little man who looked in at the door by now, and quivered like a leaf when he zeed ye and heard your song!'

'His teeth chattered, and the breath went out of his body,' said the dairyman.

'And his heart seemed to sink within him like a stone,' said Oliver Giles.

'And he bolted as if he'd been shot at,' said the hedge-carpenter.

'True – his teeth chattered, and his heart seemed to sink; and he bolted as if he'd been shot at,' slowly summed up the man in the chimney-corner.

'I didn't notice it,' remarked the hangman.

'We were all a-wondering what made him run off in such a fright,' faltered one of the women against the wall, 'and now 'tis explained!'

The firing of the alarm-gun went on at intervals, low and sullenly, and their suspicions became a certainty. The sinister gentleman in cinder-grey roused himself. 'Is there a constable here?' he asked, in thick tones. 'If so, let him step forward.'

The engaged man of fifty stepped quavering out from the wall, his betrothed beginning to sob on the back of the chair.

'You are a sworn constable?'

'I be, sir.'

'Then pursue the criminal at once, with assistance, and bring him back here. He can't have gone far.'

'I will, sir, I will – when I've got my staff. I'll go home and get it, and come sharp here, and start in a body.'

'Staff! – never mind your staff; the man'll be gone!'

'But I can't do nothing without my staff – can I, William, and John, and Charles Jake? No; for there's the king's royal crown a painted on en in yaller and gold, and the lion and the unicorn, so as when I raise en up and hit my prisoner, 'tis made a lawful blow thereby. I wouldn't 'tempt to take up a man without my staff – no, not I. If I hadn't the law to gie me courage, why, instead o' my taking up him he might take up me!'

'Now, I'm a king's man myself, and can give you authority enough for this,' said the formidable officer in grey. 'Now then, all of ye, be ready. Have ye any lanterns?'

'Yes – have ye any lanterns? – I demand it!' said the constable.

'And the rest of you able-bodied –'

'Able-bodied men – yes – the rest of ye!' said the constable.

'Have you some good stout staves and pitchforks –'

'Staves and pitchforks – in the name o' the law! And take 'em in yer hands and go in quest, and do as we in authority tell ye!'

Thus aroused, the men prepared to give chase. The evidence was, indeed, though circumstantial, so convincing, that but little argument was needed to show the shepherd's guests that after what they had seen it would look very much like connivance if they did not instantly pursue the unhappy third stranger, who could not as yet have gone more than a few hundred yards over such uneven country.

A shepherd is always well provided with lanterns; and, lighting these hastily, and with hurdle-staves in their hands, they poured out of the door, taking a direction along the crest of the hill, away from the town, the rain having fortunately a little abated.

Disturbed by the noise, or possibly by unpleasant dreams of her baptism, the child who had been christened began to cry heart-brokenly in the room overhead. These notes of grief came down through the chinks of the floor to the ears of the women below, who jumped up one by one, and seemed glad of the excuse to ascend and comfort the baby, for the incidents of the last half-hour greatly oppressed them. Thus in the space of two or three minutes the room on the ground-floor was deserted quite.

But it was not for long. Hardly had the sound of footsteps died away when a man returned round the corner of the house from the direction the pursuers had taken. Peeping in at the door, and seeing nobody there, he entered leisurely. It was the stranger of the chimney-corner, who had gone out with the rest. The motive of his return was shown by his helping himself to a cut piece of skimmer-cake that lay on a ledge beside where he had sat, and which he had apparently forgotten to take with him. He also poured out half a cup more mead from the quantity that remained, ravenously eating and drinking these as he stood. He had not finished when another figure came in just as quietly – his friend in cinder-grey.

'O – you here?' said the latter, smiling. 'I thought you had gone to help in the capture.' And this speaker also revealed the object of his return by looking solicitously round for the fascinating mug of old mead.

'And I thought you had gone,' said the other, continuing his skimmer-cake with some effort.

'Well, on second thoughts, I felt there were enough without me,' said the first confidentially, 'and such a night as it is, too. Besides, 'tis the business o' the Government to take care of its criminals – not mine.'

'True; so it is. And I felt as you did, that there were enough without me.'

'I don't want to break my limbs running over the humps and hollows of this wild country.'

'Nor I neither, between you and me.'

'These shepherd-people are used to it – simple-minded souls, you know, stirred up to anything in a moment. They'll have him ready for me before the morning, and no trouble to me at all.'

'They'll have him, and we shall have saved ourselves all labour in the matter.'

'True, true. Well, my way is to Casterbridge; and 'tis as much as my legs will do to take me that far. Going the same way?'

'No, I am sorry to say! I have to get home over there' (he nodded indefinitely to the right), 'and I feel as you do, that it is quite enough for my legs to do before bedtime.'

The other had by this time finished the mead in the mug, after which, shaking hands heartily at the door, and wishing each other well, they went their several ways.

In the meantime the company of pursuers had reached the end of the hog's-back elevation which dominated this part of the down. They had decided on no particular plan of action; and, finding that the man of the baleful trade was no longer in their company, they seemed quite unable to form any such plan now. They descended in all directions down the hill, and straightway several of the party fell into the snare set by Nature for all misguided midnight ramblers over this part of the cretaceous formation. The 'lanchets', or flint slopes, which belted the escarpment at intervals of a dozen yards, took the less cautious ones unawares, and losing their footing on the rubbly steep they slid sharply downwards, the lanterns rolling from their hands to the bottom, and there lying on their sides till the horn was scorched through.

When they had again gathered themselves together the shepherd, as the man who knew the country best, took the lead, and guided them round these treacherous inclines. The lanterns, which seemed rather to dazzle their eyes and warn the fugitive than to assist them in the exploration, were extinguished, due silence was observed; and in this more rational order they plunged into the vale. It was a grassy, briery, moist defile, affording some shelter to any person who had sought it; but the party perambulated it in vain, and ascended on the other side. Here they wandered apart, and after an interval closed together again to report progress. At the second time of closing in they found themselves near a lonely ash, the single tree on this part of the coomb, probably sown there by a passing bird some fifty years before. And here, standing a little to one side of the trunk, as motionless as the trunk itself, appeared the man they were in quest of, his outline being well defined against the sky beyond. The band noiselessly drew up and faced him.

'Your money or your life!' said the constable sternly to the still figure.

'No, no,' whispered John Pitcher. ''Tisn't our side ought to say that. That's the doctrine of vagabonds like him, and we be on the side of the law.'

'Well, well,' replied the constable impatiently; 'I must say something, mustn't I? and if you had all the weight o' this undertaking upon your mind, perhaps you'd say the wrong thing too! – Prisoner at the bar, surrender, in the name of the Father – the Crown, I mane!'

The man under the tree seemed now to notice them for the first time, and, giving them no opportunity whatever for exhibiting their courage, he strolled slowly towards them. He was, indeed, the little man, the third stranger; but his trepidation had in a great measure gone.

'Well, travellers,' he said, 'did I hear ye speak to me?'

'You did: you've got to come and be our prisoner at once!' said the constable. 'We arrest 'ee on the charge of not biding in Casterbridge jail in a decent proper manner to be hung tomorrow morning. Neighbours, do your duty, and seize the culpet!'

On hearing the charge the man seemed enlightened, and, saying not another word, resigned himself with preternatural civility to the search-party, who, with their staves in their hands, surrounded him on all sides, and marched him back towards the shepherd's cottage.

It was eleven o'clock by the time they arrived. The light shining from the open door, a sound of men's voices within, proclaimed to them as they approached the house that some new events had arisen in their absence. On entering they discovered the shepherd's living-room to be invaded by two officers from Casterbridge jail, and a well-known magistrate who lived at the nearest country-seat, intelligence of the escape having become generally circulated.

'Gentlemen,' said the constable, 'I have brought back your man – not without risk and danger; but every one must do his duty! He is inside this circle of able-bodied persons, who have lent me useful aid, considering their ignorance of Crown work. Men, bring forward your prisoner!' And the third stranger was led to the light.

'Who is this?' said one of the officials.

'The man,' said the constable.

'Certainly not,' said the turnkey; and the first corroborated his statement.

'But how can it be otherwise?' asked the constable. 'Or why was he so terrified at sight o' the singing instrument of the law who sat there?' Here he related the strange behaviour of the third stranger on entering the house during the hangman's song.

'Can't understand it,' said the officer coolly. 'All I know is that it is not the condemned man. He's quite a different character from this one; a gauntish fellow, with dark hair and eyes, rather good-looking, and with a musical bass voice that if you heard it once you'd never mistake as long as you lived.'

'Why, souls – 'twas the man in the chimney-corner!'

'Hey – what?' said the magistrate, coming forward after inquiring particulars from the shepherd in the background. 'Haven't you got the man after all?'

'Well, sir,' said the constable, 'he's the man we were in search of, that's true; and yet he's not the man we were in search of. For the man we were in search of was not the man we wanted, sir, if you understand my every-day way; for 'twas the man in the chimney-corner!'

'A pretty kettle of fish altogether!' said the magistrate. 'You had better start for the other man at once.'

The prisoner now spoke for the first time. The mention of the man in the chimney-corner seemed to have moved him as nothing else could do. 'Sir,' he said, stepping forward to the magistrate, 'take no more trouble about me. The time is come when I may as well speak. I have done nothing; my crime is that the condemned man is my brother. Early this afternoon I left home at Shottsford to tramp it all the way to Casterbridge jail to bid him farewell. I was benighted, and called here to rest and ask the way. When I opened the door I saw before me the very man, my brother, that I thought to see in the condemned cell at Casterbridge. He was in this chimney-corner; and jammed close to him, so that he could not have got out if he had tried, was the executioner who'd come to take his life, singing a song about it and not knowing that it was his victim who was close by, joining in to save appearances. My brother threw a glance of agony at me, and I knew he meant, "Don't reveal what you see; my life depends on it." I was so terror-struck that I could hardly stand, and, not knowing what I did, I turned and hurried away.'

The narrator's manner and tone had the stamp of truth, and his story made a great impression on all around.

'And do you know where your brother is at the present time?' asked the magistrate.

'I do not. I have never seen him since I closed this door.'

'I can testify to that, for we've been between ye ever since,' said the constable.

'Where does he think to fly to? – what is his occupation?'

'He's a watch-and-clock-maker, sir.'

''A said 'a was a wheelwright – a wicked rogue,' said the constable.

'The wheels of clocks and watches he meant, no doubt,' said Shepherd Fennel. 'I thought his hands were palish for's trade.'

'Well, it appears to me that nothing can be gained by retaining this poor man in custody,' said the magistrate; 'your business lies with the other, unquestionably.'

And so the little man was released off-hand; but he looked nothing the less sad on that account, it being beyond the power of magistrate or constable to raze out the written troubles in his brain, for they concerned another whom he regarded with more solicitude than himself. When this was done, and the man had gone his way, the night was found to be so far advanced that it was deemed useless to renew the search before the next morning.

Next day, accordingly, the quest for the clever sheep-stealer became general and keen, to all appearance at least. But the intended punishment was cruelly disproportioned to the transgression, and the sympathy of a great many country-folk in that district was strongly on the side of the fugitive. Moreover, his marvellous coolness and daring in hob-and-nobbing with the hangman, under the unprecedented circumstances of the shepherd's party, won their admiration. So that it may be questioned if all those who ostensibly made themselves so busy in exploring woods and fields and lanes were quite so thorough when it came to the private examination of their own lofts and out-houses. Stories were afloat of a mysterious figure being occasionally seen in some old over-grown trackway or other, remote from turnpike roads; but when a search was instituted in any of these suspected quarters nobody was found. Thus the days and weeks passed without tidings.

In brief, the bass-voiced man of the chimney-corner was never recaptured. Some said that he went across the sea, others that he did not, but buried himself in the depths of a populous city. At any rate, the gentleman in cinder-grey never did his morning's work at Casterbridge, nor met anywhere at all, for business purposes, the genial comrade with whom he had passed an hour of relaxation in the lonely house on the slope of the coomb.

The grass has long been green on the graves of Shepherd Fennel and his frugal wife; the guests who made up the christening party have mainly followed their entertainers to the tomb; the baby in whose honour they all had met is a matron in the sere and yellow leaf. But the arrival of the three strangers at the shepherd's that night, and the details connected therewith, is a story as well-known as ever in the country about Higher Crowstairs.

March 1883

The Withered Arm

I. A Lorn Milkmaid

It was an eighty-cow dairy, and the troop of milkers, regular and supernumerary, were all at work; for, though the time of year was as yet but early April, the feed lay entirely in water-meadows, and the cows were 'in full pail'. The hour was about six in the evening, and three-fourths of the large, red, rectangular animals having been finished off, there was opportunity for a little conversation.

'He do bring home his bride tomorrow, I hear. They've come as far as Anglebury today.'

The voice seemed to proceed from the belly of the cow called Cherry, but the speaker was a milking-woman, whose face was buried in the flank of that motionless beast.

'Hav' anybody seen her?' said another.

There was a negative response from the first. 'Though they say she's a rosy-cheeked, tisty-tosty little body enough,' she added; and as the milkmaid spoke she turned her face so that she could glance past her cow's tail to the other side of the barton, where a thin, fading woman of thirty milked somewhat apart from the rest.

'Years younger than he, they say,' continued the second, with also a glance of reflectiveness in the same direction.

'How old do you call him, then?'

'Thirty or so.'

'More like forty,' broke in an old milkman near, in a long white pinafore or 'wropper', and with the brim of his hat tied down, so that he looked like a woman. ''A was born before our Great Weir was builded, and I hadn't man's wages when I laved water there.'

The discussion waxed so warm that the purr of the milk-streams became jerky, till a voice from another cow's belly cried with authority, 'Now then, what the Turk do it matter to us about Farmer Lodge's age, or Farmer Lodge's new mis'ess? I shall have to pay him nine pound a year for the rent of every one of these milchers, whatever his age or hers. Get on with your work, or 'twill be dark afore we have done. The evening is pinking in a'ready.' This speaker was the dairyman himself, by whom the milkmaids and men were employed.

Nothing more was said publicly about Farmer Lodge's wedding, but the first woman murmured under her cow to her next neighbour, ''Tis hard for *she*,' signifying the thin worn milkmaid aforesaid.

'O no,' said the second. 'He ha'n't spoke to Rhoda Brook for years.'

When the milking was done they washed their pails and hung them on a many-forked stand made as usual of the peeled limb of an oak-tree, set upright in the earth, and resembling a colossal antlered horn. The majority then dispersed in various directions homeward. The thin woman who had not spoken was joined by a boy of twelve or thereabout, and the twain went away up the field also.

Their course lay apart from that of the others, to a lonely spot high above the water-meads, and not far from the border of Egdon Heath, whose dark countenance was visible in the distance as they drew nigh to their home.

'They've just been saying down in barton that your father brings his young wife home from Anglebury tomorrow,' the woman observed. 'I shall want to send you for a few things to market, and you'll be pretty sure to meet 'em.'

'Yes, mother,' said the boy. 'Is father married then?'

'Yes. . . . You can give her a look, and tell me what she's like, if you do see her.'

'Yes, mother.'

'If she's dark or fair, and if she's tall – as tall as I. And if she seems like a woman who has ever worked for a living, or one that has been always well off, and has never done anything, and shows marks of the lady on her, as I expect she do.'

'Yes.'

They crept up the hill in the twilight and entered the cottage. It was built of mud-walls, the surface of which had been washed by many rains into channels and depressions that left none of the original flat face visible; while here and there in the thatch above a rafter showed like a bone protruding through the skin.

She was kneeling down in the chimney-corner, before two pieces of turf laid together with the heather inwards, blowing at the red-hot ashes with her breath till the turves flamed. The radiance lit her pale cheek, and made her dark eyes, that had once been handsome, seem handsome anew. 'Yes,' she resumed, 'see if she is dark or fair, and if you can, notice if her hands be white; if not, see if they look as though she had ever done housework, or are milker's hands like mine.'

The boy again promised, inattentively this time, his mother not observing that he was cutting a notch with his pocket-knife in the beech-backed chair.

II. The Young Wife

The road from Anglebury to Holmstoke is in general level; but there is one place where a sharp ascent breaks its monotony. Farmers homeward-bound from the former market-town, who trot all the rest of the way, walk their horses up this short incline.

The next evening while the sun was yet bright a handsome new gig, with a lemon-coloured body and red wheels, was spinning westward along the level highway at the heels of a powerful mare. The driver was a yeoman in the prime of life, cleanly shaven like an actor, his face being toned to that bluish-vermilion hue which so often graces a thriving farmer's features when returning home after successful dealings in the town. Beside him sat a woman, many years his junior – almost, indeed, a girl. Her face too was fresh in colour, but it was of a totally different quality – soft and evanescent, like the light under a heap of rose-petals.

Few people travelled this way, for it was not a main road,

and the long white riband of gravel that stretched before them was empty, save of one small scarce-moving speck, which presently resolved itself into the figure of a boy, who was creeping on at a snail's pace, and continually looking behind him – the heavy bundle he carried being some excuse for, if not the reason of, his dilatoriness. When the bouncing gig-party slowed at the bottom of the incline above mentioned, the pedestrian was only a few yards in front. Supporting the large bundle by putting one hand on his hip, he turned and looked straight at the farmer's wife as though he would read her through and through, pacing along abreast of the horse.

The low sun was full in her face, rendering every feature, shade, and contour distinct, from the curve of her little nostril to the colour of her eyes. The farmer, though he seemed annoyed at the boy's persistent presence, did not order him to get out of the way; and thus the lad preceded them, his hard gaze never leaving her, till they reached the top of the ascent, when the farmer trotted on with relief in his lineaments – having taken no outward notice of the boy whatever.

'How that poor lad stared at me!' said the young wife.

'Yes, dear; I saw that he did.'

'He is one of the village, I suppose?'

'One of the neighbourhood. I think he lives with his mother a mile or two off.'

'He knows who we are, no doubt?'

'O yes. You must expect to be stared at just at first, my pretty Gertrude.'

'I do, – though I think the poor boy may have looked at us in the hope we might relieve him of his heavy load, rather than from curiosity.'

'O no,' said her husband off-handedly. 'These country lads will carry a hundredweight once they get it on their backs; besides, his pack had more size than weight in it. Now, then, another mile and I shall be able to show you our house in the distance – if it is not too dark before we get there.' The wheels spun round, and particles flew from their periphery as before, till a white house of ample dimensions revealed itself, with farm-buildings and ricks at the back.

Meanwhile the boy had quickened his pace, and turning up
a by-lane some mile and half short of the white farmstead,
ascended towards the leaner pastures, and so on to the cottage
of his mother.

She had reached home after her day's milking at the outlying
dairy, and was washing cabbage at the doorway in the
declining light. 'Hold up the net a moment,' she said, without
preface, as the boy came up.

He flung down his bundle, held the edge of the cabbage-net,
and as she filled its meshes with the dripping leaves she went
on, 'Well, did you see her?'

'Yes; quite plain.'

'Is she ladylike?'

'Yes; and more. A lady complete.'

'Is she young?'

'Well, she's growed up, and her ways be quite a woman's.'

'Of course. What colour is her hair and face?'

'Her hair is lightish, and her face as comely as a live doll's.'

'Her eyes, then, are not dark like mine?'

'No – of a bluish turn, and her mouth is very nice and red;
and when she smiles, her teeth show white.'

'Is she tall?' said the woman sharply.

'I couldn't see. She was sitting down.'

'Then do you go to Holmstoke church tomorrow morning:
she's sure to be there. Go early and notice her walking in, and
come home and tell me if she's taller than I.'

'Very well, mother. But why don't you go and see for
yourself?'

'*I* go to see her! I wouldn't look up at her if she were to pass
my window this instant. She was with Mr Lodge, of course.
What did he say or do?'

'Just the same as usual.'

'Took no notice of you?'

'None.'

Next day the mother put a clean shirt on the boy, and started
him off for Holmstoke church. He reached the ancient little
pile when the door was just being opened and he was the first
to enter. Taking his seat by the font, he watched all the

parishioners file in. The well-to-do Farmer Lodge came nearly last, and his young wife, who accompanied him, walked up the aisle with the shyness natural to a modest woman who had appeared thus for the first time. As all other eyes were fixed upon her, the youth's stare was not noticed now.

When he reached home his mother said, 'Well?' before he had entered the room.

'She is not tall. She is rather short,' he replied.

'Ah!' said his mother, with satisfaction.

'But she's very pretty — very. In fact, she's lovely.' The youthful freshness of the yeoman's wife had evidently made an impression even on the somewhat hard nature of the boy.

'That's all I want to hear,' said his mother quickly. 'Now, spread the tablecloth. The hare you wired is very tender; but mind that nobody catches you. — You've never told me what sort of hands she had.'

'I have never seen 'em. She never took off her gloves.'

'What did she wear this morning?'

'A white bonnet and a silver-coloured gownd. It whewed and whistled so loud when it rubbed against the pews that the lady coloured up more than ever for very shame at the noise, and pulled it in to keep it from touching; but when she pushed into her seat, it whewed more than ever. Mr Lodge, he seemed pleased, and his waistcoat stuck out, and his great golden seals hung like a lord's; but she seemed to wish her noisy gownd anywhere but on her.'

'Not she! However, that will do now.'

These descriptions of the newly-married couple were continued from time to time by the boy at his mother's request, after any chance encounter he had had with them. But Rhoda Brook, though she might easily have seen young Mrs Lodge for herself by walking a couple of miles, would never attempt an excursion towards the quarter where the farmhouse lay. Neither did she, at the daily milking in the dairyman's yard on Lodge's outlying second farm, ever speak on the subject of the recent marriage. The dairyman, who rented the cows of Lodge, and knew perfectly the tall milkmaid's history, with manly kindliness always kept the gossip in the cow-barton from annoying Rhoda. But the atmosphere thereabout was full of the subject during the first days of Mrs Lodge's arrival, and from her boy's description and the casual words of the other milkers, Rhoda Brook could raise a mental image of the unconscious Mrs Lodge that was realistic as a photograph.

III. A Vision

One night, two or three weeks after the bridal return, when the boy was gone to bed, Rhoda sat a long time over the turf ashes that she had raked out in front of her to extinguish them. She contemplated so intently the new wife, as presented to her in her mind's eye over the embers, that she forgot the lapse of time. At last, wearied with her day's work, she too retired.

But the figure which had occupied her so much during this and the previous days was not to be banished at night. For the first time Gertrude Lodge visited the supplanted woman in her dreams. Rhoda Brook dreamed – since her assertion that she really saw, before falling asleep, was not to be believed – that the young wife, in the pale silk dress and white bonnet, but with features shockingly distorted, and wrinkled as by age, was sitting upon her chest as she lay. The pressure of Mrs Lodge's person grew heavier; the blue eyes peered cruelly into her face, and then the figure thrust forward its left hand mockingly, so as to make the wedding-ring it wore glitter in Rhoda's eyes. Maddened mentally, and nearly suffocated by pressure, the sleeper struggled; the incubus, still regarding her, withdrew to the foot of the bed, only, however, to come forward by degrees, resume her seat, and flash her left hand as before.

Gasping for breath, Rhoda, in a last desperate effort, swung out her right hand, seized the confronting spectre by its obtrusive left arm, and whirled it backward to the floor, starting up herself as she did so with a low cry.

'O, merciful heaven!' she cried, sitting on the edge of the bed in a cold sweat; 'that was not a dream – she was here!'

She could feel her antagonist's arm with her grasp even now – the very flesh and bone of it, as it seemed. She looked on the floor whither she had whirled the spectre, but there was nothing to be seen.

Rhoda Brook slept no more that night, and when she went milking at the next dawn they noticed how pale and haggard she looked. The milk that she drew quivered into the pail: her hand had not calmed even yet, and still retained the feel of the arm. She came home to breakfast as wearily as if it had been supper-time.

'What was that noise in your chimmer, mother, last night?' said her son. 'You fell off the bed, surely?'

'Did you hear anything fall? At what time?'

'Just when the clock struck two.'

She could not explain, and when the meal was done went silently about her household work, the boy assisting her, for he hated going afield on the farms, and she indulged his reluctance. Between eleven and twelve the garden-gate clicked, and she lifted her eyes to the window. At the bottom of the garden, within the gate, stood the woman of her vision. Rhoda seemed transfixed.

'Ah, she said she would come!' exclaimed the boy, also observing her.

'Said so – when? How does she know us?'

'I have seen and spoken to her. I talked to her yesterday.'

'I told you,' said the mother, flushing indignantly, 'never to speak to anybody in that house, or go near the place.'

'I did not speak to her till she spoke to me. And I did not go near the place. I met her in the road.'

'What did you tell her?'

'Nothing. She said, "Are you the poor boy who had to bring the heavy load from market?" And she looked at my boots, and said they would not keep my feet dry if it came on wet, because they were so cracked. I told her I lived with my mother, and we had enough to do to keep ourselves, and that's how it was; and she said then, "I'll come and bring you some better boots, and see your mother." She gives away things to other folks in the meads besides us.'

Mrs Lodge was by this time close to the door – not in her silk, as Rhoda had dreamt of in the bed-chamber, but in a morning hat, and gown of common light material, which became her better than silk. On her arm she carried a basket.

The impression remaining from the night's experience was still strong. Brook had almost expected to see the wrinkles, the scorn, and the cruelty on her visitor's face. She would have escaped an interview had escape been possible. There was, however, no backdoor to the cottage, and in an instant the boy had lifted the latch to Mrs Lodge's gentle knock.

'I see I have come to the right house,' said she, glancing at the lad, and smiling. 'But I was not sure till you opened the door.'

The figure and action were those of the phantom; but her voice was so indescribably sweet, her glance so winning, her smile so tender, so unlike that of Rhoda's midnight visitant, that the latter could hardly believe the evidence of her senses. She was truly glad that she had not hidden away in sheer aversion, as she had been inclined to do. In her basket Mrs Lodge brought the pair of boots that she had promised to the boy, and other useful articles.

At these proofs of a kindly feeling towards her and hers Rhoda's heart reproached her bitterly. This innocent young thing should have her blessing and not her curse. When she left them a light seemed gone from the dwelling. Two days later she came again to know if the boots fitted, and less than a fortnight after that paid Rhoda another call. On this occasion the boy was absent.

'I walk a good deal,' said Mrs Lodge, 'and your house is the nearest outside our own parish. I hope you are well. You don't look quite well.'

Rhoda said she was well enough, and, indeed, though the paler of the two, there was more of the strength that endures in her well-defined features and large frame than in the soft-cheeked young woman before her. The conversation became quite confidential as regarded their powers and weaknesses; and when Mrs Lodge was leaving, Rhoda said, 'I hope you will find this air agree with you, ma'am, and not suffer from the damp of the water-meads.'

The younger one replied that there was not much doubt of it, her general health being usually good. 'Though, now you remind me,' she added, 'I have one little ailment which puzzles me. It is nothing serious, but I cannot make it out.'

She uncovered her left hand and arm, and their outline confronted Rhoda's gaze as the exact original of the limb she had beheld and seized in her dream. Upon the pink round surface of the arm were faint marks of an unhealthy colour, as if produced by a rough grasp. Rhoda's eyes became riveted on the discolorations; she fancied that she discerned in them the shape of her own four fingers.

'How did it happen?' she said mechanically.

'I cannot tell,' replied Mrs Lodge, shaking her head. 'One night when I was sound asleep, dreaming I was away in some strange place, a pain suddenly shot into my arm there, and was so keen as to awaken me. I must have struck it in the daytime, I suppose, though I don't remember doing so.' She added, laughing, 'I tell my dear husband that it looks just as if he had flown into a rage and struck me there. O, I daresay it will soon disappear.'

'Ha, ha! Yes. . . . On what night did it come?'

Mrs Lodge considered, and said it would be a fortnight ago on the morrow. 'When I awoke I could not remember where I was,' she added, 'till the clock striking two reminded me.'

She had named the night and the hour of Rhoda's spectral encounter, and Brook felt like a guilty thing. The artless disclosure startled her; she did not reason on the freaks of coincidence, and all the scenery of that ghastly night returned with double vividness to her mind.

'O, can it be,' she said to herself, when her visitor had departed, 'that I exercise a malignant power over people against my own will?' She knew that she had been slily called a witch since her fall; but never having understood why that particular stigma had been attached to her, it had passed disregarded. Could this be the explanation, and had such things as this ever happened before?

IV. A Suggestion

The summer drew on, and Rhoda Brook almost dreaded to meet Mrs Lodge again, notwithstanding that her feeling for the young wife amounted wellnigh to affection. Something in her own individuality seemed to convict Rhoda of crime. Yet a fatality sometimes would direct the steps of the latter to the outskirts of Holmstoke whenever she left her house for any other purpose than her daily work, and hence it happened that their next encounter was out of doors. Rhoda could not avoid the subject which had so mystified her, and after the first few words she stammered, 'I hope your – arm is well again, ma'am?' She had perceived with consternation that Gertrude Lodge carried her left arm stiffly.

'No; it is not quite well. Indeed, it is no better at all; it is rather worse. It pains me dreadfully sometimes.'

'Perhaps you had better go to a doctor, ma'am.'

She replied that she had already seen a doctor. Her husband had insisted upon her going to one. But the surgeon had not seemed to understand the afflicted limb at all; he had told her to bathe it in hot water, and she had bathed it, but the treatment had done no good.

'Will you let me see it?' said the milkwoman.

Mrs Lodge pushed up her sleeve and disclosed the place, which was a few inches above the wrist. As soon as Rhoda Brook saw it, she could hardly preserve her composure. There was nothing of the nature of a wound, but the arm at that point had a shrivelled look, and the outline of the four fingers appeared more distinct than at the former time. Moreover, she fancied that they were imprinted in precisely the relative position of her clutch upon the arm in the trance: the first finger towards Gertrude's wrist, and the fourth towards her elbow.

What the impress resembled seemed to have struck Gertrude herself since their last meeting. 'It looks almost like finger-marks,' she said; adding with a faint laugh, 'My husband says it is as if some witch, or the devil himself, had taken hold of me there, and blasted the flesh.'

Rhoda shivered. 'That's fancy,' she said hurriedly. 'I wouldn't mind it, if I were you.'

'I shouldn't so much mind it,' said the younger, with hesitation, 'if – if I hadn't a notion that it makes my husband –

dislike me – no, love me less. Men think so much of personal appearance.'

'Some do – he for one.'

'Yes; and he was very proud of mine, at first.'

'Keep your arm covered from his sight.'

'Ah – he knows the disfigurement is there!' She tried to hide the tears that filled her eyes.

'Well, ma'am, I earnestly hope it will go away soon.'

And so the milkwoman's mind was chained anew to the subject by a horrid sort of spell as she returned home. The sense of having been guilty of an act of malignity increased, affect as she might to ridicule her superstition. In her secret heart Rhoda did not altogether object to a slight diminution of her successor's beauty, by whatever means it had come about; but she did not wish to inflict upon her physical pain. For though this pretty young woman had rendered impossible any reparation which Lodge might have made Rhoda for his past conduct, everything like resentment at the unconscious usurpation had quite passed away from the elder's mind.

If the sweet and kindly Gertrude Lodge only knew of the dream-scene in the bed-chamber, what would she think? Not to inform her of it seemed treachery in the presence of her friendliness; but tell she could not of her own accord – neither could she devise a remedy.

She mused upon the matter the greater part of the night, and the next day, after the morning milking, set out to obtain another glimpse of Gertrude Lodge if she could, being held to her by a gruesome fascination. By watching the house from a distance the milkmaid was presently able to discern the farmer's wife in a ride she was taking alone – probably to join her husband in some distant field. Mrs Lodge perceived her, and cantered in her direction.

'Good morning, Rhoda!' Gertrude said, when she had come up. 'I was going to call.'

Rhoda noticed that Mrs Lodge held the reins with some difficulty.

'I hope – the bad arm,' said Rhoda.

'They tell me there is possibly one way by which I might be

able to find out the cause, and so perhaps the cure, of it,'
replied the other anxiously. 'It is by going to some clever man
over in Egdon Heath. They did not know if he was still alive –
and I cannot remember his name at this moment; but they said
that you knew more of his movements than anybody else
hereabout, and could tell me if he were still to be consulted.
Dear me – what was his name? But you know.'

'Not Conjuror Trendle?' said her thin companion, turning
pale.

'Trendle – yes. Is he alive?'

'I believe so,' said Rhoda, with reluctance.

'Why do you call him conjuror?'

'Well – they say – they used to say he was a – he had powers
other folks have not.'

'Oh, how could my people be so superstitious as to
recommend a man of that sort! I thought they meant some
medical man. I shall think no more of him.'

Rhoda looked relieved, and Mrs Lodge rode on. The
milkwoman had inwardly seen, from the moment she heard of
her having been mentioned as a reference for this man, that
there must exist a sarcastic feeling among the workfolk that a
sorceress would know the whereabouts of the exorcist. They
suspected her, then. A short time ago this would have given no
concern to a woman of her common sense. But she had a
haunting reason to be superstitious now; and she had been
seized with sudden dread that this Conjuror Trendle might
name her as the malignant influence which was blasting the
fair person of Gertrude and so lead her friend to hate her for
ever, and to treat her as some fiend in human shape.

But all was not over. Two days after, a shadow intruded into
the window-pattern thrown on Rhoda Brook's floor by the
afternoon sun. The woman opened the door at once, almost
breathlessly.

'Are you alone?' said Gertrude. She seemed to be no less
harassed and anxious than Brook herself.

'Yes,' said Rhoda.

'The place on my arm seems worse, and troubles me!' the
young farmer's wife went on. 'It is so mysterious! I do hope it

will not be an incurable wound. I have again been thinking of what they said about Conjuror Trendle. I don't really believe in such men, but I should not mind just visiting him, for curiosity – though on no account must my husband know. Is it far to where he lives?'

'Yes – five miles,' said Rhoda backwardly. 'In the heart of Egdon.'

'Well, I should have to walk. Could not you go with me to show the way – say tomorrow afternoon?'

'O, not I – that is,' the milkwoman murmured, with a start of dismay. Again the dread seized her that something to do with her fierce act in the dream might be revealed, and her character in the eyes of the most useful friend she had ever had be ruined irretrievably.

Mrs Lodge urged, and Rhoda finally assented, though with much misgiving. Sad as the journey would be to her, she could not conscientiously stand in the way of a possible remedy for her patron's strange affliction. It was agreed that, to escape suspicion of their mystic intent, they should meet at the edge of the heath at the corner of a plantation which was visible from the spot where they now stood.

V. Conjuror Trendle

By the next afternoon Rhoda would have done anything to escape this inquiry. But she had promised to go. Moreover, there was a horrid fascination at times in becoming instrumental in throwing such possible light on her own character as would reveal her to be something greater in the occult world than she had ever herself suspected.

She started just before the time of day mentioned between them, and half-an-hour's brisk walking brought her to the south-eastern extension of the Egdon tract of country, where the fir plantation was. A slight figure, cloaked and veiled, was already there. Rhoda recognized, almost with a shudder, that Mrs Lodge bore her left arm in a sling.

They hardly spoke to each other, and immediately set out on their climb into the interior of this solemn country, which stood high above the rich alluvial soil they had left half-an-hour before. It was a long walk; thick clouds made the atmosphere dark, though it was as yet only early afternoon; and the wind howled dismally over the slopes of the heath – not improbably the same heath which had witnessed the agony of the Wessex King Ina, presented to after-ages as Lear. Gertrude Lodge talked most, Rhoda replying with mono-syllabic preoccupation. She had a strange dislike to walking on the side of her companion where hung the afflicted arm, moving round to the other when inadvertently near it. Much heather had been brushed by their feet when they descended upon a cart-track, beside which stood the house of the man they sought.

He did not profess his remedial practices openly, or care anything about their continuance, his direct interests being those of a dealer in furze, turf, 'sharp sand', and other local products. Indeed, he affected not to believe largely in his own powers, and when warts that had been shown him for cure miraculously disappeared – which it must be owned they infallibly did – he would say lightly, 'O, I only drink a glass of grog upon 'em at your expense – perhaps it's all chance,' and immediately turn the subject.

He was at home when they arrived, having in fact seen them descending into his valley. He was a grey-bearded man, with a reddish face, and he looked singularly at Rhoda the first moment he beheld her. Mrs Lodge told him her errand; and then with words of self-disparagement he examined her arm.

'Medicine can't cure it,' he said promptly. ''Tis the work of an enemy.'

Rhoda shrank into herself, and drew back.

'An enemy? What enemy?' asked Mrs Lodge.

He shook his head. 'That's best known to yourself,' he said. 'If you like, I can show the person to you, though I shall not myself know who it is. I can do no more; and don't wish to do that.'

She pressed him; on which he told Rhoda to wait outside where she stood, and took Mrs Lodge into the room. It opened immediately from the door; and, as the latter remained ajar,

Rhoda Brook could see the proceedings without taking part in them. He brought a tumbler from the dresser, nearly filled it with water, and fetching an egg, prepared it in some private way; after which he broke it on the edge of the glass, so that the white went in and the yolk remained. As it was getting gloomy, he took the glass and its contents to the window, and told Gertrude to watch the mixture closely. They leant over the table together, and the milkwoman could see the opaline hue of the egg-fluid changing form as it sank in the water, but she was not near enough to define the shape that it assumed.

'Do you catch the likeness of any face or figure as you look?' demanded the conjuror of the young woman.

She murmured a reply, in tones so low as to be inaudible to Rhoda, and continued to gaze intently into the glass. Rhoda turned, and walked a few steps away.

When Mrs Lodge came out, and her face was met by the light, it appeared exceedingly pale – as pale as Rhoda's – against the sad dun shades of the upland's garniture. Trendle shut the door behind her, and they at once started homeward together. But Rhoda perceived that her companion had quite changed.

'Did he charge much?' she asked tentatively.

'O no – nothing. He would not take a farthing,' said Gertrude.

'And what did you see?' inquired Rhoda.

'Nothing I – care to speak of.' The constraint in her manner was remarkable; her face was so rigid as to wear an oldened aspect, faintly suggestive of the face in Rhoda's bed-chamber.

'Was it you who first proposed coming here?' Mrs Lodge suddenly inquired, after a long pause. 'How very odd, if you did!'

'No. But I am not sorry we have come, all things considered,' she replied. For the first time a sense of triumph possessed her, and she did not altogether deplore that the young thing at her side should learn that their lives had been antagonized by other influences than their own.

The subject was no more alluded to during the long and dreary walk home. But in some way or other a story was whispered about the many-dairied lowland that winter that Mrs Lodge's gradual loss of the use of her left arm was owing to her being 'overlooked' by Rhoda Brook. The latter kept her own counsel about the incubus, but her face grew sadder and thinner; and in the spring she and her boy disappeared from the neighbourhood of Holmstoke.

VI. A Second Attempt

Half a dozen years passed away, and Mr and Mrs Lodge's married experience sank into prosiness, and worse. The farmer was usually gloomy and silent; the woman whom he had wooed for her grace and beauty was contorted and disfigured in the left limb; moreover, she had brought him no child, which rendered it likely that he would be the last of a family who had occupied that valley for some two hundred years. He thought of Rhoda Brook and her son; and feared this might be a judgment from heaven upon him.

The once blithe-hearted and enlightened Gertrude was changing into an irritable, superstitious woman, whose whole time was given to experimenting upon her ailment with every quack remedy she came across. She was honestly attached to her husband, and was ever secretly hoping against hope to win back his heart again by regaining some at least of her personal beauty. Hence it arose that her closet was lined with bottles, packets and ointment-pots of every description – nay, bunches of mystic herbs, charms, and books of necromancy, which in her schoolgirl time she would have ridiculed as folly.

'Damned if you won't poison yourself with these apothecary messes and witch mixtures some time or other,' said her husband, when his eyes chanced to fall upon the multitudinous array.

She did not reply, but turned her sad, soft glance upon him in such heart-swollen reproach that he looked sorry for his words, and added, 'I only meant it for your good, you know Gertrude.'

'I'll clear out the whole lot, and destroy them,' she said huskily, 'and try such remedies no more!'

'You want somebody to cheer you,' he observed. 'I once thought of adopting a boy; but he is too old now. And he is gone away I don't know where.'

She guessed to whom he alluded; for Rhoda Brook's story had in the course of years become known to her; though not a word had ever passed between her husband and herself on the subject. Neither had she ever spoken to him of her visit to Conjuror Trendle, and of what was revealed to her, or she thought was revealed to her, by that solitary heathman.

She was now five-and-twenty; but she seemed older. 'Six years of marriage, and only a few months of love,' she sometimes whispered to herself. And then she thought of the apparent cause, and said, with a tragic glance at her withering limb, 'If I could only again be as I was when he first saw me!'

She obediently destroyed her nostrums and charms; but there remained a hankering wish to try something else – some other sort of cure altogether. She had never revisited Trendle since she had been conducted to the house of the solitary by Rhoda against her will; but it now suddenly occurred to Gertrude that she would, in a last desperate effort at deliverance from this seeming curse, again seek out the man, if he yet lived. He was entitled to a certain credence, for the indistinct form he had raised in the glass had undoubtedly resembled the only woman in the world who – as she now knew, though not then – could have a reason for bearing her ill-will. The visit should be paid.

This time she went alone, though she nearly got lost on the heath, and roamed a considerable distance out of her way. Trendle's house was reached at last, however; he was not indoors, and instead of waiting at the cottage, she went to where his bent figure was pointed out to her at work a long way off. Trendle remembered her, and laying down the handful of furze-roots which he was gathering and throwing into a heap, he offered to accompany her in her homeward direction, as the distance was considerable and the days were short. So they walked together, his head bowed nearly to the earth, and his form of a colour with it.

'You can send away warts and other excrescences, I know,'

she said; 'why can't you send away this?' And the arm was uncovered.

'You think too much of my powers!' said Trendle; 'and I am old and weak now, too. No, no; it is too much for me to attempt in my own person. What have ye tried?'

She named to him some of the hundred medicaments and counter-spells which she had adopted from time to time. He shook his head.

'Some were good enough,' he said approvingly; 'but not many of them for such as this. This is of the nature of a blight, not of the nature of a wound, and if you ever do throw it off, it will be all at once.'

'If I only could!'

'There is only one chance of doing it known to me. It has never failed in kindred afflictions – that I can declare. But it is hard to carry out, and especially for a woman.'

'Tell me!' said she.

'You must touch with the limb the neck of a man who's been hanged.'

She started a little at the image he had raised.

'Before he's cold – just after he's cut down,' continued the conjuror impassively.

'How can that do good?'

'It will turn the blood and change the constitution. But, as I say, to do it is hard. You must go to the jail when there's a hanging, and wait for him when he's brought off the gallows. Lots have done it, though perhaps not such pretty women as you. I used to send dozens for skin complaints. But that was in former times. The last I sent was in '13 – near twelve years ago.'

He had no more to tell her, and, when he had put her into a straight track homeward, turned and left her, refusing all money as at first.

VII. A Ride

The communication sank deep into Gertrude's mind. Her nature was rather a timid one; and probably of all remedies that the white wizard could have suggested there was not one which would have filled her with so much aversion as this, not to speak of the immense obstacles in the way of its adoption.

Casterbridge, the county-town, was a dozen or fifteen miles off; and though in those days, when men were executed for horse-stealing, arson, and burglary, an assize seldom passed without a hanging, it was not likely that she could get access to the body of the criminal unaided. And the fear of her husband's anger made her reluctant to breathe a word of Trendle's suggestion to him or to anybody about him.

She did nothing for months, and patiently bore her disfigurement as before. But her woman's nature, craving for renewed love, through the medium of renewed beauty (she was but twenty-five), was ever stimulating her to try what, at any rate, could hardly do her any harm. 'What came by a spell will go by a spell surely,' she would say. Whenever her imagination pictured the act she shrank in terror from the possibility of it; then the words of the conjuror, 'It will turn your blood,' were seen to be capable of a scientific no less than a ghastly interpretation; the mastering desire returned, and urged her on again.

There was at this time but one county paper, and that her husband only occasionally borrowed. But old-fashioned days had old-fashioned means, and news was extensively conveyed by word of mouth from market to market, or from fair to fair, so that, whenever such an event as execution was about to take place, few within a radius of twenty miles were ignorant of the coming sight; and so far as Holmstoke was concerned, some enthusiasts had been known to walk all the way to Casterbridge and back in one day, solely to witness the spectacle. The next assizes were in March; and when Gertrude Lodge heard that they had been held, she inquired stealthily at the inn as to the result, as soon as she could find opportunity.

She was, however, too late. The time at which the sentences were to be carried out had arrived, and to make the journey and obtain admission at such short notice required at least her husband's assistance. She dared not tell him, for she had found by delicate experiment that these smouldering village beliefs made him furious if mentioned, partly because he half entertained them himself. It was therefore necessary to wait for another opportunity.

Her determination received a fillip from learning that two epileptic children had attended from this very village of Holmstoke many years before with beneficial results, though the experiment had been strongly condemned by the neighbouring clergy. April, May, June passed; and it is no overstatement to say that by the end of the last-named month Gertrude wellnigh longed for the death of a fellow-creature. Instead of her formal prayers each night, her unconscious prayer was, 'O Lord, hang some guilty or innocent person soon!'

This time she made earlier inquiries, and was altogether more systematic in her proceedings. Moreover, the season was summer, between the haymaking and the harvest, and in the leisure thus afforded him her husband had been holiday-taking away from home.

The assizes were in July, and she went to the inn as before. There was to be one execution – only one – for arson.

Her greatest problem was not how to get to Casterbridge, but what means she should adopt for obtaining admission to the jail. Though access for such purposes had formerly never been denied, the custom had fallen into desuetude; and in contemplating her possible difficulties, she was again almost driven to fall back upon her husband. But, on sounding him about the assizes, he was so uncommunicative, so more than usually cold, that she did not proceed, and decided that whatever she did she would do alone.

Fortune, obdurate hitherto, showed her unexpected favour. On the Thursday before the Saturday fixed for the execution, Lodge remarked to her that he was going away from home for another day or two on business at a fair, and that he was sorry he could not take her with him.

She exhibited on this occasion so much readiness to stay at home that he looked at her in surprise. Time had been when she would have shown deep disappointment at the loss of such a jaunt. However, he lapsed into his usual taciturnity, and on the day named left Holmstoke.

It was now her turn. She at first had thought of driving, but on reflection held that driving would not do, since it would necessitate her keeping to the turnpike-road, and so increase by tenfold the risk of her ghastly errand being found out. She decided to ride, and avoid the beaten track, notwithstanding that in her husband's stables there was no animal just at present which by any stretch of imagination could be considered a lady's mount, in spite of his promise before marriage to always keep a mare for her. He had, however, many cart-horses, fine ones of their kind; and among the rest was a serviceable creature, an equine Amazon, with a back as broad as a sofa, on which Gertrude had occasionally taken an airing when unwell. This horse she chose.

On Friday afternoon one of the men brought it round. She was dressed, and before going down looked at her shrivelled arm. 'Ah!' she said to it, 'if it had not been for you this terrible ordeal would have been saved me!'

When strapping up the bundle in which she carried a few articles of clothing, she took occasion to say to the servant, 'I take these in case I should not get back tonight from the person I am going to visit. Don't be alarmed if I am not in by ten, and close up the house as usual. I shall be at home tomorrow for certain.' She meant then to tell her husband privately; the deed accomplished was not like the deed projected. He would almost certainly forgive her.

And then the pretty palpitating Gertrude Lodge went from her husband's homestead; but though her goal was Caster-bridge she did not take the direct route thither through Stickleford. Her cunning course at first was in precisely the opposite direction. As soon as she was out of sight, however, she turned to the left, by a road which led into Egdon, and on entering the heath wheeled round, and set out in the true course, due westerly. A more private way down the county could not be imagined; and as to direction, she had merely to keep her horse's head to a point a little to the right of the sun. She knew that she would light upon a furze-cutter or cottager of some sort from time to time, from whom she might correct her bearing.

Though the date was comparatively recent, Egdon was much less fragmentary in character than now. The attempts – successful and otherwise – at cultivation on the lower slopes, which intrude and break up the original heath into small detached heaths, had not been carried far; Enclosure Acts had not taken effect, and the banks and fences which now exclude the cattle of those villagers who formerly enjoyed rights of commonage thereon, and the carts of those who had turbary privileges which kept them in firing all the year round, were not erected. Gertrude, therefore, rode along with no other obstacles than the prickly furze-bushes, the mats of heather, the white water-courses, and the natural steeps and declivities of the ground.

Her horse was sure, if heavy-footed and slow, and though a draught animal, was easy-paced; had it been otherwise, she was not a woman who could have ventured to ride over such a bit of country with a half-dead arm. It was therefore nearly eight o'clock when she drew rein to breathe her bearer on the last outlying high point of heath-land towards Casterbridge, previous to leaving Egdon for the cultivated valleys.

She halted before a pool called Rushy-pond, flanked by the ends of two hedges; a railing ran through the centre of the pond, dividing it in half. Over the railing she saw the low green country; over the green trees the roofs of the town; over the roofs a white flat façade, denoting the entrance to the county jail. On the roof of this front specks were moving about; they seemed to be workmen erecting something. Her flesh crept. She descended slowly, and was soon amid corn-fields and pastures. In another half-hour, when it was almost dark, Gertrude reached the White Hart, the first inn of the town on that side.

Little surprise was excited by her arrival; farmers' wives rode on horseback then more than they do now; though, for that matter, Mrs Lodge was not imagined to be a wife at all; the innkeeper supposed her some harum-skarum young woman who had come to attend 'hang-fair' next day. Neither her husband nor herself ever dealt in Casterbridge market, so that she was unknown. While dismounting she beheld a crowd of boys standing at the door of a harness-maker's shop just above the inn, looking inside it with deep interest.

'What is going on there?' she asked of the ostler.

'Making the rope for tomorrow.'

She throbbed responsively, and contracted her arm.

''Tis sold by the inch afterwards,' the man continued. 'I could get you a bit, miss, for nothing, if you'd like?'

She hastily repudiated any such wish, all the more from a curious creeping feeling that the condemned wretch's destiny was becoming interwoven with her own; and having engaged a room for the night, sat down to think.

Up to this time she had formed but the vaguest notions about her means of obtaining access to the prison. The words of the cunning-man returned to her mind. He had implied that she should use her beauty, impaired though it was, as a pass-key. In her inexperience she knew little about jail functionaries; she had heard of a high-sheriff and an under-sheriff, but dimly only. She knew, however, that there must be a hangman, and to the hangman she determined to apply.

VIII. A Water-Side Hermit

At this date, and for several years after, there was a hangman to almost every jail. Gertrude found, on inquiry, that the Casterbridge official dwelt in a lonely cottage by a deep slow river flowing under the cliff on which the prison buildings were situate – the stream being the self-same one, though she did not know it, which watered the Stickleford and Holmstoke meads lower down in its course.

Having changed her dress, and before she had eaten or drunk – for she could not take her ease till she had ascertained some particulars – Gertrude pursued her way by a path along the water-side to the cottage indicated. Passing thus the outskirts of the jail, she discerned on the level roof over the gateway three rectangular lines against the sky, where the specks had been moving in her distant view; she recognized what the erection was, and passed quickly on. Another hundred yards brought her to the executioner's house, which a boy pointed out. It stood close to the same stream, and was hard by a weir, the waters of which emitted a steady roar.

While she stood hesitating the door opened, and an old man came forth, shading a candle with one hand. Locking the door on the outside, he turned to a flight of wooden steps fixed against the end of the cottage, and began to ascend them, this being evidently the staircase to his bedroom. Gertrude hastened forward, but by the time she reached the foot of the ladder he was at the top. She called to him loudly enough to be heard above the roar of the weir; he looked down and said, 'What d'ye want here?'

'To speak to you a minute.'

The candlelight, such as it was, fell upon her imploring, pale, upturned face, and Davies (as the hangman was called) backed down the ladder. 'I was just going to bed,' he said. ' "Early to bed and early to rise," but I don't mind stopping a minute for such a one as you. Come into house.' He reopened the door, and preceded her to the room within.

The implements of his daily work, which was that of a jobbing gardener, stood in a corner, and seeing probably that she looked rural, he said, 'If you want me to undertake country work I can't come, for I never leave Casterbridge for gentle nor simple – not I. My real calling is officer of justice,' he added formally.

'Yes, yes! That's it. Tomorrow!'

'Ah! I thought so. Well, what's the matter about that? 'Tis no use to come here about the knot – folks do come continually, but I tell 'em one knot is as merciful as another if ye keep it under the ear. Is the unfortunate man a relation; or, I should say, perhaps' (looking at her dress) 'a person who's been in your employ?'

'No. What time is the execution?'

'The same as usual – twelve o'clock, or as soon after as the London mail-coach gets in. We always wait for that, in case of a reprieve.'

'O – a reprieve – I hope not!' she said involuntarily.

'Well, – hee, hee! – as a matter of business, so do I! But still, if ever a young fellow deserved to be let off, this one does; only just turned eighteen, and only present by chance when the rick was fired. Howsomever, there's not much risk of it, as they are obliged to make an example of him, there having been so much destruction of property that way lately.'

'I mean,' she explained, 'that I want to touch him for a charm, a cure of an affliction, by the advice of a man who has proved the virtue of the remedy.'

'O yes, miss! Now I understand. I've had such people come in past years. But it didn't strike me that you looked of a sort to require blood-turning. What's the complaint? The wrong kind for this, I'll be bound.'

'My arm.' She reluctantly showed the withered skin.

'Ah! – 'tis all a-scram!' said the hangman, examining it.

'Yes,' said she.

'Well,' he continued, with interest, 'that *is* the class o' subject, I'm bound to admit! I like the look of the wownd; it is truly as suitable for the cure as any I ever saw. 'Twas a knowing-man that sent 'ee, whoever he was.'

'You can contrive for me all that's necessary?' she said breathlessly.

'You should really have gone to the governor of the jail, and your doctor with 'ee, and given your name and address – that's how it used to be done, if I recollect. Still, perhaps, I can manage it for a trifling fee.'

'O, thank you! I would rather do it this way, as I should like it kept private.'

'Lover not to know, eh?'

'No – husband.'

'Aha! Very well. I'll get 'ee a touch of the corpse.'

'Where is it now?' she said, shuddering.

'It? – *he*, you mean; he's living yet. Just inside that little small winder up there in the glum.' He signified the jail on the cliff above.

She thought of her husband and her friends. 'Yes, of course,' she said; 'and how am I to proceed?'

He took her to the door. 'Now, do you be waiting at the little wicket in the wall, that you'll find up there in the lane, not later than one o'clock. I will open it from the inside, as I shan't come

home to dinner till he's cut down. Good-night. Be punctual;
and if you don't want anybody to know 'ee, wear a veil. Ah –
once I had such a daughter as you!'

She went away, and climbed the path above, to assure
herself that she would be able to find the wicket next day. Its
outline was soon visible to her – a narrow opening in the outer
wall of the prison precincts. The steep was so great that, having
reached the wicket, she stopped a moment to breathe; and,
looking back upon the water-side cot, saw the hangman again
ascending his outdoor staircase. He entered the loft or
chamber to which it led, and in a few minutes extinguished his
light.

The town clock struck ten, and she returned to the White
Hart as she had come.

IX. A Rencounter

It was one o'clock on Saturday. Gertrude Lodge, having been
admitted to the jail as above described, was sitting in a
waiting-room within the second gate, which stood under a
classic archway of ashlar, then comparatively modern, and
bearing the inscription, 'COVNTY JAIL; 1793'. This had been
the facade she saw from the heath the day before. Near at hand
was a passage to the roof on which the gallows stood.

The town was thronged, and the market suspended; but
Gertrude had seen scarcely a soul. Having kept her room till
the hour of the appointment, she had proceeded to the spot by
a way which avoided the open space below the cliff where the
spectators had gathered; but she could, even now, hear the
multitudinous babble of their voices, out of which rose at
intervals the hoarse croak of a single voice uttering the words,
'Last dying speech and confession!' There had been no
reprieve, and the execution was over; but the crowd still
waited to see the body taken down.

Soon the persistent woman heard a trampling overhead,
then a hand beckoned to her, and, following directions, she
went out and crossed the inner paved court beyond the
gatehouse, her knees trembling so that she could scarcely walk.

One of her arms was out of its sleeve, and only covered by her shawl.

On the spot at which she had now arrived were two trestles, and before she could think of their purpose she heard heavy feet descending stairs somewhere at her back. Turn her head she would not, or could not, and, rigid in this position, she was conscious of a rough coffin passing her shoulder, borne by four men. It was open, and in it lay the body of a young man, wearing the smockfrock of a rustic, and fustian breeches. The corpse had been thrown into the coffin so hastily that the skirt of the smockfrock was hanging over. The burden was temporarily deposited on the trestles.

By this time the young woman's state was such that a grey mist seemed to float before her eyes, on account of which, and the veil she wore, she could scarcely discern anything: it was as though she had nearly died, but was held up by a sort of galvanism.

'Now!' said a voice close at hand, and she was just conscious that the word had been addressed to her.

By a last strenuous effort she advanced, at the same time hearing persons approaching behind her. She bared her poor curst arm; and Davies, uncovering the face of the corpse, took Gertrude's hand, and held it so that her arm lay across the dead man's neck, upon a line the colour of an unripe blackberry, which surrounded it.

Gertrude shrieked: 'the turn o' the blood', predicted by the conjuror, had taken place. But at that moment a second shriek rent the air of the enclosure: it was not Gertrude's, and its effect upon her was to make her start round.

Immediately behind her stood Rhoda Brook, her face drawn, and her eyes red with weeping. Behind Rhoda stood Gertrude's own husband; his countenance lined, his eyes dim, but without a tear.

'D—n you! what are you doing here?' he said hoarsely.

'Hussy – to come between us and our child now!' cried Rhoda. 'This is the meaning of what Satan showed me in the vision! You are like her at last!' And clutching the bare arm of the younger woman, she pulled her unresistingly back against the wall. Immediately Brook had loosened her hold the fragile young Gertrude slid down against the feet of her husband. When he lifted her up she was unconscious.

The mere sight of the twain had been enough to suggest to her that the dead young man was Rhoda's son. At that time the relatives of an executed convict had the privilege of claiming the body for burial, if they chose to do so; and it was for this purpose that Lodge was awaiting the inquest with Rhoda. He had been summoned by her as soon as the young man was taken in the crime, and at different times since; and he had attended in court during the trial. This was the 'holiday' he had been indulging in of late. The two wretched parents had wished to avoid exposure; and hence had come themselves for the body, a waggon and sheet for its conveyance and covering being in waiting outside.

Gertrude's case was so serious that it was deemed advisable to call to her the surgeon who was at hand. She was taken out of the jail into the town; but she never reached home alive. Her delicate vitality, sapped perhaps by the paralyzed arm, collapsed under the double shock that followed the severe strain, physical and mental, to which she had subjected herself during the previous twenty-four hours. Her blood had been 'turned' indeed – too far. Her death took place in the town three days after.

Her husband was never seen in Casterbridge again; once only in the old market-place at Anglebury, which he had so much frequented, and very seldom in public anywhere. Burdened at first with moodiness and remorse, he eventually changed for the better, and appeared as a chastened and thoughtful man. Soon after attending the funeral of his poor young wife he took steps towards giving up the farms in Holmstoke and the adjoining parish, and, having sold every head of his stock, he went away to Port-Bredy, at the other end of the county, living there in solitary lodgings till his death two years later of a painless decline. It was then found that he had bequeathed the whole of his not inconsiderable property to a reformatory for boys, subject to the payment of a small annuity to Rhoda Brook, if she could be found to claim it.

For some time she could not be found; but eventually she reappeared in her old parish, – absolutely refusing, however, to have anything to do with the provision made for her. Her monotonous milking at the dairy was resumed, and followed for many long years, till her form became bent, and her once abundant dark hair white and worn away at the forehead – perhaps by long pressure against the cows. Here, sometimes, those who knew her experiences would stand and observe her, and wonder what sombre thoughts were beating inside that impassive, wrinkled brow, to the rhythm of the alternating milk-streams.

'Blackwood's Magazine',
January 1888

The Melancholy Hussar of the German Legion

I

Here stretch the downs, high and breezy and green, absolutely unchanged since those eventful days. A plough has never disturbed the turf, and the sod that was uppermost then is uppermost now. Here stood the camp; here are distinct traces of the banks thrown up for the horses of the cavalry, and spots where the midden-heaps lay are still to be observed. At night, when I walk across the lonely place, it is impossible to avoid hearing, amid the scourings of the wind over the grass-bents and thistles, the old trumpet and bugle calls, the rattle of the halters; to help seeing rows of spectral tents and the *impedimenta* of the soldiery. From within the canvases come guttural syllables of foreign tongues, and broken songs of the fatherland; for they were mainly regiments of the King's German Legion that slept round the tent-poles hereabouts at that time.

It was nearly ninety years ago. The British uniform of the period, with its immense epaulettes, queer cocked-hat, breeches, gaiters, ponderous cartridge-box, buckled shoes, and what not, would look strange and barbarous now. Ideas have changed; invention has followed invention. Soldiers were monumental objects then. A divinity still hedged kings here and there; and war was considered a glorious thing.

Secluded old manor-houses and hamlets lie in the ravines and hollows among these hills, where a stranger had hardly ever been seen till the King chose to take the baths yearly at the sea-side watering-place a few miles to the south; as a consequence of which battalions descended in a cloud upon the open country around. Is it necessary to add that the echoes of many characteristic tales, dating from that picturesque time, still linger about here in more or less fragmentary form, to be caught by the attentive ear? Some of them I have repeated; most of them I have forgotten; one I have never repeated, and assuredly can never forget.

Phyllis told me the story with her own lips. She was then an old lady of seventy-five, and her auditor a lad of fifteen. She enjoined silence as to her share in the incident, till she should be 'dead, buried, and forgotten'. Her life was prolonged twelve years after the day of her narration, and she has now been dead nearly twenty. The oblivion which in her modesty and humility she courted for herself has only partially fallen on her, with the unfortunate result of inflicting an injustice upon her memory; since such fragments of her story as got abroad at the time, and have been kept alive ever since, are precisely those which are most unfavourable to her character.

It all began with the arrival of the York Hussars, one of the foreign regiments above alluded to. Before that day scarcely a soul had been seen near her father's house for weeks. When a noise like the brushing skirt of a visitor was heard on the doorstep, it proved to be a scudding leaf; when a carriage seemed to be nearing the door, it was her father grinding his sickle on the stone in the garden for his favourite relaxation of trimming the box-tree borders to the plots. A sound like luggage thrown down from the coach was a gun far away at sea; and what looked like a tall man by the gate at dusk was a yew bush cut into a quaint and attenuated shape. There is no such solitude in country places now as there was in those old days.

Yet all the while King George and his Court were at his favourite sea-side resort, not more than five miles off.

The daughter's seclusion was great, but beyond the seclusion of the girl lay the seclusion of the father. If her social condition was twilight, his was darkness. Yet he enjoyed his darkness, while her twilight oppressed her. Dr Grove had been a professional man whose taste for lonely meditation over metaphysical questions had diminished his practice till it no longer paid him to keep it going; after which he had relinquished it and hired at a nominal rent the small, dilapidated, half farm, half manor-house of this obscure inland nook, to make a sufficiency of an income which in a town would have been inadequate for their maintenance. He stayed in his garden the greater part of the day, growing more and more irritable with the lapse of time, and the increasing perception that he had wasted his life in the pursuit of illusions. He saw his friends less and less frequently. Phyllis became so shy that if she met a stranger anywhere in her short rambles she felt ashamed at his gaze, walked awkwardly, and blushed to her shoulders.

Yet Phyllis was discovered even here by an admirer, and her hand most unexpectedly asked in marriage.

The King, as aforesaid, was at the neighbouring town, where he had taken up his abode at Gloucester Lodge; and his presence in the town naturally brought many county people thither. Among these idlers – many of whom professed to have connections and interests with the Court – was one Humphrey Gould, a bachelor; a personage neither young nor old; neither good-looking nor positively plain. Too steady-going to be 'a buck' (as fast and unmarried men were then called), he was an approximately fashionable man of a mild type. This bachelor of thirty found his way to the village on the down: beheld Phyllis; made her father's acquaintance in order to make hers; and by some means or other she sufficiently inflamed his heart to lead him in that direction almost daily; till he became engaged to marry her.

As he was of an old local family, some of whose members were held in respect in the county, Phyllis, in bringing him to her feet, had accomplished what was considered a brilliant move for one in her constrained position. How she had done it was not quite known to Phyllis herself. In those days unequal marriages were regarded rather as a violation of the laws of nature than as a mere infringement of convention, the more modern view, and hence when Phyllis, of the watering-place *bourgeoisie*, was chosen by such a gentlemanly fellow, it was as if she were going to be taken to heaven, though perhaps the uninformed would have seen no great difference in the respective positions of the pair, the said Gould being as poor as a crow.

This pecuniary condition was his excuse – probably a true one – for postponing their union, and as the winter drew nearer, and the King departed for the season, Mr Humphrey Gould set out for Bath, promising to return to Phyllis in a few weeks. The winter arrived, the date of his promise passed, yet Gould postponed his coming, on the ground that he could not very easily leave his father in the city of their sojourn, the elder having no other relative near him. Phyllis, though lonely in the extreme, was content. The man who had asked her in marriage was a desirable husband for her in many ways; her father highly approved of his suit; but this neglect of her was awkward, if not painful, for Phyllis. Love him in the true sense of the word she assured me she never did, but she had a genuine regard for him; admired a certain methodical and dogged way in which he sometimes took his pleasure; valued his knowledge of what the Court was doing, had done, or was about to do; and she was not without a feeling of pride that he had chosen her when he might have exercised a more ambitious choice.

But he did not come; and the spring developed. His letters were regular though formal; and it is not to be wondered that the uncertainty of her position, linked with the fact that there was not much passion in her thoughts of Humphrey, bred an indescribable dreariness in the heart of Phyllis Grove. The spring was soon summer, and the summer brought the King; but still no Humphrey Gould. All this while the engagement by letter was maintained intact.

At this point of time a golden radiance flashed in upon the lives of people here, and charged all youthful thought with emotional interest. This radiance was the aforesaid York Hussars.

II

The present generation has probably but a very dim notion of the celebrated York Hussars of ninety years ago. They were one of the regiments of the King's German Legion, and (though they somewhat degenerated later on) their brilliant uniform, their splendid horses, and above all, their foreign air and mustachios (rare appendages then), drew crowds of admirers of both sexes wherever they went. These with other regiments had come to encamp on the downs and pastures, because of the presence of the King in the neighbouring town.

The spot was high and airy, and the view extensive, commanding Portland – the Isle of Slingers – in front, and reaching to St Aldhelm's Head eastward, and almost to the Start on the west.

Phyllis, though not precisely a girl of the village, was as interested as any of them in this military investment. Her father's home stood somewhat apart, and on the highest point of ground to which the lane ascended, so that it was almost level with the top of the church tower in the lower part of the parish. Immediately from the outside of the garden-wall the grass spread away to a great distance, and it was crossed by a path which came close to the wall. Ever since her childhood it had been Phyllis's pleasure to clamber up this fence and sit on the top – a feat not so difficult as it may seem, the walls in this district being built of rubble, without mortar, so that there were plenty of crevices for small toes.

She was sitting up here one day, listlessly surveying the pasture without, when her attention was arrested by a solitary figure walking along the path. It was one of the renowned German Hussars, and he moved onward with his eyes on the ground, and with the manner of one who wished to escape company. His head would probably have been bent like his eyes but for his stiff neck-gear. On nearer view she perceived that his face was marked with deep sadness. Without observing her, he advanced by the footpath till it brought him almost immediately under the wall.

Phyllis was much surprised to see a fine, tall soldier in such a mood as this. Her theory of the military, and of the York Hussars in particular (derived entirely from hearsay, for she had never talked to a soldier in her life), was that their hearts were as gay as their accoutrements.

At this moment the Hussar lifted his eyes and noticed her on her perch, the white muslin neckerchief which covered her shoulders and neck where left bare by her low gown, and her white raiment in general, showing conspicuously in the bright sunlight of this summer day. He blushed a little at the suddenness of the encounter, and without halting a moment from his pace passed on.

All that day the foreigner's face haunted Phyllis; its aspect was so striking, so handsome, and his eyes were so blue, and sad, and abstracted. It was perhaps only natural that on some following day at the same hour she should look over that wall again, and wait till he had passed a second time. On this occasion he was reading a letter, and at the sight of her his manner was that of one who had half expected or hoped to discover her. He almost stopped, smiled, and made a courteous salute. The end of the meeting was that they exchanged a few words. She asked him what he was reading, and he readily informed her that he was re-perusing letters from his mother in Germany; he did not get them often, he said, and was forced to read the old ones a great many times. This was all that passed at the present interview, but others of the same kind followed.

Phyllis used to say that his English, though not good, was quite intelligible to her, so that their acquaintance was never hindered by difficulties of speech. Whenever the subject became too delicate, subtle, or tender, for such words of English as were at his command, the eyes no doubt helped out the tongue, and – though this was later on – the lips helped out the eyes. In short, this acquaintance, unguardedly made, and rash enough on her part, developed and ripened. Like Desdemona, she pitied him, and learnt his history.

His name was Matthäus Tina, and Saarbrück his native town, where his mother was still living. His age was twenty-two, and he had already risen to the grade of corporal, though he had not long been in the army. Phyllis used to assert that no such refined or well-educated young man could have been found in the ranks of the purely English regiments, some of these foreign soldiers having rather the graceful manner and presence of our native officers than of our rank and file.

She by degrees learnt from her foreign friend a circumstance about himself and his comrades which Phyllis would least have expected from the York Hussars. So far from being as gay as its uniform, the regiment was pervaded by a dreadful melancholy, a chronic home-sickness, which depressed many of the men to such an extent that they could hardly attend to their drill. The worst sufferers were the younger soldiers who had not been over here long. They hated England and English life; they took no interest whatever in King George and his island kingdom, and they only wished to be out of it and never to see it any more. Their bodies were here, but their hearts and minds were always far away in their dear fatherland, of which – brave men and stoical as they were in many ways – they would speak with tears in their eyes. One of the worst of the sufferers from his home-woe, as he called it in his own tongue, was Matthäus Tina, whose dreamy musing nature felt the gloom of exile still more intensely from the fact that he had left a lonely mother at home with nobody to cheer her.

Though Phyllis, touched by all this, and interested in his history, did not disdain her soldier's acquaintance, she declined (according to her own account, at least) to permit the young man to overstep the line of mere friendship for a long while – as long, indeed, as she considered herself likely to become the possession of another; though it is probable that she had lost her heart to Matthäus before she was herself aware. The stone wall of necessity made anything like intimacy difficult; and he had never ventured to come, or to ask to come, inside the garden, so that all their conversation had been overtly conducted across this boundary.

III

But news reached the village from a friend of Phyllis's father concerning Mr Humphrey Gould, her remarkably cool and patient betrothed. This gentleman had been heard to say in Bath that he considered his overtures to Miss Phyllis Grove to have reached only the stage of a half-understanding; and in view of his enforced absence on his father's account, who was too great an invalid now to attend to his affairs, he thought it best that there should be no definite promise as yet on either side. He was not sure, indeed, that he might not cast his eyes elsewhere.

This account – though only a piece of hearsay, and as such entitled to no absolute credit – tallied so well with the infrequency of his letters and their lack of warmth, that Phyllis did not doubt its truth for one moment; and from that hour she felt herself free to bestow her heart as she should choose. Not so her father; he declared the whole story to be a fabrication. He had known Mr Gould's family from his boyhood; and if there was one proverb which expressed the matrimonial aspect of that family well, it was 'Love me little, love me long'. Humphrey was an honourable man, who would not think of treating his engagement so lightly. 'Do you wait in patience,' he said; 'all will be right enough in time.'

From these words Phyllis at first imagined that her father was in correspondence with Mr Gould; and her heart sank within her; for in spite of her original intentions she had been relieved to hear that her engagement had come to nothing. But she presently learnt that her father had heard no more of Humphrey Gould than she herself had done; while he would not write and address her affianced directly on the subject, lest it should be deemed an imputation on that bachelor's honour.

'You want an excuse for encouraging one or other of those foreign fellows to flatter you with his unmeaning attentions,' her father exclaimed, his mood having of late been a very unkind one towards her. 'I see more than I say. Don't you ever set foot outside that garden-fence without my permission. If you want to see the camp I'll take you myself some Sunday afternoon.'

Phyllis had not the smallest intention of disobeying him in her actions, but she assumed herself to be independent with respect to her feelings. She no longer checked her fancy for the Hussar, though she was far from regarding him as her lover in the serious sense in which an Englishman might have been regarded as such. The young foreign soldier was almost an ideal being to her, with none of the appurtenances of an ordinary house-dweller; one who had descended she knew not whence, and would disappear she knew not whither; the subject of a fascinating dream – no more.

They met continually now – mostly at dusk – during the brief interval between the going down of the sun and the minute at which the last trumpet-call summoned him to his tent. Perhaps her manner had become less restrained latterly; at any rate that of the Hussar was so; he had grown more tender every day, and at parting after these hurried interviews she reached down her hand from the top of the wall that he might press it. One evening he held it such a while that she exclaimed, 'The wall is white, and somebody in the field may see your shape against it!'

He lingered so long that night that it was with the greatest difficulty that he could run across the intervening stretch of ground and enter the camp in time. On the next occasion of his awaiting her she did not appear in her usual place at the usual hour. His disappointment was unspeakably keen; he remained staring blankly at the spot, like a man in a trance. The trumpets and tattoo sounded, and still he did not go.

She had been delayed purely by an accident. When she arrived she was anxious because of the lateness of the hour, having heard as well as he the sounds denoting the closing of the camp. She implored him to leave immediately.

'No,' he said gloomily. 'I shall not go in yet – the moment you come – I have thought of your coming all day.'

'But you may be disgraced at being after time?'

'I don't mind that. I should have disappeared from the world some time ago if it had not been for two persons – my beloved, here, and my mother in Saarbrück. I hate the army. I care more for a minute of your company than for all the promotion in the world.'

Thus he stayed and talked to her, and told her interesting details of his native place, and incidents of his childhood, till she was in a simmer of distress at his recklessness in remaining. It was only because she insisted on bidding him good-night, and leaving the wall, that he returned to his quarters.

The next time that she saw him he was without the stripes that had adorned his sleeve. He had been broken to the level of private for his lateness that night; and as Phyllis considered herself to be the cause of his disgrace her sorrow was great.

But the position was now reversed; it was his turn to cheer her.

'Don't grieve, meine Liebliche!' he said. 'I have got a remedy for whatever comes. First, even supposing I regain my stripes, would your father allow you to marry a non-commissioned officer in the York Hussars?'

She flushed. This practical step had not been in her mind in relation to such an unrealistic person as he was; and a moment's reflection was enough for it. 'My father would not — certainly would not,' she answered unflinchingly. 'It cannot be thought of! My dear friend, please do forget me: I fear I am ruining you and your prospects!'

'Not at all!' said he. 'You are giving this country of yours just sufficient interest to me to make me care to keep alive in it. If my dear land were here also, and my old parent, with you, I could be happy as I am, and would do my best as a soldier. But it is not so. And now listen. This is my plan. That you go with me to my own country, and be my wife there, and live there with my mother and me. I am not a Hanoverian, as you know, though I entered the army as such; my country is by the Saar, and is at peace with France, and if I were once in it I should be free.'

'But how get there?' she asked. Phyllis had been rather amazed than shocked at his proposition. Her position in her father's house was growing irksome and painful in the extreme; his parental affection seemed to be quite dried up. She was not a native of the village, like all the joyous girls around her; and in some way Matthäus Tina had infected her with his own passionate longing for his country, and mother, and home.

'But how?' she repeated, finding that he did not answer. 'Will you buy your discharge?'

'Ah, no,' he said. 'That's impossible in these times. No; I came here against my will; why should I not escape? Now is the time, as we shall soon be striking camp, and I might see you no more. This is my scheme. I will ask you to meet me on the highway two miles off, on some calm night next week that may be appointed. There will be nothing unbecoming in it, or to cause you shame; you will not fly alone with me, for I will bring with me my devoted young friend, Christoph, an Alsatian, who has lately joined the regiment, and who has agreed to assist in this enterprise. We shall have come from yonder harbour, where we shall have examined the boats, and found one suited to our purpose. Christoph has already a chart of the Channel, and we will then go to the harbour, and at midnight cut the boat from her moorings, and row away round the point out of sight; and by the next morning we are on the coast of France, near Cherbourg. The rest is easy, for I have saved money for the land journey, and can get a change of clothes. I will write to my mother, who will meet us on the way.'

He added details in reply to her inquiries, which left no doubt in Phyllis's mind of the feasibility of the undertaking. But its magnitude almost appalled her; and it is questionable if she would ever have gone further in the wild adventure if, on entering the house that night, her father had not accosted her in the most significant terms.

'How about the York Hussars?' he said.

'They are still at the camp; but they are soon going away, I believe.'

'It is useless for you to attempt to cloak your actions in that way. You have been meeting one of those fellows; you have been seen walking with him – foreign barbarians, not much better than the French themselves! I have made up my mind – don't speak a word till I have done, please! – I have made up my mind that you shall stay here no longer while they are on the spot. You shall go to your aunt's.'

It was useless for her to protest that she had never taken a walk with any soldier or man under the sun except himself. Her protestations were feeble, too, for though he was not literally correct in his assertion, he was virtually only half in error.

The house of her father's sister was a prison to Phyllis. She had quite recently undergone experience of its gloom; and when her father went on to direct her to pack what would be necessary for her to take, her heart died within her. In afteryears she never attempted to excuse her conduct during this week of agitation; but the result of her self-communing was that she decided to join in the scheme of her lover and his friend, and fly to the country which he had coloured with such lovely hues in her imagination. She always said that the one feature in his proposal which overcame her hesitation was the obvious purity and straightforwardness of his intentions. He showed himself to be so virtuous and kind; he treated her with a respect to which she had never before been accustomed; and she was braced to the obvious risks of the voyage by her confidence in him.

IV

It was on a soft, dark evening of the following week that they engaged in the adventure. Tina was to meet her at a point in the highway at which the lane to the village branched off. Christoph was to go ahead of them to the harbour where the boat lay, row it round the Nothe – or Look-out as it was called in those days – and pick them up on the other side of the promontory, which they were to reach by crossing the harbour-bridge on foot, and climbing over the Look-out hill.

As soon as her father had ascended to his room she left the house, and, bundle in hand, proceeded at a trot along the lane. At such an hour not a soul was afoot anywhere in the village, and she reached the junction of the lane with the highway unobserved. Here she took up her position in the obscurity formed by the angle of a fence, whence she could discern every one who approached along the turnpike-road, without being herself seen.

She had not remained thus waiting for her lover longer than a minute – though from the tension of her nerves the lapse of even that short time was trying – when, instead of the expected footsteps, the stage-coach could be heard descending the hill. She knew that Tina would not show himself till the road was clear, and waited impatiently for the coach to pass. Nearing the corner where she was it slackened speed, and, instead of going by as usual, drew up within a few yards of her. A passenger alighted, and she heard his voice. It was Humphrey Gould's.

He had brought a friend with him, and luggage. The luggage was deposited on the grass, and the coach went on its route to the royal watering-place.

'I wonder where that young man is with the horse and trap?' said her former admirer to his companion. 'I hope we shan't have to wait here long. I told him half-past nine o'clock precisely.'

'Have you got her present safe?'

'Phyllis's? O, yes. It is in this trunk. I hope it will please her.'

'Of course it will. What woman would not be pleased with such a handsome peace-offering?'

'Well – she deserves it. I've treated her rather badly. But she has been in my mind these last two days much more than I should care to confess to everybody. Ah, well; I'll say no more about that. It cannot be that she is so bad as they make out. I am quite sure that a girl of her good wit would know better than to get entangled with any of those Hanoverian soldiers. I won't believe it of her, and there's an end on't.'

More words in the same strain were casually dropped as the two men waited; words which revealed to her, as by a sudden illumination, the enormity of her conduct. The conversation was at length cut off by the arrival of the man with the vehicle. The luggage was placed in it, and they mounted, and were driven on in the direction from which she had just come.

Phyllis was so conscience-stricken that she was at first inclined to follow them; but a moment's reflection led her to feel that it would only be bare justice to Matthäus to wait till he arrived, and explain candidly that she had changed her mind – difficult as the struggle would be when she stood face to face with him. She bitterly reproached herself for having believed reports which represented Humphrey Gould as false to his engagement, when, from what she now heard from his own lips, she gathered that he had been living full of trust in her. But she knew well enough who had won her love. Without him her life seemed a dreary prospect, yet the more she looked at his proposal the more she feared to accept it – so wild as it was, so vague, so venturesome. She had promised Humphrey Gould, and it was only his assumed faithlessness which had led her to treat that promise as nought. His solicitude in bringing her these gifts touched her; her promise must be kept, and esteem must take the place of love. She would preserve her selfrespect. She would stay at home, and marry him, and suffer.

Phyllis had thus braced herself to an exceptional fortitude when, a few minutes later, the outline of Matthäus Tina appeared behind a field-gate, over which he lightly leapt as she stepped forward. There was no evading it, he pressed her to his breast.

'It is the first and last time!' she wildly thought as she stood encircled by his arms.

How Phyllis got through the terrible ordeal of that night she could never clearly recollect. She always attributed her success in carrying out her resolve to her lover's honour, for as soon as she declared to him in feeble words that she had changed her mind, and felt that she could not, dared not, fly with him, he forbore to urge her, grieved as he was at her decision. Unscrupulous pressure on his part, seeing how romantically she had become attached to him, would no doubt have turned the balance in his favour. But he did nothing to tempt her unduly or unfairly.

On her side, fearing for his safety, she begged him to remain. This, he declared, could not be. 'I cannot break faith with my friend,' said he. Had he stood alone he would have abandoned his plan. But Christoph, with the boat and compass and chart, was waiting on the shore; the tide would soon turn; his mother had been warned of his coming; go he must.

Many precious minutes were lost while he tarried, unable to tear himself away. Phyllis held to her resolve, though it cost her many a bitter pang. At last they parted, and he went down the hill. Before his footsteps had quite died away she felt a desire to behold at least his outline once more, and running noiselessly after him regained view of his diminishing figure. For one moment she was sufficiently excited to be on the point of rushing forward and linking her fate with his. But she could not. The courage which at the critical instant failed Cleopatra of Egypt could scarcely be expected of Phyllis Grove.

A dark shape, similar to his own, joined him in the highway.

It was Christoph, his friend. She could see no more; they had hastened on in the direction of the town and harbour, four miles ahead. With a feeling akin to despair she turned and slowly pursued her way homeward.

Tattoo sounded in the camp; but there was no camp for her now. It was as dead as the camp of the Assyrians after the passage of the Destroying Angel.

She noiselessly entered the house, seeing nobody, and went to bed. Grief, which kept her awake at first, ultimately wrapped her in a heavy sleep. The next morning her father met her at the foot of the stairs.

'Mr Gould is come!' he said triumphantly.

Humphrey was staying at the inn, and had already called to inquire for her. He had brought her a present of a very handsome looking-glass in a frame of *repoussé* silverwork, which her father held in his hand. He had promised to call again in the course of an hour, to ask Phyllis to walk with him.

Pretty mirrors were rarer in country-houses at that day than they are now, and the one before her won Phyllis's admiration. She looked into it, saw how heavy her eyes were, and endeavoured to brighten them. She was in that wretched state of mind which leads a woman to move mechanically onward in what she conceives to be her allotted path. Mr Humphrey had, in his undemonstrative way, been adhering all along to the old understanding; it was for her to do the same, and to say not a word of her own lapse. She put on her bonnet and tippet, and when he arrived at the hour named she was at the door awaiting him.

V

Phyllis thanked him for his beautiful gift; but the talking was soon entirely on Humphrey's side as they walked along. He told her of the latest movements of the world of fashion – a subject which she willingly discussed to the exclusion of anything more personal – and his measured language helped to still her disquieted heart and brain. Had not her own sadness been what it was she must have observed his embarrassment. At last he abruptly changed the subject.

'I am glad you are pleased with my little present,' he said. 'The truth is that I brought it to propitiate 'ee, and to get you to help me out of a mighty difficulty.'

It was inconceivable to Phyllis that this independent bachelor – whom she admired in some respects – could have a difficulty.

'Phyllis – I'll tell you my secret at once; for I have a monstrous secret to confide before I can ask your counsel. The case is, then, that I am married: yes, I have privately married a dear young belle; and if you knew her, and I hope you will, you would say everything in her praise. But she is not quite the one that my father would have chose for me – you know the paternal idea as well as I – and I have kept it secret. There will be a terrible noise, no doubt; but I think that with your help I may get over it. If you would only do me this good turn – when I have told my father, I mean – say that you never could have married me, you know, or something of that sort – 'pon my life it will help to smooth the way vastly. I am so anxious to win him round to my point of view, and not to cause any estrangement.'

What Phyllis replied she scarcely knew, or how she counselled him as to his unexpected situation. Yet the relief that his announcement brought her was perceptible. To have confided her trouble in return was what her aching heart longed to do; and had Humphrey been a woman she would instantly have poured out her tale. But to him she feared to confess; and there was a real reason for silence, till a sufficient time had elapsed to allow her lover and his comrade to get out of harm's way.

As soon as she reached home again she sought a solitary place, and spent the time in half regretting that she had not gone away, and in dreaming over the meetings with Matthäus Tina from their beginning to their end. In his own country, amongst his own countrywomen, he would possibly soon forget her, even to her very name.

Her listlessness was such that she did not go out of the house for several days. There came a morning which broke in fog and mist, behind which the dawn could be discerned in greenish grey; and the outlines of the tents, and the rows of horses at the ropes. The smoke from the canteen fires drooped heavily.

The spot at the bottom of the garden where she had been accustomed to climb the wall to meet Matthäus was the only inch of English ground in which she took any interest; and in spite of the disagreeable haze prevailing she walked out there till she reached the well-known corner. Every blade of grass was weighted with little liquid globes, and slugs and snails had crept out upon the plots. She could hear the usual faint noises from the camp, and in the other direction the trot of farmers on the road to the town, for it was market-day. She observed that her frequent visits to this corner had quite trodden down the grass in the angle of the wall, and left marks of garden soil on the stepping-stones by which she had mounted to look over the top. Seldom having gone there till dusk, she had not considered that her traces might be visible by day. Perhaps it was these which had revealed her trysts to her father.

While she paused in melancholy regard, she fancied that the customary sounds from the tents were changing their character. Indifferent as Phyllis was to camp doings now, she mounted by the steps to the old place. What she beheld at first awed and perplexed her; then she stood rigid, her fingers hooked to the wall, her eyes staring out of her head, and her face as if hardened to stone.

On the open green stretching before her all the regiments in the camp were drawn up in line, in the mid-front of which two empty coffins lay on the ground. The unwonted sounds which she had noticed came from an advancing procession. It consisted of the band of the York Hussars playing a dead march; next two soldiers of that regiment in a mourning coach, guarded on each side, and accompanied by two priests. Behind came a crowd of rustics who had been attracted by the event. The melancholy procession marched along the front of the line, returned to the centre, and halted beside the coffins, where the two condemned men were blindfolded, and each placed kneeling on his coffin; a few minutes' pause was now given while they prayed.

A firing-party of twenty-four men stood ready with levelled carbines. The commanding officer, who had his sword drawn, waved it through some cuts of the sword-exercise till he reached the downward stroke, whereat the firing-party discharged their volley. The two victims fell, one upon his face across his coffin, the other backwards.

As the volley resounded there arose a shriek from the wall of Dr Grove's garden, and some one fell down inside; but nobody among the spectators without noticed it at the time. The two executed Hussars were Matthäus Tina and his friend Christoph. The soldiers on guard placed the bodies in the coffins almost instantly; but the colonel of the regiment, an Englishman, rode up and exclaimed in a stern voice: 'Turn them out – as an example to the men!'

The coffins were lifted endwise, and the dead Germans flung out upon their faces on the grass. Then all the regiments wheeled in sections, and marched past the spot in slow time. When the survey was over the corpses were again coffined, and borne away.

Meanwhile Dr Grove, attracted by the noise of the volley, had rushed out into his garden, where he saw his wretched daughter lying motionless against the wall. She was taken indoors, but it was long before she recovered consciousness; and for weeks they despaired for her reason.

It transpired that the luckless deserters from the York Hussars had cut the boat from her moorings in the adjacent harbour, according to their plan, and with two other comrades who were smarting under ill-treatment from their colonel, had sailed in safety across the Channel. But mistaking their bearings they steered into Jersey, thinking that island the French coast. Here they were perceived to be deserters, and delivered up to the authorities. Matthäus and Christoph interceded for the other two at the court-martial, saying that it was entirely by the former's representations that these were induced to go. Their sentence was accordingly commuted to flogging, the death punishment being reserved for their leaders.

The visitor to the well-known old Georgian watering-place

who may care to ramble to the neighbouring village under the hills and examine the register of burials, will there find two entries in these words: —

'Matth: Tina (Corpl) in His Majesty's Regmt of York Hussars, and Shot for Desertion, was Buried 30 June 1801, aged 22 years. Born in the town of Sarrbruk, Germany.

'Christoph Bless, belonging to His Majesty's Regmt of York Hussars, who was Shot for Desertion, was Buried 30 June 1801, aged 22 years. Born at Lothaargen, Alsatia.'

Their graves were dug at the back of the little church, near the wall. There is no memorial to mark the spot, but Phyllis pointed it out to me. While she lived she used to keep their mounds neat; but now they are overgrown with nettles, and sunk nearly flat. The older villagers, however, who know of the episode from their parents, still recollect the place where the soldiers lie. Phyllis lies near.

October 1889

Dame the Third
The Marchioness of Stonehenge

In Hardy's book of short stories, 'A Group of Noble Dames', members of the Wessex Field and Antiquarian Club tell stories of noble ladies of the past.

The rural dean thought that such cases as that related by the surgeon were rather an illustration of passion electrified back to life than of a latent, true affection. The story had suggested that he should try to recount to them one which he had used to hear in his youth, and which afforded an instance of the latter and better kind of feeling, his heroine being also a lady who had married beneath her, though he feared his narrative would be of a much slighter kind than the surgeon's. The Club begged him to proceed, and the parson began.

I would have you know, then, that a great many years ago there lived in a classical mansion with which I used to be familiar, standing not a hundred miles from the city of Melchester, a lady whose personal charms were so rare and unparalleled that she was courted, flattered, and spoilt by almost all the young noblemen and gentlemen in that part of Wessex. For a time these attentions pleased her well. But as, in the words of good Robert South (whose sermons might be read much more than they are), the most passionate lover of sport, if tied to follow his hawks and hounds every day of his life, would find the pursuit the greatest torment and calamity, and would fly to the mines and galleys for his recreation, so did this lofty and beautiful lady after a while become satiated with the constant iteration of what she had in its novelty enjoyed; and by an almost natural revulsion turned her regards absolutely netherward, socially speaking. She perversely and passionately centred her affection on quite a plain-looking young man of humble birth and no position at all; though it is true that he was gentle and delicate in nature, of good address, and guileless heart. In short, he was the parish-clerk's son, acting as assistant to the land-steward for her father the Earl of Avon, with the hope of becoming some day a land-steward himself. It should be said that perhaps the Lady Caroline (as she was called) was a little stimulated in this passion by the discovery that a young girl of the village already loved the young man fondly, and that he had paid some attentions to her, though merely of a casual and good-natured kind.

Since his occupation brought him frequently to the manor-house and its environs, Lady Caroline could make ample opportunities of seeing and speaking to him. She had, in Chaucer's phrase, 'all the craft of fine loving' at her fingers' ends, and the young man, being of a readily-kindling heart, was quick to notice the tenderness in her eyes and voice. He could not at first believe in his good fortune, having no understanding of her weariness of more artificial men; but a time comes when the stupidest sees in an eye the glance of his other half; and it came to him, who was quite the reverse of dull. As he gained confidence accidental encounters led to encounters by design; till at length when they were alone together there was no reserve on the matter. They whispered tender words as other lovers do, and were as devoted a pair as ever was seen. But not a ray or symptom of this attachment was allowed to show itself to the outer world.

Now, as she became less and less scrupulous towards him under the influence of her affection, and he became more and more reverential under the influence of his, and they looked the situation in the face together, their condition seemed intolerable in its hopelessness. That she could ever ask to be allowed to marry him, or could hold her tongue and quietly renounce him, was equally beyond conception. They resolved upon a third course, possessing neither of the disadvantages of these two: to wed secretly, and live on in outward appearance the same as before. In this they differed from the lovers of my friend's story.

Not a soul in the parental mansion guessed, when Lady Caroline came coolly into the hall one day after a visit to her aunt, that, during the visit, her lover and herself had found an opportunity of uniting themselves till death should part them.

Yet such was the fact; the young woman who rode fine horses, and drove in pony-chaises, and was saluted deferentially by every one, and the young man who trudged about, and directed the tree-felling, and the laying out of fish-ponds in the park, were husband and wife.

As they had planned, so they acted to the letter for the space of a month and more, clandestinely meeting when and where they best could do so; both being supremely happy and content. To be sure, towards the latter part of that month, when the first wild warmth of her love had gone off, the Lady Caroline sometimes wondered within herself how she, who might have chosen a peer of the realm, baronet, knight; or, if serious-minded, a bishop or judge of the more gallant sort who prefer young wives, could have brought herself to do a thing so rash as to make this marriage; particularly when, in their private meetings, she perceived that though her young husband was full of ideas, and fairly well read, they had not a single social experience in common. It was his custom to visit her after nightfall, in her own house, when he could find no opportunity for an interview elsewhere; and to further this course she would contrive to leave unfastened a window on the ground-floor overlooking the lawn, by entering which a back staircase was accessible; so that he could climb up to her apartments, and gain audience of his lady when the house was still.

One dark midnight, when he had not been able to see her during the day, he made use of this secret method, as he had done many times before; and when they had remained in company about an hour he declared that it was time for him to descend.

He would have stayed longer but that the interview had been a somewhat painful one. What she had said to him that night had much excited and angered him, for it had revealed a change in her; cold reason had come to his lofty wife; she was beginning to have more anxiety about her own position and prospects than ardour for him. Whether from the agitation of this perception or not, he was seized with a spasm; he gasped, rose, and in moving towards the window for air he uttered in a short thick whisper, 'O, my heart!'

With his hand upon his chest he sank down to the floor before he had gone another step. By the time that she had relighted the candle, which had been extinguished in case any eye in the opposite grounds should witness his egress, she found that his poor heart had ceased to beat; and there rushed upon her mind what his cottage-friends had once told her, that he was liable to attacks of heart-failure, one of which, the doctor had informed them, might some day carry him off.

Accustomed as she was to doctoring the other parishioners, nothing that she could effect upon him in that kind made any difference whatever; and his stillness, and the increasing coldness of his feet and hands, disclosed too surely to the affrighted young woman that her husband was dead indeed. For more than an hour, however, she did not abandon her efforts to restore him; when she fully realized the fact that he was a corpse she bent over his body, distracted and bewildered as to what step she next should take.

Her first feelings had undoubtedly been those of passionate grief at the loss of him; her second thoughts were concern at her own position as the daughter of an earl. 'O, why, why, my unfortunate husband, did you die in my chamber at this hour!' she said piteously to the corpse. 'Why not have died in your own cottage if you would die! Then nobody would ever have known of our imprudent union, and no syllable would have been breathed of how I mismated myself for love of you!'

The clock in the courtyard striking the solitary hour of one aroused Lady Caroline from the stupor into which she had fallen, and she stood up, and went towards the door. To awaken and tell her mother seemed her only way out of this terrible situation; yet when she put her hand on the key to unlock it she withdrew herself again. It would be impossible to call even her mother's assistance without risking a revelation to all the world through the servants; while if she could remove the body unassisted to a distance she might avert suspicion of her union even now. This thought of immunity from the social consequences of her rash act, of renewed freedom, was indubitably a relief to her, for, as has been said, the constraint and riskiness of her position had begun to tell upon the Lady Caroline's nerves.

She braced herself for the effort, and hastily dressed herself, and then dressed him. Tying his dead hands together with a handkerchief, she laid his arms round her shoulders, and bore him to the landing and down the narrow stairs. Reaching the bottom by the window, she let his body slide slowly over the sill till it lay on the ground without. She then climbed over the window-sill herself, and, leaving the sash open, dragged him on the lawn with a rustle not louder than the rustle of a broom. There she took a securer hold, and plunged with him under the trees, still dragging him by his tied hands.

Away from the precincts of the house she could apply herself more vigorously to her task, which was a heavy one enough for her, robust as she was; and the exertion and fright she had already undergone began to tell upon her by the time she reached the corner of a beech-plantation which intervened between the manor-house and the village. Here she was so nearly exhausted that she feared she might have to leave him on the spot. But she plodded on after a while, and keeping upon the grass at every opportunity she stood at last opposite the poor young man's garden-gate, where he lived with his father, the parish-clerk. How she accomplished the end of her task Lady Caroline never quite knew; but, to avoid leaving traces in the road, she carried him bodily across the gravel, and laid him down at the door. Perfectly aware of his ways of coming and going, she searched behind the shutter for the cottage door-key, which she placed in his cold hand. Then she kissed his face for the last time, and with silent little sobs bade him farewell.

Lady Caroline retraced her steps, and reached the mansion without hindrance; and to her great relief found the window open just as she had left it. When she had climbed in she listened attentively, fastened the window behind her, and ascending the stairs noiselessly to her room, set everything in order, and returned to bed.

The next morning it was speedily echoed around that the amiable and gentle young villager had been found dead outside his father's door, which he had apparently been in the act of unlocking when he fell. The circumstances were sufficiently exceptional to justify an inquest, at which syncope from heart disease was ascertained to be beyond doubt the explanation of his death, and no more was said about the matter then. But, after the funeral, it was rumoured that some man who had been returning late from a distant horse-fair had seen in the gloom of night a person, apparently a woman, dragging a heavy body of some sort towards the cottage-gate, which, by the light of after events, would seem to have been the corpse of the young fellow. His clothes were thereupon examined more particularly than at first, with the result that marks of friction were visible upon them here and there, precisely resembling such as would be left by dragging on the ground.

Our beautiful and ingenious Lady Caroline was now in great consternation; and began to think that, after all, it might have been better to honestly confess the truth. But having reached this stage without discovery or suspicion, she determined to make another effort towards concealment; and a bright idea struck her as a means of securing it. I think I mentioned that, before she cast eyes on the unfortunate steward's clerk, he had been the beloved of a certain village damsel, the woodman's daughter, his neighbour, to whom he had paid some attentions; and possibly he was beloved of her still. At any rate, the Lady Caroline's influence on the estates of her father being considerable, she resolved to seek an interview with the young girl in furtherance of her plan to save her reputation, about which she was now exceedingly anxious; for by this time, the fit being over, she began to be ashamed of her mad passion for her late husband, and almost wished she had never seen him.

In the course of her parish-visiting she lighted on the young girl without much difficulty, and found her looking pale and sad, and wearing a simple black gown, which she had put on out of respect for the young man's memory, whom she had tenderly loved, though he had not loved her.

'Ah, you have lost your lover, Milly,' said Lady Caroline.

The young woman could not repress her tears. 'My lady, he was not quite my lover,' she said. 'But I was his – and now he is dead I don't care to live any more!'

'Can you keep a secret about him?' asks the lady; 'one in which his honour is involved – which is known to me alone, but should be known to you?'

The girl readily promised, and, indeed, could be safely trusted on such a subject, so deep was her affection for the youth she mourned.

'Then meet me at his grave tonight, half-an-hour after sunset, and I will tell it to you,' says the other.

In the dusk of that spring evening the two shadowy figures of the young women converged upon the assistant-steward's newly-turfed mound; and at that solemn place and hour, which she had chosen on purpose, the one of birth and beauty unfolded her tale: how she had loved him and married him secretly; how he had died in her chamber; and how, to keep her secret, she had dragged him to his own door.

'Married him, my lady!' said the rustic maiden, starting back.

'I have said so,' replied Lady Caroline. 'But it was a mad thing, and a mistaken course. He ought to have married you. You, Milly, were peculiarly his. But you lost him.'

'Yes,' said the poor girl; 'and for that they laughed at me. "Ha – ha, you mid love him, Milly," they said; "but he will not love you!" '

'Victory over such unkind jeerers would be sweet,' said Lady Caroline. 'You lost him in life; but you may have him in death *as if* you had had him in life; and so turn the tables upon them.'

'How?' said the breathless girl.

The young lady then unfolded her plan, which was that Milly should go forward and declare that the young man had contracted a secret marriage (as he truly had done); that it was with her, Milly, his sweetheart; that he had been visiting her in her cottage on the evening of his death; when, on finding he was a corpse, she had carried him to his house to prevent discovery by her parents, and that she had meant to keep the whole matter a secret till the rumours afloat had forced it from her.

'And how shall I prove this?' said the woodman's daughter, amazed at the boldness of the proposal.

'Quite sufficiently. You can say, if necessary, that you were married to him at the church of St Something, in Bath City, in my name, as the first that occurred to you, to escape detection. That was where he married me. I will support you in this.'

'O – I don't quite like –'

'If you will do so,' said the lady peremptorily, 'I will always be your father's friend and yours; if not, it will be otherwise. And I will give you my wedding-ring, which you shall wear as yours.'

'Have you worn it, my lady?'

'Only at night.'

There was not much choice in the matter, and Milly consented. Then this noble lady took from her bosom the ring she had never been able openly to exhibit, and, grasping the young girl's hand, slipped it upon her finger as she stood upon her lover's grave.

Milly shivered, and bowed her head, saying, 'I feel as if I had become a corpse's bride!'

But from that moment the maiden was heart and soul in the substitution. A blissful repose came over her spirit. It seemed to her that she had secured in death him whom in life she had vainly idolized; and she was almost content. After that the lady handed over to the young man's new wife all the little mementoes and trinkets he had given herself, even to a brooch containing his hair.

The next day the girl made her so-called confession, which the simple mourning she had already worn, without stating for whom, seemed to bear out; and soon the story of the little romance spread through the village and country-side, almost as far as Melchester. It was a curious psychological fact that, having once made the avowal, Milly seemed possessed with a spirit of ecstasy at her position. With the liberal sum of money supplied to her by Lady Caroline she now purchased the garb of a widow, and duly appeared at church in her weeds, her simple face looking so sweet against its margin of crape that she was almost envied her state by the other village-girls of her age. And when a woman's sorrow for her beloved can maim her young life so obviously as it had done Milly's there was, in truth, little subterfuge in the case. Her explanation tallied so well with the details of her lover's latter movements – those strange absences and sudden returnings, which had occasionally puzzled his friends – that nobody supposed for a moment that the second actor in these secret nuptials was other than she. The actual and whole truth would indeed have seemed a preposterous assertion beside this plausible one, by reason of the lofty demeanour of the Lady Caroline and the unassuming habits of the late villager. There being no inheritance in question, not a soul took the trouble to go to the city church, forty miles off, and search the registers for marriage signatures bearing out so humble a romance.

In a short time Milly caused a decent tombstone to be erected over her nominal husband's grave, whereon appeared the statement that it was placed there by his heartbroken widow, which, considering that the payment for it came from Lady Caroline and the grief from Milly, was as truthful as such inscriptions usually are, and only required pluralizing to render it yet more nearly so.

The impressionable and complaisant Milly, in her character of widow, took delight in going to his grave every day, and indulging in sorrow which was a positive luxury to her. She placed fresh flowers on his grave, and so keen was her emotional imaginativeness that she almost believed herself to have been his wife indeed as she walked to and fro in her garb of woe. One afternoon, Milly being busily engaged in this labour of love at the grave, Lady Caroline passed outside the churchyard wall with some of her visiting friends, who, seeing Milly there, watched her actions with interest, remarked upon the pathos of the scene, and upon the intense affection the young man must have felt for such a tender creature as Milly. A strange light, as of pain, shot from the Lady Caroline's eye, as if for the first time she begrudged to the young girl the position she had been at such pains to transfer to her; it showed that a slumbering affection for her husband still had life in Lady Caroline, obscured and stifled as it was by social considerations.

An end was put to this smooth arrangement by the sudden

appearance in the churchyard one day of the Lady Caroline, when Milly had come there on her usual errand of laying flowers. Lady Caroline had been anxiously awaiting her behind the chancel, and her countenance was pale and agitated.

'Milly!' she said, 'come here! I don't know how to say to you what I am going to say. I am half dead!'

'I am sorry for your ladyship,' says Milly, wondering.

'Give me that ring!' says the lady, snatching at the girl's left hand.

Milly drew it quickly away.

'I tell you give it to me!' repeated Caroline, almost fiercely. 'O – but you don't know why? I am in a grief and a trouble I did not expect!' And Lady Caroline whispered a few words to the girl.

'O my lady!' said the thunderstruck Milly. 'What *will* you do?'

'You must say that your statement was a wicked lie, an invention, a scandal, a deadly sin – that I told you to make it to screen me! That it was I whom he married at Bath. In short, we must tell the truth, or I am ruined – body, mind, and reputation – for ever!'

But there is a limit to the flexibility of gentle-souled women. Milly by this time had so grown to the idea of being one flesh with this young man, of having the right to bear his name as she bore it; had so thoroughly come to regard him as her husband, to dream of him as her husband, to speak of him as her husband, that she could not relinquish him at a moment's peremptory notice.

'No, no,' she said desperately, 'I cannot, I will not give him up! Your ladyship took him away from me alive, and gave him back to me only when he was dead. Now I will keep him! I am truly his widow. More truly than you, my lady! for I love him and mourn for him, and call myself by his dear name, and your ladyship does neither!'

'I *do* love him!' cries Lady Caroline with flashing eyes, 'and I cling to him, and won't let him go to such as you! How can I, when he is the father of this poor child that's coming to me? I must have him back again! Milly, Milly, can't you pity and understand me, perverse girl that you are, and the miserable plight that I am in? O, this precipitancy – it is the ruin of women! Why did I not consider, and wait! Come, give me back all that I have given you, and assure me you will support me in confessing the truth!'

'Never, never!' persisted Milly, with woe-begone passionateness. 'Look at this headstone! Look at my gown and bonnet of crape – this ring: listen to the name they call me by! My character is worth as much to me as yours is to you! After declaring my Love mine, myself his, taking his name, making his death my own particular sorrow, how can I say it was not so? No such dishonour for me! I will outswear you, my lady; and I shall be believed. My story is so much the more likely that yours will be thought false. But, O please, my lady, do not drive me to this! In pity let me keep him!'

The poor nominal widow exhibited such anguish at a proposal which would have been truly a bitter humiliation to her, that Lady Caroline was warmed to pity in spite of her own condition.

'Yes, I see your position,' she answered. 'But think of mine! What can I do? Without your support it would seem an invention to save me from disgrace; even if I produced the register, the love of scandal in the world is such that the multitude would slur over the fact, say it was a fabrication, and believe your story. I do not know who were the witnesses, or the name of the church, or anything!'

In a few minutes these two poor young women felt, as so many in a strait have felt before, that union was their greatest strength, even now; and they consulted calmly together. The result of their deliberations was that Milly went home as usual, and Lady Caroline also, the latter confessing that very night to the Countess her mother of the marriage, and to nobody else in the world. And, some time after, Lady Caroline and her mother went away to London, where a little while later still they were joined by Milly, who was supposed to have left the village to proceed to a watering-place in the North for the benefit of her health, at the expense of the ladies of the Manor, who had been much interested in her state of lonely and defenceless widowhood.

Early the next year the ostensible widow Milly came home with an infant in her arms, the family at the Manor House having meanwhile gone abroad. They did not return from their tour till the autumn ensuing, by which time Milly and the child had again departed from the cottage of her father the woodman, Milly having attained to the dignity of dwelling in a cottage of her own, many miles to the eastward of her native village; a comfortable little allowance had moreover been settled on her and the child for life, through the instrumentality of Lady Caroline and her mother.

Two or three years passed away, and the Lady Caroline married a nobleman – the Marquis of Stonehenge – considerably her senior, who had wooed her long and phlegmatically. He was not rich, but she led a placid life with him for many years, though there was no child of the marriage. Meanwhile Milly's boy, as the youngster was called, and as Milly herself considered him, grew up, and throve wonderfully, and loved her as she deserved to be loved for her devotion to him, in whom she every day traced more distinctly the lineaments of the man who had won her girlish heart, and kept it even in the tomb.

She educated him as well as she could with the limited means at her disposal, for the allowance had never been increased, Lady Caroline, or the Marchioness of Stonehenge as she now was, seeming by degrees to care little what had become of them. Milly became extremely ambitious on the boy's account; she pinched herself almost of necessaries to send him to the Grammar School in the town to which they retired, and at twenty he enlisted in the cavalry regiment, joining it with a deliberate intent of making the Army his profession, and not in a freak of idleness. His exceptional attainments, his manly bearing, his steady conduct, speedily won him promotion, which was furthered by the serious war in which this country was at that time engaged. On his return to England after the peace he had risen to the rank of riding-master, and was soon after advanced another stage, and made quartermaster, though still a young man.

His mother – his corporeal mother, that is, the Marchioness of Stonehenge – heard tidings of this unaided progress; it reawakened her maternal instincts, and filled her with pride. She became keenly interested in her successful soldier-son; and as she grew older much wished to see him again, particularly when, the Marquis dying, she was left a solitary and childless widow. Whether or not she would have gone to him of her own impulse I cannot say; but one day, when she was driving in an open carriage in the outskirts of a neighbouring town, the troops lying at the barracks hard by passed her in marching order. She eyed them narrowly, and in the finest of the horsemen recognized her son from his likeness to her first husband.

This sight of him doubly intensified the motherly emotions which had lain dormant in her for so many years, and she wildly asked herself how she could so have neglected him? Had she possessed the true courage of affection she would have owned to her first marriage, and have reared him as her own! What would it have mattered if she had never obtained this precious coronet of pearls and gold leaves, by comparison with the gain of having the love and protection of such a noble and worthy son? These and other sad reflections cut the gloomy and solitary lady to the heart; and she repented of her pride in disclaiming her first husband more bitterly than she had ever repented of her infatuation in marrying him.

Her yearning was so strong that at length it seemed to her that she could not live without announcing herself to him as his mother. Come what might, she would do it: late as it was, she would have him away from that woman whom she began to hate with the fierceness of a deserted heart for having taken her place as the mother of her only child. She felt confidently enough that her son would only too gladly exchange a cottage-mother for one who was a peeress of the realm. Being now, in her widowhood, free to come and go as she chose, without question from anybody, Lady Stonehenge started next day for the little town where Milly yet lived, still in her robes of sable for the lost lover of her youth.

'He is *my* son,' said the Marchioness, as soon as she was

alone in the cottage with Milly. 'You must give him back to me, now that I am in a position in which I can defy the world's opinion. I suppose he comes to see you continually?'

'Every month since he returned from the war, my lady. And sometimes he stays two or three days, and takes me about seeing sights everywhere!' She spoke with quiet triumph.

'Well, you will have to give him up,' said the Marchioness calmly. 'It shall not be the worse for you – you may see him when you choose. I am going to avow my first marriage, and have him with me.'

'You forget that there are two to be reckoned with, my lady. Not only me, but himself.'

'That can be arranged. You don't suppose that he wouldn't –' But not wishing to insult Milly by comparing their positions, she said, 'He is my own flesh and blood, not yours.'

'Flesh and blood's nothing!' said Milly, flashing with as much scorn as a cottager could show to a peeress, which, in this case, was not so little as may be supposed. 'But I will agree to put it to him, and let him settle it for himself.'

'That's all I require,' said Lady Stonehenge. 'You must ask him to come, and I will meet him here.'

The soldier was written to, and the meeting took place. He was not so much astonished at the disclosure of his parentage as Lady Stonehenge had been led to expect, having known for years that there was a little mystery about his birth. His manner towards the Marchioness, though respectful, was less warm than she could have hoped. The alternatives as to his choice of a mother were put before him. His answer amazed and stupefied her.

'No, my lady,' said the quartermaster. 'Thank you much, but I prefer to let things be as they have been. My father's name is mine in any case. You see, my lady, you cared little for me when I was weak and helpless; why should I come to you now I am strong? She, dear devoted soul [pointing to Milly], tended me from my birth, watched over me, nursed me when I was ill, and deprived herself of many a little comfort to push me on. I cannot love another mother as I love her. She *is* my mother, and I will always be her son!' As he spoke he put his manly arm around Milly's neck, and kissed her with the tenderest affection.

The agony of the poor Marchioness was pitiable. 'You kill me!' she said, between her shaking sobs. 'Cannot you – love – me – too?'

'No, my lady. If I must say it, you were once ashamed of my poor father, who was a sincere and honest man; therefore, I am now ashamed of you.'

Nothing would move him; and the suffering woman at last gasped, 'Cannot – O, cannot you give one kiss to me – as you did to her? It is not much – it is all I ask – all!'

'Certainly,' he replied.

He kissed her, but with a difference – quite coldly; and the painful scene came to an end. That day was the beginning of death to the unfortunate Marchioness of Stonehenge. It was in the perverseness of her human heart that his denial of her should add fuel to the fire of her craving for his love. How long afterwards she lived I do not know with any exactness, but it was no great length of time. That anguish that is sharper than a serpent's tooth wore her out soon. Utterly reckless of the world, its ways, and its opinions, she allowed her story to become known; and when the welcome end supervened (which, I grieve to say, she refused to lighten by the consolations of religion), a broken heart was the truest phrase in which to sum up its cause.

The rural dean having concluded, some observations upon his tale were made in due course. The sentimental member said that Lady Caroline's history afforded a sad instance of how an honest human affection will become shamefaced and mean under the frost of class-division and social prejudices. She probably deserved some pity; though her offspring, before he grew up to man's estate, had deserved more. There was no pathos like the pathos of childhood, when a child found itself in a world where it was not wanted, and could not understand the reason why.

1890

A Few Crusted Characters

FROM LIFE'S LITTLE IRONIES

Introduction

It is a Saturday afternoon of blue and yellow autumn-time, and the scene is the High Street of a well-known market-town. A large carrier's van stands in the quadrangular fore-court of the White Hart Inn, upon the sides of its spacious tilt being painted, in weather-beaten letters: 'Burthen, Carrier to Longpuddle'. These vans, so numerous hereabout, are a respectable, if somewhat lumbering, class of conveyance, much resorted to by decent travellers not overstocked with money, the better among them roughly corresponding to the old French *diligences*.

The present one is timed to leave the town at four in the afternoon precisely, and it is now half-past three by the clock in the turret at the top of the street. In a few seconds errand-boys from the shops begin to arrive with packages, which they fling into the vehicle, and turn away whistling, and care for the packages no more. At twenty minutes to four an elderly woman places her basket upon the shafts, slowly mounts, takes up a seat inside, and folds her hands and her lips. She has secured her corner for the journey, though there is as yet no sign of a horse being put in, nor of a carrier. At the three-quarters, two other women arrive, in whom the first recognizes the postmistress of Upper Longpuddle and the registrar's wife, they recognizing her as the aged groceress of the same village. At five minutes to the hour there approach Mr Profitt, the schoolmaster, in a soft felt hat, and Christopher Twink, the master-thatcher; and as the hour strikes there rapidly drop in the parish clerk and his wife, the seedsman and his aged father, the registrar; also Mr Day, the world-ignored local landscape-painter, an elderly man who resides in his native place, and has never sold a picture outside it, though his pretensions to art have been nobly supported by his fellow-villagers, whose confidence in his genius has been as remarkable as the outer neglect of it, leading them to buy his paintings so extensively (at the price of a few shillings each, it is true) that every dwelling in the parish exhibits three or four of those admired productions on its walls.

Burthen, the carrier, is by this time seen bustling round the vehicle; the horses are put in, the proprietor arranges the reins and springs up into his seat as if he were used to it – which he is.

'Is everybody here?' he asks preparatorily over his shoulder to the passengers within.

As those who were not there did not reply in the negative the muster was assumed to be complete, and after a few hitches and hindrances the van with its human freight was got under way. It jogged on at an easy pace till it reached the bridge which formed the last outpost of the town. The carrier pulled up suddenly.

'Bless my soul!' he said, 'I've forgot the curate!'

All who could do so gazed from the little back-window of the van, but the curate was not in sight.

'Now I wonder where that there man is?' continued the carrier.

'Poor man, he ought to have a living at his time of life.'

'And he ought to be punctual,' said the carrier. ' "Four o'clock sharp is my time for starting," I said to 'en. And he said, "I'll be there." Now he's not here; and as a serious old church-minister he ought to be as good as his word. Perhaps Mr Flaxton knows, being in the same line of life?' He turned to the parish clerk.

'I was talking an immense deal with him, that's true, half an hour ago,' replied that ecclesiastic, as one of whom it was no erroneous supposition that he should be on intimate terms with another of the cloth. 'But he didn't say he would be late.'

The discussion was cut off by the appearance round the corner of the van of rays from the curate's spectacles, followed hastily by his face and a few white whiskers, and the swinging tails of his long gaunt coat. Nobody reproached him, seeing how he was reproaching himself; and he entered breathlessly and took his seat.

'Now be we all here?' said the carrier again. They started a second time, and moved on till they were about three hundred yards out of the town, and had nearly reached the second bridge, behind which, as every native remembers, the road takes a turn, and travellers by this highway disappear finally from the view of gazing burghers.

'Well, as I'm alive!' cried the postmistress from the interior of the conveyance, peering through the little square back-window along the road townward.

'What?' said the carrier.

'A man hailing us!'

Another sudden stoppage. 'Somebody else?' the carrier asked.

'Ay, sure!' All waited silently, while those who could gaze out did so.

'Now, who can that be?' Burthen continued. 'I just put it to ye, neighbours, can any man keep time with such hindrances? Bain't we full a'ready? Who in the world can the man be?'

'He's a sort of gentleman,' said the schoolmaster, his position commanding the road more comfortably than that of his comrades.

The stranger, who had been holding up his umbrella to attract their notice, was walking forward leisurely enough, now that he found, by their stopping, that it had been secured. His clothes were decidedly not a local cut, though it was difficult to point out any particular mark of difference. In his left hand he carried a small leather travelling-bag. As soon as he had overtaken the van he glanced at the inscription on its side, as if to assure himself that he had hailed the right conveyance, and asked if they had room.

The carrier replied that though they were pretty well laden he supposed they could carry one more, whereupon the stranger mounted, and took the seat cleared for him within. And then the horses made another move, this time for good, and swung along with their burden of fourteen souls all told.

'You bain't one of these parts, sir?' said the carrier. 'I could tell that as far as I could see 'ee.'

'Yes, I am one of these parts,' said the stranger.

'Oh? H'm.'

The silence which followed seemed to imply a doubt of the truth of the new-comer's assertion. 'I was speaking of Upper Longpuddle, more particular,' continued the carrier hardily, 'and I think I know most faces of that valley.'

'I was born at Longpuddle, and nursed at Longpuddle, and my father and grandfather before me,' said the passenger quietly.

'Why, to be sure,' said the aged groceress in the background, 'it isn't John Lackland's son – never – it can't be – he who went to foreign parts five-and-thirty years ago with his wife and family? Yet – what do I hear? – that's his father's voice!'

'That's the man,' replied the stranger. 'John Lackland was my father, and I am John Lackland's son. Five-and-thirty years ago, when I was a boy of eleven, my parents emigrated across the seas, taking me and my sister with them. Kytes's boy Tony was the one who drove us and our belongings to Casterbridge on the morning we left; and his was the last Longpuddle face I saw. We sailed the same week across the ocean, and there we've been ever since, and there I've left those I went with – all three.'

'Alive or dead?'

'Dead,' he replied in a low voice. 'And I have come back to the old place, having nourished a thought – not a definite intention, but just a thought – that I should like to return here in a year or two, to spend the remainder of my days.'

'Married man, Mr Lackland?'

'No.'

'And have the world used 'ee well, sir – or rather John, knowing 'ee as a child? In these rich new countries that we hear of so much, you've got rich with the rest?'

'I am not very rich,' Mr Lackland said. 'Even in new countries, you know, there are failures. The race is not always to the swift, nor the battle to the strong; and even if it sometimes is, you may be neither swift nor strong. However, that's enough about me. Now, having answered your inquiries, you must answer mine; for being in London, I have come down here entirely to discover what Longpuddle is looking like, and who are living there. That was why I preferred a seat in your van to hiring a carriage for driving across.'

'Well, as for Longpuddle, we rub on there much as usual. Old figures have dropped out o' their frames, so to speak it, and new ones have been put in their places. You mentioned Tony Kytes as having been the one to drive your family and your goods to Casterbridge in his father's waggon when you left. Tony is, I believe, living still, but not at Longpuddle. He went away and settled at Lewgate, near Mellstock, after his marriage. Ah, Tony was a sort o' man!'

'His character had hardly come out when I knew him.'

'No. But 'twas well enough, as far as that goes – except as to women. I shall never forget his courting – never!'

The returned villager waited silently, and the carrier went on: –

[*The carrier then tells his story of 'Tony Kytes, the Arch-Deceiver'; the parish clerk 'The History of the Hardcomes'; the seedsman's father 'The Superstitious Man's Story'; and there follows the master-thatcher's story of 'Andrey Satchel and the Parson and Clerk'.*]

Andrey Satchel and the Parson and Clerk

'It all arose, you must know, from Andrey being fond of a drop of drink at that time – though he's a sober enough man now by all account, so much the better for him. Jane, his bride, you see, was somewhat older than Andrey; how much older I don't pretend to say; she was not one of our parish, and the register alone may be able to tell that. But, at any rate, her being a little ahead of her young man in mortal years, coupled with other bodily circumstances owing to that young man –'

('Ah, poor thing!' sighed the women.)

'– made her very anxious to get the thing done before he changed his mind; and 'twas with a joyful countenance (they say) that she, with Andrey and his brother and sister-in-law, marched off to church one November morning as soon as 'twas day a'most to be made one with Andrey for the rest of her life. He had left our place long before it was light, and the folks that were up all waved their lanterns at him, and flung up their hats as he went.

'The church of her parish was a mile and more from where she lived, and, as it was a wonderful fine day for the time of year, the plan was that as soon as they were married they would make out a holiday by driving straight off to Port Bredy, to see the ships and the sea and the sojers, instead of coming back to a meal at the house of the distant relation she lived wi', and moping about there all the afternoon.

'Well, some folks noticed that Andrey walked with rather wambling steps to church that morning; the truth o't was that his nearest neighbour's child had been christened the day before, and Andrey, having stood godfather, had stayed all night keeping up the christening, for he had said to himself, "Not if I live to be a thousand shall I again be made a godfather one day, and a husband the next, and perhaps a father the next, and therefore I'll make the most of the blessing." So that when he started from home in the morning he had not been in bed at all. The result was, as I say, that when he and his bride-to-be walked up the church to get married, the pa'son (who was a very strict man inside the church, whatever he was outside) looked hard at Andrey, and said, very sharp:

' "How's this, my man? You are in liquor. And so early, too. I'm ashamed of you!"

' "Well, that's true, sir," says Andrey. "But I can walk straight enough for practical purposes. I can walk a chalk line," he says (meaning no offence), "as well as some other folk: and" – (getting hotter) – "I reckon that if you, Pa'son Billy Toogood, had kept up a christening all night so thoroughly as I have done, you wouldn't be able to stand at all; d—me if you would!"

'This answer made Pa'son Billy – as they used to call him –rather spitish, not to say hot, for he was a warm-tempered man if provoked, and he said, very decidedly: "Well, I cannot marry you in this state; and I will not! Go home and get sober!" And he slapped the book together like a rat-trap.

'Then the bride burst out crying as if her heart would break, for very fear that she would lose Andrey after all her hard work to get him, and begged and implored the pa'son to go on with the ceremony. But no.

' "I won't be a party to your solemnizing matrimony with a tipsy man," says Mr Toogood. "It is not right and decent. I am sorry for you, my young woman, seeing the condition you are in, but you'd better go home again. I wonder how you could think of bringing him here drunk like this!"

' "But if – if he don't come drunk he won't come at all, sir!" she says, through her sobs.

' "I can't help that," says the pa'son; and plead as she might, it did not move him. Then she tried him another way.

' "Well, then, if you'll go home, sir, and leave us here, and come back to the church in an hour or two, I'll undertake to say that he shall be as sober as a judge," she cries. "We'll bide here, with your permission; for if he once goes out of this here church unmarried, all Van Amburgh's horses won't drag him back again!"

' "Very well," says the pa'son. "I'll give you two hours, and then I'll return."

' "And please, sir, lock the door, so that we can't escape!" says she.

' "Yes," says the pa'son.

' "And let nobody know that we are here."

'The pa'son then took off his clane white surplice, and went away; and the others consulted upon the best means for keeping the matter a secret, which it was not a very hard thing to do, the place being so lonely, and the hour so early. The witnesses, Andrey's brother and brother's wife, neither one o' which cared about Andrey's marrying Jane, and had come rather against their will, said they couldn't wait two hours in that hole of a place, wishing to get home to Longpuddle before dinner-time. They were altogether so crusty that the clerk said there was no difficulty in their doing as they wished. They could go home as if their brother's wedding had actually taken place and the married couple had gone onward for their day's pleasure jaunt to Port Bredy as intended. He, the clerk, and any casual passer-by would act as witnesses when the pa'son came back.

'This was agreed to, and away Andrey's relations went, nothing loath, and the clerk shut the church door and prepared to lock in the couple. The bride went up and whispered to him, with her eyes a-streaming still.

' "My dear good clerk," she says, "if we bide here in the church, folk may see us through the windows, and find out what has happened; and 'twould cause such a talk and scandal that I never should get over it: and perhaps, too, dear Andrey might try to get out and leave me! Will ye lock us up in the tower, my dear good clerk?" she says. "I'll tole him in there if you will."

'The clerk had no objection to do this to oblige the poor young woman, and they toled Andrey into the tower, and the clerk locked 'em both up straightway, and then went home, to return at the end of the two hours.

'Pa'son Toogood had not been long in his house after leaving the church when he saw a gentleman in pink and top-boots ride past his windows, and with a sudden flash of heat he called to mind that the hounds met that day just on the edge of his parish. The pa'son was one who dearly loved sport, and much he longed to be there.

'In short, except o' Sundays and at tide-times in the week, Pa'son Billy was the life o' the hunt. 'Tis true that he was poor, and that he rode all of a heap, and that his black mare was rat-tailed and old, and his tops older, and all over of one colour, whitey-brown, and full o' cracks. But he'd been in at the death of three thousand foxes. And – being a bachelor man – every time he went to bed in summer he used to open the bed at bottom and crawl up head foremost, to mind en of the coming winter and the good sport he'd have, and the foxes going to earth. And whenever there was a christening at the Squire's, and he had dinner there afterwards, as he always did, he never failed to christen the chiel over again in a bottle of port wine.

'Now the clerk was the pa'son's groom and gardener and

general manager, and had just got back to his work in the garden when he, too, saw the hunting man pass, and presently saw lots more of 'em, noblemen and gentry, and then he saw the hounds, the huntsman, Jim Treadhedge, the whipper-in, and I don't know who besides. The clerk loved going to cover as frantical as the pa'son, so much so that whenever he saw or heard the pack he could no more rule his feelings than if they were the winds of heaven. He might be bedding, or he might be sowing – all was forgot. So he throws down his spade and rushes in to the pa'son, who was by this time as frantical to go as he.

' "That there mare of yours, sir, do want exercise bad, very bad, this morning!" the clerk says, all of a tremble. "Don't ye think I'd better trot her round the downs for an hour, sir?'

' "To be sure, she does want exercise badly. I'll trot her round myself," says the pa'son.

' "Oh – you'll trot her yerself? Well, there's the cob, sir. Really that cob is getting oncontrollable through biding in a stable so long! If you wouldn't mind my putting on the saddle –"

' "Very well. Take him out, certainly," says the pa'son, never caring what the clerk did so long as he himself could get off immediately. So, scrambling into his riding-boots and breeches as quick as he could, he rode off towards the meet, intending to be back in an hour. No sooner was he gone than the clerk mounted the cob, and was off after him. When the pa'son got to the meet he found a lot of friends, and was as jolly as he could be: the hounds found a'most as soon as they threw off, and there was great excitement. So, forgetting that he had meant to go back at once, away rides the pa'son with the rest o' the hunt, all across the fallow ground that lies between Lippet Wood and Green's Copse; and as he galloped he looked behind for a moment, and there was the clerk close to his heels.

' "Ha, ha, clerk – you here?" he says.

' "Yes, sir, here be I," says t'other.

' "Fine exercise for the horses!"

' "Ay, sir – hee, hee!" says the clerk.

'So they went on and on, into Green's Copse, then across to

Higher Jirton; then on across this very turnpike-road to Waterston Ridge, then away towards Yalbury Wood: up hill and down dale, like the very wind, the clerk close to the pa'son, and the pa'son not far from the hounds. Never was there a finer run knowed with that pack than they had that day; and neither pa'son nor clerk thought one word about the unmarried couple locked up in the church tower waiting to get j'ined.

' "These hosses of yours, sir, will be much improved by this!" says the clerk as he rode along, just a neck behind the pa'son. "'Twas a happy thought of your reverent mind to bring 'em out today. Why, it may be frosty and slippery in a day or two, and then the poor things mid not be able to leave the stable for weeks."

' "They may not, they may not, it is true. A merciful man is merciful to his beast," says the pa'son.

' "Hee, hee!" says the clerk, glancing sly into the pa'son's eye.

' "Ha, ha!" says the pa'son, a-glancing back into the clerk's. "Halloo!" he shouts, as he sees the fox break cover at that moment.

' "Halloo!" cries the clerk. "There he goes! Why, dammy, there's two foxes —"

' "Hush, clerk, hush! Don't let me hear that word again! Remember our calling."

' "True, sir, true. But really, good sport do carry away a man so, that he's apt to forget his high persuasion!" And the next minute the corner of the clerk's eye shot again into the corner of the pa'son's, and the pa'son's back again to the clerk's. "Hee, hee!" said the clerk.

' "Ha, ha!" said Pa'son Toogood.

' "Ah, sir," says the clerk again, "this is better than crying Amen to your Ever-and-ever on a winter's morning!"

' "Yes, indeed, clerk! To everything there's a season," says Pa'son Toogood, quite pat, for he was a learned Christian man when he liked, and had chapter and ve'se at his tongue's end, as a pa'son should.

'At last, late in the day, the hunting came to an end by the fox running into a' old woman's cottage, under her table, and up the clock-case. The pa'son and clerk were among the first in at the death, their faces a-staring in at the old woman's winder, and the clock striking as he'd never been heard to strik' before. Then came the question of finding their way home.

'Neither the pa'son nor the clerk knowed how they were going to do this, for their beasts were wellnigh tired down to the ground. But they started back-along as well as they could, though they were so done up that they could only drag along at a' amble, and not much of that at a time.

' "We shall never, never get there!" groaned Mr Toogood, quite bowed down.

' "Never!" groans the clerk. " 'Tis a judgment upon us for our iniquities!"

' "I fear it is," murmurs the pa'son.

'Well, 'twas quite dark afore they entered the pa'sonage gate, having crept into the parish as quiet as if they'd stole a hammer, little wishing their congregation to know what they'd been up to all day long. And as they were so dog-tired, and so anxious about the horses, never once did they think of the unmarried people. As soon as ever the horses had been stabled and fed, and the pa'son and clerk had had a bit and a sup theirselves, they went to bed.

'Next morning when Pa'son Toogood was at breakfast, thinking of the glorious sport he'd had the day before, the clerk came in a hurry to the door and asked to see him.

' "It has just come into my mind, sir, that we've forgot all about the couple that we was to have married yesterday!"

'The half-chawed victuals dropped from the pa'son's mouth as if he'd been shot. "Bless my soul," says he, "so we have! How very awkward!"

' "It is, sir; very. Perhaps we've ruined the 'ooman!"

' "Ah – to be sure – I remember! She ought to have been married before."

' "If anything has happened to her up in that there tower, and no doctor or nuss –" '

('Ah – poor thing!' sighed the women.)

' "– 'twill be a quarter-sessions matter for us, not to speak of the disgrace to the Church!"

' "Good God, clerk, don't drive me wild!" says the pa'son. "Why the hell didn't I marry 'em, drunk or sober!" (Pa'sons used to cuss in them days like plain honest men.) "Have you been to the church to see what happened to them, or inquired in the village?"

' "Not I, sir! It only came into my head a moment ago, and I always like to be second to you in church matters. You could have knocked me down with a sparrow's feather when I thought o't, sir; I assure 'ee you could!"

'Well, the pa'son jumped up from his breakfast, and together they went off to the church.

' "It is not at all likely that they are there now," says Mr Toogood, as they went; "and indeed I hope they are not. They be pretty sure to have escaped and gone home."

'However, they opened the church-hatch, entered the churchyard, and looking up at the tower there they seed a little small white face at the belfry-winder, and a little small hand waving. 'Twas the bride.

' "God my life, clerk," says Mr Toogood. "I don't know how to face 'em!" And he sank down upon a tombstone. "How I wish I hadn't been so cussed particular!"

' "Yes – 'twas a pity we didn't finish it when we'd begun," the clerk said. "Still, since the feelings of your holy priestcraft wouldn't let ye, the couple must put up with it."

' "True, clerk, true! Does she look as if anything premature had took place?"

' "I can't see her no lower down than her arm-pits, sir."

' "Well – how do her face look?"

' "It do look mighty white!"

' "Well, we must know the worst! Dear me, how the small of my back do ache from that ride yesterday! . . . But to more godly business!"

'They went on into the church, and unlocked the tower stairs, and immediately poor Jane and Andrey busted out like starved mice from a cupboard, Andrey limp and sober enough now, and his bride pale and cold, but otherwise as usual.

' "What," says the pa'son with a great breath of relief, "you haven't been here ever since?"

' "Yes, we have, sir!" says the bride, sinking down upon a seat in her weakness. "Not a morsel, wet or dry, have we had since! It was impossible to get out without help, and here we've stayed!"

' "But why didn't you shout, good souls?" said the pa'son.

' "She wouldn't let me," says Andrey.

' "Because we were so ashamed at what had led to it," sobs Jane. "We felt that if it were noised abroad it would cling to us all our lives! Once or twice Andrey had a good mind to toll the bell, but then he said: 'No; I'll starve first. I won't bring disgrace on my name and yours, my dear.' And so we waited and waited, and walked round and round; but never did you come till now!"

' "To my regret!" says the pa'son. "Now, then, we will soon get it over."

' "I – I should like some victuals," said Andrey; "'twould gie me courage to do it, if it is only a crust o' bread and a' onion; for I am that leery that I can feel my stomach rubbing against my backbone."

' "I think we had better get it done," said the bride, a bit anxious in manner; "since we are all here convenient, too!"

'Andrey gave way about the victuals, and the clerk called in a second witness who wouldn't be likely to gossip about it, and soon the knot was tied, and the bride looked smiling and calm forthwith, and Andrey limper than ever.

' "Now," said Pa'son Toogood, "you two must come to my house, and have a good lining put to your insides before you go a step further."

'They were very glad of the offer, and went out of the churchyard by one path while the pa'son and clerk went out by the other, and so did not attract notice, it being still early. They entered the rectory as if they'd just come back from their trip to Port Bredy; and then they knocked in the victuals and drink till they could hold no more.

'It was a long while before the story of what they had gone through was known, but it was talked of in time, and they themselves laugh over it now; though what Jane got for her pains was no great bargain after all. 'Tis true she saved her name.'

*

'Was that the same Andrey who went to the squire's house as one of the Christmas fiddlers?' asked the seedsman.

'No, no,' replied Mr Profitt, the schoolmaster. 'It was his father did that. Ay, it was all owing to his being such a man for eating and drinking.' Finding that he had the ear of the audience, the schoolmaster continued without delay: –

Old Andrey's Experience as a Musician

'I was one of the quire-boys at that time, and we and the players were to appear at the manor-house as usual that Christmas week, to play and sing in the hall to the Squire's people and visitors (among 'em being the archdeacon, Lord and Lady Baxby, and I don't know who); afterwards going, as we always did, to have a good supper in the servants' hall. Andrew knew this was the custom, and meeting us when we were starting to go, he said to us: "Lord, how I should like to join in that meal of beef, and turkey, and plum-pudding, and ale, that you happy ones be going to just now! One more or less will make no difference to the Squire. I am too old to pass as a singing boy, and too bearded to pass as a singing girl; can ye lend me a fiddle, neighbours, that I may come with ye as a bandsman?"

'Well, we didn't like to be hard upon him, and lent him an old one, though Andrew knew no more of music than the Giant o' Cernel; and armed with the instrument he walked up to the Squire's house with the others of us at the time appointed, and went in boldly, his fiddle under his arm. He made himself as natural as he could in opening the music-books and moving the candles to the best points for throwing light upon the notes; and all went well till we had played and sung "While shepherds watch", and "Star, arise", and "Hark the glad sound". Then the Squire's mother, a tall gruff old lady, who was much interested in church-music, said quite unexpectedly to Andrew: "My man, I see you don't play your instrument with the rest. How is that?"

'Every one of the quire was ready to sink into the earth with concern at the fix Andrew was in. We could see that he had fallen into a cold sweat, and how he would get out of it we did not know.

' "I've had a misfortune, mem," he says, bowing as meek as a child. "Coming along the road I fell down and broke my bow."

' "O, I am sorry to hear that," says she. "Can't it be mended?"

' "O no, mem," says Andrew. "'Twas broke all to splinters."

' "I'll see what I can do for you," says she.

'And then it seemed all over, and we played "Rejoice, ye drowsy mortals all", in D and two sharps. But no sooner had we got through it than she says to Andrew: ' "I've sent up into the attic, where we have some old musical instruments, and found a bow for you." And she hands the bow to poor wretched Andrew, who didn't even know which end to take hold of. "Now we shall have the full accompaniment," says she.

'Andrew's face looked as if it were made of rotten apple as he stood in the circle of players in front of his book; for if there was one person in the parish that everybody was afraid of, 'twas this hook-nosed old lady. However, by keeping a little behind the next man he managed to make pretence of beginning, sawing away with his bow without letting it touch the strings, so that it looked as if he were driving into the tune with heart and soul. 'Tis a question if he wouldn't have got through all right if one of the Squire's visitors (no other than the archdeacon) hadn't noticed that he held the fiddle upside down, the nut under his chin, and the tail-piece in his hand; and they began to crowd round him, thinking 'twas some new way of performing.

'This revealed everything; the Squire's mother had Andrew turned out of the house as a vile impostor, and there was great interruption to the harmony of the proceedings, the Squire declaring he should have notice to leave his cottage that day fortnight. However, when we got to the servants' hall there sat Andrew, who had been let in at the back door by the orders of the Squire's wife, after being turned out at the front by the orders of the Squire, and nothing more was heard about his leaving his cottage. But Andrew never performed in public as a musician after that night; and now he's dead and gone, poor man, as we all shall be!'

'I had quite forgotten the old choir, with their fiddles and bass-viols,' said the home-comer, musingly. 'Are they still going on the same as of old?'

'Bless the man!' said Christopher Twink, the master-thatcher; 'why, they've been done away with these twenty year. A young teetotaller plays the organ in church now, and plays it very well; though 'tis not quite such good music as in old times, because the organ is one of them that go with a winch, and the young teetotaller says he can't always throw the proper feeling into the tune without wellnigh working his arms off.'

'Why did they make the change, then?'

'Well, partly because of fashion, partly because the old musicians got into a sort of scrape. A terrible scrape 'twas, too – wasn't it, John? I shall never forget it – never! They lost their character as officers of the church as complete as if they'd never had any character at all.'

'That was very bad for them.'

'Yes.' The master-thatcher attentively regarded past times as if they lay about a mile off, and went on: –

Absent-Mindedness in a Parish Choir

'It happened on Sunday after Christmas – the last Sunday ever they played in Longpuddle church gallery, as it turned out, though they didn't know it then. As you may know, sir, the players formed a very good band – almost as good as the Mellstock parish players that were led by the Dewys; and that's saying a great deal. There was Nicholas Puddingcome, the leader, with the first fiddle; there was Timothy Thomas, the bass-viol man; John Biles, the tenor fiddler, Dan'l Hornhead, with the serpent; Robert Dowdle, with the clarionet; and Mr Nicks, with the oboe – all sound and powerful musicians, and strong-winded men – they that blowed. For that reason they were much in demand Christmas week for little reels and dancing parties: for they could turn a jig or a hornpipe out of hand as well as ever they could turn out a psalm, and perhaps better, not to speak irreverent. In short, one half-hour they could be playing a Christmas carol in the Squire's hall to the ladies and gentlemen, and drinking tay and coffee with 'em as modest as saints; and the next, at The Tinker's Arms, blazing away like wild horses with the ''Dashing White Sergeant'' to nine couple of dancers and more, and swallowing rum-and-cider hot as flame.

'Well, this Christmas they'd been out to one rattling randy after another every night, and had got next to no sleep at all. Then came the Sunday after Christmas, their fatal day. 'Twas so mortal cold that year that they could hardly sit in the gallery; for though the congregation down in the body of the church had a stove to keep off the frost, the players in the gallery had nothing at all. So Nicholas said at morning service, when 'twas freezing an inch an hour, "Please the Lord I won't stand this numbing weather no longer: this afternoon we'll have something in our insides to make us warm, if it cost a king's ransom."

'So he brought a gallon of hot brandy and beer, ready mixed, to church with him in the afternoon, and by keeping the jar well wrapped up in Timothy Thomas's bass-viol bag it kept drinkably warm till they wanted it, which was just a thimbleful in the Absolution, and another after the Creed, and the remainder at the beginning o' the sermon. When they'd had the last pull they felt quite comfortable and warm, and as the sermon went on – most unfortunately for 'em it was a long one that afternoon – they fell asleep, every man jack of 'em; and there they slept on as sound as rocks.

''Twas a very dark afternoon, and by the end of the sermon all you could see of the inside of the church were the pa'son's two candles alongside of him in the pulpit, and his spaking face behind 'em. The sermon being ended at last, the pa'son gie'd out the Evening Hymn. But no quire set about sounding up the tune, and the people began to turn their heads to learn the reason why, and then Levi Limpet, a boy who sat in the gallery, nudged Timothy and Nicholas, and said, "Begin! begin!"

' "Hey? what?" says Nicholas, starting up; and the church being so dark and his head so muddled he thought he was at the party they had played at all the night before, and away he went, bow and fiddle, at "The Devil among the Tailors", the favourite jig of our neighbourhood at that time. The rest of the band, being in the same state of mind and nothing doubting, followed their leader with all their strength, according to custom. They poured out that there tune till the lower bass notes of "The Devil among the Tailors" made the cobwebs in the roof shiver like ghosts; then Nicholas, seeing nobody moved, shouted out as he scraped (in his usual commanding way at dances when the folk didn't know the figures), "Top couples cross hands! And when I make the fiddle squeak at the end, every man kiss his pardner under the mistletoe!"

'The boy Levi was so frightened that he bolted down the gallery stairs and out homeward like lightning. The pa'son's hair fairly stood on end when he heard the evil tune raging through the church, and thinking the quire had gone crazy he held up his hand and said: "Stop, stop, stop! Stop, stop! What's this?" But they didn't hear'n for the noise of their own playing, and the more he called the louder they played.

'Then the folks came out of their pews, wondering down to the ground, and saying: "What do they mean by such wickedness! We shall be consumed like Sodom and Gomorrah!"

'And the Squire, too, came out of his pew lined wi' green baize, where lots of lords and ladies visiting at the house were worshipping along with him, and went and stood in front of the gallery, and shook his fist in the musicians' faces, saying, "What! In this reverent edifice! What!"

'And at last they heard'n through their playing, and stopped.

' "Never such an insulting, disgraceful thing – never!" says the Squire, who couldn't rule his passion.

' "Never!" says the pa'son, who had come down and stood beside him.

' "Not if the Angels of Heaven," says the Squire (he was a

wickedish man, the Squire was, though now for once he happened to be on the Lord's side) – "not if the Angels of Heaven come down," he says, "shall one of you villainous players ever sound a note in this church again; for the insult to me, and my family, and my visitors, and the pa'son, and God Almighty, that you've a-perpetrated this afternoon!"

'Then the unfortunate church band came to their senses, and remembered where they were; and 'twas a sight to see Nicholas Puddingcome and Timothy Thomas and John Biles creep down the gallery stairs with their fiddles under their arms, and poor Dan'l Hornhead with his serpent, and Robert Dowdle with his clarionet, all looking as little as ninepins; and out they went. The pa'son might have forgi'ed 'em when he learned the truth o't, but the Squire would not. That very week he sent for a barrel-organ that would play two-and-twenty new psalm-tunes, so exact and particular that, however sinful inclined you was, you could play nothing but psalm-tunes whatsomever. He had a really respectable man to turn the winch, as I said, and the old players played no more.'

[*After the groceress' story of 'The Winters and the Palmleys' and the registrar's 'Incident in the Life of Mr George Crookhill', 'A Few Crusted Characters' ends with the landscape-painter's tale of 'Netty Sargent's Copyhold'.*]

Netty Sargent's Copyhold

'She continued to live with her uncle, in the lonely house by the copse, just as at the time you knew her; a tall spry young woman. Ah, how well one can remember her black hair and dancing eyes at that time, and her sly way of screwing up her mouth when she meant to tease ye! Well, she was hardly out of short frocks before the chaps were after her, and by long and by late she was courted by a young man whom perhaps you did not know – Jasper Cliff was his name – and, though she might have had many a better fellow, he so greatly took her fancy that 'twas Jasper or nobody for her. He was a selfish customer, always thinking less of what he was going to do than of what he was going to gain by his doings. Jasper's eyes might have been fixed upon Netty, but his mind was upon her uncle's house; though he was fond of her in his way – I admit that.

'This house, built by her great-great-grandfather, with its garden and little field, was copyhold – granted upon lives in the old way, and had been so granted for generations. Her uncle's was the last life upon the property; so that at his death, if there was no admittance of new lives, it would all fall into the hands of the lord of the manor. But 'twas easy to admit – a slight "fine", as 'twas called, of a few pounds, was enough to entitle him to a new deed o' grant by the custom of the manor; and the lord could not hinder it.

'Now there could be no better provision for his niece and only relative than a sure house over her head, and Netty's uncle should have seen to the renewal in time, owing to the peculiar custom of forfeiture by the dropping of the last life before the new fine was paid; for the Squire was very anxious to get hold of the house and land; and every Sunday when the old man came into the church and passed the Squire's pew, the Squire would say, "A little weaker in his knees, a little crookeder in his back – and the re-admittance not applied for: ha! ha! I shall be able to make a complete clearing of that corner of the manor some day!"

''Twas extraordinary, now we look back upon it, that old Sargent should have been so dilatory; yet some people are like it; and he put off calling at the Squire's agent's office with the fine week after week, saying to himself, "I shall have more time next market-day than I have now." One unfortunate hindrance was that he didn't very well like Jasper Cliff, and as Jasper kept urging Netty, and Netty on that account kept urging her uncle, the old man was inclined to postpone the reliving as long as he could, to spite the selfish young lover. At last old Mr Sargent fell ill, and then Jasper could bear it no longer: he produced the fine-money himself, and handed it to Netty, and spoke to her plainly.

' "You and your uncle ought to know better. You should press him more. There's the money. If you let the house and ground slip between ye, I won't marry; hang me if I will! For folks won't deserve a husband that can do such things."

'The worried girl took the money and went home, and told her uncle that it was no house no husband for her. Old Mr Sargent pooh-poohed the money, for the amount was not worth consideration, but he did now bestir himself, for he saw she was bent upon marrying Jasper, and he did not wish to make her unhappy, since she was so determined. It was much to the Squire's annoyance that he found Sargent had moved in the matter at last; but he could not gainsay it, and the documents were prepared (for on this manor the copyholders had writings with their holdings, though on some manors they had none). Old Sargent being now too feeble to go to the agent's house, the deed was to be brought to his house signed, and handed over as a receipt for the money; the counterpart to be signed by Sargent, and sent back to the Squire.

'The agent had promised to call on old Sargent for this purpose at five o'clock, and Netty put the money into her desk to have it close at hand. While doing this she heard a slight cry from her uncle, and turning round, saw that he had fallen forward in his chair. She went and lifted him, but he was unconscious; and unconscious he remained. Neither medicine nor stimulants would bring him to himself. She had been told that he might possibly go off in that way, and it seemed as if the end had come. Before she had started for the doctor his face and extremities grew quite cold and white, and she saw that help would be useless. He was stone-dead.

'Netty's situation rose upon her distracted mind in all its seriousness. The house, garden, and field were lost – by a few hours – and with them a home for herself and her lover. She would not think so meanly of Jasper as to suppose that he would adhere to the resolution declared in a moment of impatience; but she trembled, nevertheless. Why could not her uncle have lived a couple of hours longer, since he had lived so long? It was now past three o'clock; at five the agent was to call, and, if all had gone well, by ten minutes past five the house and holding would have been securely hers for her own and Jasper's lives, these being two of the three proposed to be added by paying the fine. How that wretched old Squire would rejoice at getting the little tenancy into his hands! He did not really require it, but constitutionally hated these tiny copy-holds and leaseholds and freeholds, which made islands of independence in the fair, smooth ocean of his estates.

'Then an idea struck into the head of Netty how to accomplish her object in spite of her uncle's negligence. It was a dull December afternoon: and the first step in her scheme – so the story goes, and I see no reason to doubt it –'

''Tis true as the light,' affirmed Christopher Twink. 'I was just passing by.'

'The first step in her scheme was to fasten the outer door, to make sure of not being interrupted. Then she set to work by placing her uncle's small, heavy oak table before the fire; then she went to her uncle's corpse, sitting in the chair as he had died – a stuffed armchair, on casters, and rather high in the seat, so it was told me – and wheeled the chair, uncle and all, to the table, placing him with his back towards the window, in the attitude of bending over the said oak table, which I knew as a boy as well as I know any piece of furniture in my own house. On the table she laid the large family Bible open before him, and placed his forefinger on the page; and then she opened his eyelids a bit, and put on him his spectacles, so that from behind he appeared for all the world as if he were reading the Scriptures. Then she unfastened the door and sat down, and when it grew dark she lit a candle, and put it on the table beside her uncle's book.

'Folk may well guess how the time passed with her till the agent came, and how, when his knock sounded upon the door, she nearly started out of her skin – at least that's as it was told me. Netty promptly went to the door.

' "I am sorry, sir," she says, under her breath; "my uncle is not so well tonight, and I'm afraid he can't see you."

' "H'm! – that's a pretty tale," says the steward. "So I've come all this way about this trumpery little job for nothing!"

' "O no, sir – I hope not," says Netty. "I suppose the business of granting the new deed can be done just the same?"

' "Done? Certainly not. He must pay the renewal money, and sign the parchment in my presence."

'She looked dubious. "Uncle is so dreadful nervous about

law business," says she, "that, as you know, he's put it off and put it off for years; and now today really I've feared it would verily drive him out of his mind. His poor three teeth quite chattered when I said to him that you would be here soon with the parchment writing. He always was afraid of agents, and folks that come for rent, and such-like."

' "Poor old fellow – I'm sorry for him. Well, the thing can't be done unless I see him and witness his signature."

' "Suppose, sir, that you see him sign, and he don't see you looking at him! I'd soothe his nerves by saying you weren't strict about the form of witnessing, and didn't wish to come in. So that it was done in your bare presence it would be sufficient, would it not? As he's such an old, shrinking, shivering man, it would be a great considerateness on your part if that would do."

' "In my bare presence would do, of course – that's all I come for. But how can I be a witness without his seeing me?"

' "Why, in this way, sir; if you'll oblige me by just stepping here." She conducted him a few yards to the left, till they were opposite the parlour window. The blind had been left up purposely, and the candle-light shone out upon the garden bushes. Within the agent could see, at the other end of the room, the back and side of the old man's head, and his shoulders and arm, sitting with the book and candle before him, and his spectacles on his nose, as she had placed him.

' "He's reading his Bible, as you see, sir," she says, quite in her meekest way.

' "Yes. I thought he was a careless sort of man in matters of religion?"

' "He always was fond of his Bible," Netty assured him. "Though I think he's nodding over it just at this moment. However, that's natural in an old man, and unwell. Now you could stand here and see him sign, couldn't you, sir, as he's such an invalid?"

' "Very well," said the agent, lighting a cigar. "You have ready by you the merely nominal sum you'll have to pay for the admittance, of course?"

' "Yes," said Netty. "I'll bring it out." She fetched the cash, wrapped in paper, and handed it to him, and when he had counted it the steward took from his breast pocket the precious parchments and gave one to her to be signed.

' "Uncle's hand is a little paralyzed," she said. "And what with his being half asleep, too, really I don't know what sort of a signature he'll be able to make."

' "Doesn't matter, so that he signs."

' "Might I hold his hand?"

' "Ay, hold his hand, my young woman – that will be near enough."

'Netty re-entered the house, and the agent continued smoking outside the window. Now came the ticklish part of Netty's performance. The steward saw her put the inkhorn – "horn", says I in my old-fashioned way – the inkstand, before her uncle, and touch his elbow as if to arouse him, and speak to him, and spread out the deed; when she had pointed to show him where to sign she dipped the pen and put it into his hand. To hold his hand she artfully stepped behind him, so that the agent could only see a little bit of his head, and the hand she held; but he saw the old man's hand trace his name on the document. As soon as 'twas done she came out to the steward with the parchment in her hand, and the steward signed as witness by the light from the parlour window. Then he gave her the deed signed by the Squire, and left; and next morning Netty told the neighbours that her uncle was dead in his bed.'

'She must have undressed him and put him there.'

'She must. O, that girl had a nerve, I can tell ye! Well, to cut a long story short, that's how she got back the house and field that were, strictly speaking, gone from her; and by getting them, got her a husband.

'Every virtue has its reward, they say. Netty had hers for her ingenious contrivance to gain Jasper. Two years after they were married he took to beating her – not hard, you know; just a smack or two, enough to set her in a temper, and let out to the neighbours what she had done to win him, and how she repented of her pains. When the old Squire was dead, and his son came into the property, this confession of hers began to be whispered about. But Netty was a pretty young woman, and the Squire's son was a pretty young man at that time, and wider-minded than his father, having no objection to little holdings; and he never took any proceedings against her.'

There was now a lull in the discourse, and soon the van descended the hill leading into the long straggling village. When the houses were reached the passengers dropped off one by one, each at his or her own door. Arrived at the inn, the returned emigrant secured a bed, and having eaten a light meal, sallied forth upon the scene he had known so well in his early days. Though flooded with the light of the rising moon, none of the objects wore the attractiveness in this their real presentation that had ever accompanied their images in the field of his imagination when he was more than two thousand miles removed from them. The peculiar charm attaching to an old village in an old country, as seen by the eyes of an absolute foreigner, was lowered in his case by magnified expectations from infantine memories. He walked on, looking at this chimney and that old wall, till he came to the churchyard, which he entered.

The head-stones, whitened by the moon, were easily decipherable; and now for the first time Lackland began to feel himself amid the village community that he had left behind him five-and-thirty years before. Here, beside the Sallets, the Darths, the Pawles, the Privetts, the Sargents, and others of whom he had just heard, were names he remembered even better than those: the Jickses, and the Crosses, and the Knights, and the Olds. Doubtless representatives of these families, or some of them, were yet among the living; but to him they would all be as strangers. Far from finding his heart ready-supplied with roots and tendrils here, he perceived that in returning to this spot it would be incumbent upon him to re-establish himself from the beginning, precisely as though he had never known the place, nor it him. Time had not condescended to wait his pleasure, nor local life his greeting.

The figure of Mr Lackland was seen at the inn, and in the village street, and in the fields and lanes about Upper Longpuddle, for a few days after his arrival, and then, ghost-like, it silently disappeared. He had told some of the villagers that his immediate purpose in coming had been fulfilled by a sight of the place, and by conversation with its inhabitants; but that his ulterior purpose – of coming to spend his latter days among them – would probably never be carried out. It is now a dozen or fifteen years since his visit was paid, and his face has not again been seen.

March 1891

An Imaginative Woman

When William Marchmill had finished his inquiries for lodgings at the well-known watering-place of Solentsea in Upper Wessex, he returned to the hotel to find his wife. She, with the children, had rambled along the shore, and Marchmill followed in the direction indicated by the military-looking hall-porter.

'By Jove, how far you've gone! I am quite out of breath,' Marchmill said, rather impatiently, when he came up with his wife, who was reading as she walked, the three children being considerably further ahead with the nurse.

Mrs Marchmill started out of the reverie into which the book had thrown her. 'Yes,' she said, 'you've been such a long time. I was tired of staying in that dreary hotel. But I am sorry if you have wanted me, Will.'

'Well, I have had trouble to suit myself. When you see the airy and comfortable rooms heard of, you find they are stuffy and uncomfortable. Will you come and see if what I've fixed on will do? There is not much room, I am afraid; but I can light on nothing better. The town is rather full.'

The pair left the children and nurse to continue their ramble, and went back together.

In age well-balanced, in personal appearance fairly matched, and in domestic requirements conformable, in temper this couple differed, though even here they did not often clash, he being equable, if not lymphatic, and she decidedly nervous and sanguine. It was to their tastes and fancies, those smallest, greatest particulars, that no common denominator could be applied. Marchmill considered his wife's likes and inclinations somewhat silly; she considered his sordid and material. The husband's business was that of a gunmaker in a thriving city northwards, and his soul was in that business always; the lady was best characterized by that superannuated phrase of elegance 'a votary of the muse'. An impressionable, palpitating creature was Ella, shrinking humanely from detailed knowledge of her husband's trade whenever she reflected that everything he manufactured had for its purpose the destruction of life. She could only recover her equanimity by assuring herself that some, at least, of his weapons were sooner or later used for the extermination of horrid vermin and animals almost as cruel to their inferiors in species as human beings were to theirs.

She had never antecedently regarded this occupation of his as any objection to having him for a husband. Indeed, the necessity of getting life-leased at all cost, a cardinal virtue which all good mothers teach, kept her from thinking of it at all till she had closed with William, had passed the honeymoon, and reached the reflecting stage. Then, like a person who has stumbled upon some object in the dark, she wondered what she had got; mentally walked round it, estimated it; whether it were rare or common; contained gold, silver, or lead; were a clog or a pedestal, everything to her or nothing.

She came to some vague conclusions, and since then had kept her heart alive by pitying her proprietor's obtuseness and want of refinement, pitying herself, and letting off her delicate and ethereal emotions in imaginative occupations, daydreams, and night-sighs, which perhaps would not much have disturbed William if he had known of them.

Her figure was small, elegant, and slight in build, tripping, or rather bounding, in movement. She was dark-eyed, and had that marvellously bright and liquid sparkle in each pupil which characterizes persons of Ella's cast of soul, and is too often a cause of heartache to the possessor's male friends, ultimately sometimes to herself. Her husband was a tall, long-featured man, with a brown beard; he had a pondering regard; and was, it must be added, usually kind and tolerant to her. He spoke in squarely shaped sentences, and was supremely satisfied with a condition of sublunary things which made weapons a necessity.

Husband and wife walked till they had reached the house they were in search of, which stood in a terrace facing the sea, and was fronted by a small garden of wind-proof and salt-proof evergreens, stone steps leading up to the porch. It had its number in the row, but, being rather larger than the rest, was in addition sedulously distinguished as Coburg House by its landlady, though everybody else called it 'Thirteen, New Parade'. The spot was bright and lively now; but in winter it became necessary to place sandbags against the door, and to stuff up the keyhole against the wind and rain, which had worn the paint so thin that the priming and knotting showed through.

The householder, who had been watching for the gentleman's return, met them in the passage, and showed the rooms. She informed them that she was a professional man's widow, left in needy circumstances by the rather sudden death of her husband, and she spoke anxiously of the conveniences of the establishment.

Mrs Marchmill said that she liked the situation and the house; but, it being small, there would not be accommodation enough, unless she could have all the rooms.

The landlady mused with an air of disappointment. She wanted the visitors to be her tenants very badly, she said, with obvious honesty. But unfortunately two of the rooms were occupied permanently by a bachelor gentleman. He did not pay season prices, it was true; but as he kept on his apartments all the year round, and was an extremely nice and interesting young man, who gave no trouble, she did not like to turn him out for a month's 'let', even at a high figure. 'Perhaps, however,' she added, 'he might offer to go for a time.'

They would not hear of this, and went back to the hotel, intending to proceed to the agent's to inquire further. Hardly had they sat down to tea when the landlady called. Her gentleman, she said, had been so obliging as to offer to give up his rooms for three or four weeks rather than drive the newcomers away.

'It is very kind, but we won't inconvenience him in that way,' said the Marchmills.

'O, it won't inconvenience him, I assure you!' said the landlady eloquently. 'You see, he's a different sort of young man from most – dreamy, solitary, rather melancholy – and he cares more to be here when the south-westerly gales are beating against the door, and the sea washes over the Parade, and there's not a soul in the place, than he does now in the season. He'd just as soon be where, in fact, he's going temporarily, to a little cottage on the Island opposite, for a change.' She hoped therefore that they would come.

The Marchmill family accordingly took possession of the house next day, and it seemed to suit them very well. After luncheon Mr Marchmill strolled out towards the pier, and Mrs Marchmill, having despatched the children to their outdoor amusements on the sands, settled herself in more completely, examining this and that article, and testing the reflecting powers of the mirror in the wardrobe door.

In the small back sitting-room, which had been the young bachelor's, she found furniture of a more personal nature than in the rest. Shabby books, of correct rather than rare editions, were piled up in a queerly reserved manner in corners, as if the previous occupant had not conceived the possibility that any incoming person of the season's bringing could care to look inside them. The landlady hovered on the threshold to rectify anything that Mrs Marchmill might not find to her satisfaction.

'I'll make this my own little room,' said the latter, 'because the books are here. By the way, the person who has left seems to have a good many. He won't mind my reading some of them, Mrs Hooper, I hope?'

'O dear no, ma'am. Yes, he has a good many. You see, he is in the literary line himself somewhat. He is a poet – yes, really a poet – and he has a little income of his own, which is enough to write verses on, but not enough for cutting a figure, even if he cared to.'

'A poet! Oh, I did not know that.'

Mrs Marchmill opened one of the books, and saw the owner's name written on the title-page. 'Dear me!' she continued; 'I know his name very well – Robert Trewe – of course I do; and his writings! And it is *his* rooms we have taken, and *him* we have turned out of his home?'

Ella Marchmill, sitting down alone a few minutes later,

thought with interested surprise of Robert Trewe. Her own latter history will best explain that interest. Herself the only daughter of a struggling man of letters, she had during the last year or two taken to writing poems, in an endeavour to find a congenial channel in which to let flow her painfully embayed emotions, whose former limpidity and sparkle seemed departing in the stagnation caused by the routine of a practical household and the gloom of bearing children to a commonplace father. These poems, subscribed with a masculine pseudonym, had appeared in various obscure magazines, and in two cases in rather prominent ones. In the second of the latter the page which bore her effusion at the bottom, in smallish print, bore at the top, in large print, a few verses on the same subject by this very man, Robert Trewe. Both of them had, in fact, been struck by a tragic incident reported in the daily papers, and had used it simultaneously as an inspiration, the editor remarking in a note upon the coincidence, and that the excellence of both poems prompted him to give them together.

After that event Ella, otherwise 'John Ivy', had watched with much attention the appearance anywhere in print of verse bearing the signature of Robert Trewe, who, with a man's unsusceptibility on the question of sex, had never once thought of passing himself off as a woman. To be sure, Mrs Marchmill had satisfied herself with a sort of reason for doing the contrary in her case; since nobody might believe in her inspiration if they found that the sentiments came from a pushing tradesman's wife, from the mother of three children by a matter-of-fact small-arms manufacturer.

Trewe's verse contrasted with that of the rank and file of recent minor poets in being impassioned rather than ingenious, luxuriant rather than finished. Neither *symboliste* nor *décadent*, he was a pessimist in so far as that character applies to a man who looks at the worst contingencies as well as the best in the human condition. Being little attracted by excellences of form and rhythm apart from content, he sometimes, when feeling outran his artistic speed, perpetrated sonnets in the loosely rhymed Elizabethan fashion, which every right-minded reviewer said he ought not to have done.

With sad and hopeless envy Ella Marchmill had often and often scanned the rival poet's work, so much stronger as it always was than her own feeble lines. She had imitated him, and her inability to touch his level would send her into fits of despondency. Months passed away thus, till she observed from the publisher's list that Trewe had collected his fugitive pieces into a volume, which was duly issued, and was much or little praised according to chance, and had a sale quite sufficient to pay for the printing.

This step onward had suggested to 'John Ivy' the idea of collecting her pieces also, or at any rate of making up a book of her rhymes by adding many in manuscript to the few that had seen the light, for she had been able to get no great number into print. A ruinous charge was made for costs of publication; a few reviews noticed her poor little volume; but nobody talked of it, nobody bought it, and it fell dead in a fortnight – if it had ever been alive.

The author's thoughts were diverted to another groove just then by the discovery that she was going to have a third child, and the collapse of her poetical venture had perhaps less effect upon her mind than it might have done if she had been domestically unoccupied. Her husband had paid the publisher's bill with the doctor's, and there it all had ended for the time. But, though less than a poet of her century, Ella was more than a mere multiplier of her kind, and latterly she had begun to feel the old afflatus once more. And now by an odd conjunction she found herself in the rooms of Robert Trewe.

She thoughtfully rose from her chair and searched the apartment with the interest of a fellow-tradesman. Yes, the volume of his own verse was among the rest. Though quite familiar with its contents, she read it here as if it spoke aloud to her, then called up Mrs Hooper, the landlady, for some trivial service, and inquired again about the young man.

'Well, I'm sure you'd be interested in him, ma'am, if you could see him, only he's so shy that I don't suppose you will.' Mrs Hooper seemed nothing loth to minister to her tenant's curiosity about her predecessor. 'Lived here long? Yes, nearly two years. He keeps on his rooms even when he's not here: the soft air of this place suits his chest, and he likes to be able to come back at any time. He is mostly writing or reading, and doesn't see many people, though, for the matter of that, he is such a good, kind young fellow that folks would only be too glad to be friendly with him if they knew him. You don't meet kind-hearted people every day.'

'Ah, he's kind-hearted . . . and good.'

'Yes; he'll oblige me in anything if I ask him. "Mr Trewe," I say to him sometimes, "you are rather out of spirits." "Well, I am, Mrs Hooper," he'll say, "though I don't know how you should find it out." "Why not take a little change?" I ask. Then in a day or two he'll say that he will take a trip to Paris, or Norway, or somewhere; and I assure you he comes back all the better for it.'

'Ah, indeed! His is a sensitive nature, no doubt.'

'Yes. Still he's odd in some things. Once when he had finished a poem of his composition late at night he walked up and down the room rehearsing it; and the floors being so thin – jerry-built houses, you know, though I say it myself – he kept me awake up above him till I wished him further. . . . But we get on very well.'

This was but the beginning of a series of conversations about the rising poet as the days went on. On one of these occasions Mrs Hooper drew Ella's attention to what she had not noticed before: minute scribblings in pencil on the wall-paper behind the curtains at the head of the bed.

'O! let me look,' said Mrs Marchmill, unable to conceal a rush of tender curiosity as she bent her pretty face close to the wall.

'These,' said Mrs Hooper, with the manner of a woman who knew things, 'are the very beginnings and first thoughts of his verses. He has tried to rub most of them out, but you can read them still. My belief is that he wakes up in the night, you know, with some rhyme in his head, and jots it down there on the wall lest he should forget it by the morning. Some of these very lines you see here I have seen afterwards in print in the magazines. Some are newer; indeed, I have not seen that one before. It must have been done only a few days ago.'

'O yes! . . .'

Ella Marchmill flushed without knowing why, and suddenly wished her companion would go away, now that the information was imparted. An indescribable consciousness of personal interest rather than literary made her anxious to read the inscription alone; and she accordingly waited till she could do so, with a sense that a great store of emotion would be enjoyed in the act.

Perhaps because the sea was choppy outside the Island, Ella's husband found it much pleasanter to go sailing and steaming about without his wife, who was a bad sailor, than with her. He did not disdain to go thus alone on board the steamboats of the cheap-trippers, where there was dancing by moonlight, and where the couples would come suddenly down with a lurch into each other's arms; for, as he blandly told her, the company was too mixed for him to take her amid such scenes. Thus, while this thriving manufacturer got a great deal of change and sea-air out of his sojourn here, the life, external at least, of Ella was monotonous enough, and mainly consisted in passing a certain number of hours each day in bathing and walking up and down a stretch of shore. But the poetic impulse having again waxed strong, she was possessed by an inner flame which left her hardly conscious of what was proceeding around her.

She had read till she knew by heart Trewe's last little volume of verses, and spent a great deal of time in vainly attempting to rival some of them, till, in her failure, she burst into tears. The personal element in the magnetic attraction exercised by this circum-ambient, unapproachable master of hers was so much stronger than the intellectual and abstract that she could not understand it. To be sure, she was surrounded noon and night by his customary environment, which literally whispered of him to her at every moment; but he was a man she had never seen, and that all that moved her was the instinct to specialize a waiting emotion on the first fit thing that came to hand did not, of course, suggest itself to Ella.

In the natural way of passion under the too practical conditions which civilization has devised for its fruition, her husband's love for her had not survived, except in the form of fitful friendship, any more than, or even so much as, her own for him; and, being a woman of very living ardours, that required sustenance of some sort, they were beginning to feed on this chancing material, which was, indeed, of a quality far better than chance usually offers.

One day the children had been playing hide-and-seek in a closet, whence, in their excitement, they pulled out some clothing. Mrs Hooper explained that it belonged to Mr Trewe, and hung it up in the closet again. Possessed of her fantasy, Ella went later in the afternoon, when nobody was in that part of the house, opened the closet, unhitched one of the articles, a mackintosh, and put it on, with the waterproof cap belonging to it.

'The mantle of Elijah!' she said. 'Would it might inspire me to rival him, glorious genius that he is!'

Her eyes always grew wet when she thought like that, and she turned to look at herself in the glass. *His* heart had beat inside that coat, and *his* brain had worked under that hat at levels of thought she would never reach. The consciousness of her weakness beside him made her feel quite sick. Before she had got the things off her the door opened, and her husband entered the room.

'What the devil –'

She blushed, and removed them.

'I found them in the closet here,' she said, 'and put them on in a freak. What have I else to do? You are always away!'

'Always away? Well. . . .'

That evening she had a further talk with the landlady, who might herself have nourished a half-tender regard for the poet, so ready was she to discourse ardently about him.

'You are interested in Mr Trewe, I know, ma'am,' she said; 'and he has just sent to say that he is going to call tomorrow afternoon to look up some books of his that he wants, if I'll be in, and he may select them from your room?'

'O yes!'

'You could very well meet Mr Trewe then, if you'd like to be in the way!'

She promised with secret delight, and went to bed musing of him.

Next morning her husband observed: 'I've been thinking of what you said, Ell: that I have gone about a good deal and left you without much to amuse you. Perhaps it's true. Today, as there's not much sea, I'll take you with me on board the yacht.'

For the first time in her experience of such an offer Ella was not glad. But she accepted it for the moment. The time for setting out drew near, and she went to get ready. She stood reflecting. The longing to see the poet she was now distinctly in love with overpowered all other considerations.

'I don't want to go,' she said to herself. 'I can't bear to be away! And I won't go.'

She told her husband that she had changed her mind about wishing to sail. He was indifferent, and went his way.

For the rest of the day the house was quiet, the children having gone out upon the sands. The blinds waved in the sunshine to the soft, steady stroke of the sea beyond the wall; and the notes of the Green Silesian band, a troop of foreign gentlemen hired for the season, had drawn almost all the residents and promenaders away from the vicinity of Coburg House. A knock was audible at the door.

Mrs Marchmill did not hear any servant go to answer it, and she became impatient. The books were in the room where she sat; but nobody came up. She rang the bell.

'There is some person waiting at the door,' she said.

'O no, ma'am! He's gone long ago. I answered it,' the servant replied, and Mrs Hooper came in herself.

'So disappointing!' she said. 'Mr Trewe not coming after all!'

'But I heard him knock, I fancy!'

'No; that was somebody inquiring for lodgings who came to the wrong house. I forgot to tell you that Mr Trewe sent a note just before lunch to say I needn't get any tea for him, as he should not require the books, and wouldn't come to select them.'

Ella was miserable, and for a long time could not even re-read his mournful ballad on 'Severed Lives', so aching was her erratic little heart, and so tearful her eyes. When the children came in with wet stockings, and ran up to her to tell her of their adventures, she could not feel that she cared about them half as much as usual.

* * *

'Mrs Hooper, have you a photograph of – the gentleman who lived here?' She was getting to be curiously shy in mentioning his name.

'Why, yes. It's in the ornamental frame on the mantelpiece in your own bedroom, ma'am.'

'No; the Royal Duke and Duchess are in that.'

'Yes, so they are; but he's behind them. He belongs rightly to that frame, which I bought on purpose; but as he went away he said: "Cover me up from those strangers that are coming, for God's sake. I don't want them staring at me, and I am sure they won't want me staring at them." So I slipped in the Duke and Duchess temporarily in front of him, as they had no frame, and Royalties are more suitable for letting furnished than a private young man. If you take 'em out you'll see him under. Lord, ma'am, he wouldn't mind if he knew it! He didn't think the next tenant would be such an attractive lady as you, or he wouldn't have thought of hiding himself, perhaps.'

'Is he handsome?' she asked timidly.

'*I* call him so. Some, perhaps, wouldn't.'

'Should I?' she asked, with eagerness.

'I think you would, though some would say he's more striking than handsome; a large-eyed, thoughtful fellow, you know, with a very electric flash in his eye when he looks round quickly, such as you'd expect a poet to be who doesn't get his living by it.'

'How old is he?'

'Several years older than yourself, ma'am; about thirty-one or two, I think.'

Ella was, as a matter of fact, a few months over thirty herself; but she did not look nearly so much. Though so immature in nature, she was entering on that tract of life in which emotional women begin to suspect that last love may be stronger than first love; and she would soon, alas! enter on the still more melancholy tract when at least the vainer ones of her sex shrink from receiving a male visitor otherwise than with their backs to the window or the blinds half down. She reflected on Mrs Hooper's remark, and said no more about age.

Just then a telegram was brought up. It came from her husband, who had gone down the Channel as far as Budmouth with his friends in the yacht, and would not be able to get back till next day.

After her light dinner Ella idled about the shore with the children till dusk, thinking of the yet uncovered photograph in her room, with a serene sense of something ecstatic to come. For, with the subtle luxuriousness of fancy in which this young woman was an adept, on learning that her husband was to be absent that night she had refrained from incontinently rushing upstairs and opening the picture-frame, preferring to reserve the inspection till she could be alone, and a more romantic tinge be imparted to the occasion by silence, candles, solemn sea and stars outside, than was afforded by the garish afternoon sunlight.

The children had been sent to bed, and Ella soon followed, though it was not yet ten o'clock. To gratify her passionate curiosity she now made her preparations, first getting rid of superfluous garments and putting on her dressing-gown, then arranging a chair in front of the table and reading several pages of Trewe's tenderest utterances. Next she fetched the portrait-frame to the light, opened the back, took out the likeness, and set it up before her.

It was a striking countenance to look upon. The poet wore a luxuriant black moustache and imperial, and a slouched hat which shaded the forehead. The large dark eyes described by the landlady showed an unlimited capacity for misery; they looked out from beneath well-shaped brows as if they were reading the universe in the microcosm of the confronter's face, and were not altogether overjoyed at what the spectacle portended.

Ella murmured in her lowest, richest, tenderest tone: 'And it's *you* who've so cruelly eclipsed me these many times!'

As she gazed long at the portrait she fell into thought, till her eyes filled with tears, and she touched the cardboard with her lips. Then she laughed with a nervous lightness, and wiped her eyes.

She thought how wicked she was, a woman having a husband and three children, to let her mind stray to a stranger in this unconscionable manner. No, he was not a stranger! She knew his thoughts and feelings as well as she knew her own; they were, in fact, the self-same thoughts and feelings as hers, which her husband distinctly lacked; perhaps luckily for himself, considering that he had to provide for family expenses.

'He's nearer my real self, he's more intimate with the real me than Will is, after all, even though I've never seen him,' she said.

She laid his book and picture on the table at the bedside, and when she was reclining on the pillow she re-read those of Robert Trewe's verses which she had marked from time to time as most touching and true. Putting these aside she set up the photograph on its edge upon the coverlet, and contemplated it as she lay. Then she scanned again by the light of the candle the half-obliterated pencillings on the wall-paper beside her head. There they were — phrases, couplets, *bouts-rimés*, beginnings and middles of lines, ideas in the rough, like Shelley's scraps, and the least of them so intense, so sweet, so palpitating, that it seemed as if his very breath, warm and loving, fanned her cheeks from those walls, walls that had surrounded his head times and times as they surrounded her own now. He must often have put up his hand so — with the pencil in it. Yes, the writing was sideways, as it would be if executed by one who extended his arm thus.

These inscribed shapes of the poet's world,

> Forms more real than living man,
> Nurslings of immortality,

were, no doubt, the thoughts and spirit-strivings which had come to him in the dead of night, when he could let himself go and have no fear of the frost of criticism. No doubt they had often been written up hastily by the light of the moon, the rays of the lamp, in the blue-grey dawn, in full daylight perhaps never. And now her hair was dragging where his arm had lain when he secured the fugitive fancies; she was sleeping on a poet's lips, immersed in the very essence of him, permeated by his spirit as by an ether.

While she was dreaming the minutes away thus, a footstep came upon the stairs, and in a moment she heard her husband's heavy step on the landing immediately without.

'Ell, where are you?'

What possessed her she could not have described, but, with an instinctive objection to let her husband know what she had been doing, she slipped the photograph under the pillow just as he flung open the door with the air of a man who had dined not badly.

'O, I beg pardon,' said William Marchmill. 'Have you a headache? I am afraid I have disturbed you.'

'No, I've not got a headache,' said she. 'How is it you've come?'

'Well, we found we could get back in very good time after all, and I didn't want to make another day of it, because of going somewhere else tomorrow.'

'Shall I come down again?'

'O no. I'm as tired as a dog. I've had a good feed, and I shall turn in straight off. I want to get out at six o'clock tomorrow if I can. . . . I shan't disturb you by my getting up; it will be long before you are awake.' And he came forward into the room.

While her eyes followed his movements, Ella softly pushed the photograph further out of sight.

'Surely you're not ill?' he asked, bending over her.

'No, only wicked!'

'Never mind that.' And he stooped and kissed her. 'I wanted to be with you tonight.'

Next morning Marchmill was called at six o'clock; and in waking and yawning she heard him muttering to himself: 'What the deuce is this that's been crackling under me so?' Imagining her asleep he searched round him and withdrew something. Through her half-opened eyes she perceived it to be Mr Trewe.

'Well, I'm damned!' her husband exclaimed.

'What, dear?' said she.

'O, you are awake? Ha! ha!'

'What *do* you mean?'

'Some bloke's photograph – a friend of our landlady's, I suppose. I wonder how it came here; whisked off the mantelpiece by accident perhaps when they were making the bed.'

'I was looking at it yesterday, and it must have dropped in then.'

'O, he's a friend of yours? Bless his picturesque heart!'

Ella's loyalty to the object of her admiration could not endure to hear him ridiculed. 'He's a clever man!' she said, with a tremor in her gentle voice which she herself felt to be absurdly uncalled for. 'He is a rising poet – the gentleman who occupied two of these rooms before we came, though I've never seen him.'

'How do you know, if you've never seen him?'

'Mrs Hooper told me when she showed me the photograph.'

'O, well, I must up and be off. I shall be home rather early. Sorry I can't take you today, dear. Mind the children don't go getting drowned.'

That day Mrs Marchmill inquired if Mr Trewe were likely to call at any other time.

'Yes,' said Mrs Hooper. 'He's coming this day week to stay with a friend near here till you leave. He'll be sure to call.'

Marchmill did return quite early in the afternoon; and, opening some letters which had arrived in his absence, declared suddenly that he and his family would have to leave a week earlier than they had expected to do – in short, in three days.

'Surely we can stay a week longer?' she pleaded. 'I like it here.'

'I don't. It is getting rather slow.'

'Then you might leave me and the children!'

'How perverse you are, Ell! What's the use? And have to come to fetch you! No: we'll all return together; and we'll make out our time in North Wales or Brighton a little later on. Besides, you've three days longer yet.'

It seemed to be her doom not to meet the man for whose rival talent she had a despairing admiration, and to whose person she was now absolutely attached. Yet she determined to make a last effort; and having gathered from her landlady that Trewe was living in a lonely spot not far from the fashionable town on the Island opposite, she crossed over in the packet from the neighbouring pier the following afternoon.

What a useless journey it was! Ella knew but vaguely where

the house stood, and when she fancied she had found it, and ventured to inquire of a pedestrian if he lived there, the answer returned by the man was that he did not know. And if he did live there, how could she call upon him? Some women might have the assurance to do it, but she had not. How crazy he would think her. She might have asked him to call upon her, perhaps; but she had not the courage for that, either. She lingered mournfully about the picturesque seaside eminence till it was time to return to the town and enter the steamer for recrossing, reaching home for dinner without having been greatly missed.

At the last moment, unexpectedly enough, her husband said that he should have no objection to letting her and the children stay on till the end of the week, since she wished to do so, if she felt herself able to get home without him. She concealed the pleasure this extension of time gave her; and Marchmill went off the next morning alone.

But the week passed, and Trewe did not call.

On Saturday morning the remaining members of the Marchmill family departed from the place which had been productive of so much fervour in her. The dreary, dreary train; the sun shining in moted beams upon the hot cushions; the dusty permanent way; the mean rows of wire – these things were her accompaniment: while out of the window the deep blue sea-levels disappeared from her gaze, and with them her poet's home. Heavy-hearted, she tried to read, and wept instead.

Mr Marchmill was in a thriving way of business, and he and his family lived in a large new house, which stood in rather extensive grounds a few miles outside the midland city wherein he carried on his trade. Ella's life was lonely here, as the suburban life is apt to be, particularly at certain seasons; and she had ample time to indulge her taste for lyric and elegiac composition. She had hardly got back when she encountered a piece by Robert Trewe in the new number of her favourite magazine, which must have been written almost immediately before her visit to Solentsea, for it contained the very couplet she had seen pencilled on the wallpaper by the bed, and Mrs

Hooper had declared to be recent. Ella could resist no longer, but seizing a pen impulsively, wrote to him as a brother-poet, using the name of John Ivy, congratulating him in her letter on his triumphant executions in metre and rhythm of thoughts that moved his soul, as compared with her own brow-beaten efforts in the same pathetic trade.

To this address there came a response in a few days, little as she had dared to hope for it – a civil and brief note, in which the young poet stated that, though he was not well acquainted with Mr Ivy's verse, he recalled the name as being one he had seen attached to some very promising pieces; that he was glad to gain Mr Ivy's acquaintance by letter, and should certainly look with much interest for his productions in the future.

There must have been something juvenile or timid in her own epistle, as one ostensibly coming from a man, she declared to herself; for Trewe quite adopted the tone of an elder and superior in this reply. But what did it matter? He had replied; he had written to her with his own hand from that very room she knew so well, for he was now back again in his quarters.

The correspondence thus begun was continued for two months or more, Ella Marchmill sending him from time to time some that she considered to be the best of her pieces, which he very kindly accepted, though he did not say he sedulously read them, nor did he send her any of his own in return. Ella would have been more hurt at this than she was if she had not known that Trewe laboured under the impression that she was one of his own sex.

Yet the situation was unsatisfactory. A flattering little voice told her that, were he only to see her, matters would be otherwise. No doubt she would have helped on this by making a frank confession of womanhood, to begin with, if something had not happened, to her delight, to render it unnecessary. A friend of her husband's, the editor of the most important newspaper in their city and county, who was dining with them one day, observed during their conversation about the poet that his (the editor's) brother the landscape-painter was a friend of Mr Trewe's, and that the two men were at that very moment in Wales together.

Ella was slightly acquainted with the editor's brother. The next morning down she sat and wrote, inviting him to stay at her house for a short time on his way back, and requesting him to bring with him, if practicable, his companion Mr Trewe, whose acquaintance she was anxious to make. The answer arrived after some few days. Her correspondent and his friend Trewe would have much satisfaction in accepting her invitation on their way southward, which would be on such and such a day in the following week.

Ella was blithe and buoyant. Her scheme had succeeded; her beloved though as yet unseen one was coming. 'Behold, he standeth behind our wall; he looked forth at the windows, showing himself through the lattice,' she thought ecstatically. 'And, lo, the winter is past, the rain is over and gone, the flowers appear on the earth, the time of the singing of birds is come, and the voice of the turtle is heard in our land.'

But it was necessary to consider the details of lodging and feeding him. This she did most solicitously, and awaited the pregnant day and hour.

It was about five in the afternoon when she heard a ring at the door and the editor's brother's voice in the hall. Poetess as she was, or as she thought herself, she had not been too sublime that day to dress with infinite trouble in a fashionable robe of rich material, having a faint resemblance to the *chiton* of the Greeks, a style just then in vogue among ladies of an artistic and romantic turn, which had been obtained by Ella of her Bond Street dressmaker when she was last in London. Her visitor entered the drawing-room. She looked towards his rear; nobody else came through the door. Where, in the name of the God of Love, was Robert Trewe?

'O, I'm sorry,' said the painter, after their introductory words had been spoken. 'Trewe is a curious fellow, you know, Mrs Marchmill. He said he'd come; then he said he couldn't. He's rather dusty. We've been doing a few miles with knapsacks, you know; and he wanted to get on home.'

'He – he's not coming?'

'He's not; and he asked me to make his apologies.'

'When did you p-p-part from him?' she asked, her nether lip

starting off quivering so much that it was like a *tremolo*-stop opened in her speech. She longed to run away from this dreadful bore and cry her eyes out.

'Just now, in the turnpike road yonder there.'

'What! he has actually gone past my gates?'

'Yes. When we got to them – handsome gates they are, too, the finest bit of modern wrought-iron work I have seen – when we came to them we stopped, talking there a little while, and then he wished me goodbye and went on. The truth is, he's a little bit depressed just now, and doesn't want to see anybody. He's a very good fellow, and a warm friend, but a little uncertain and gloomy sometimes; he thinks too much of things. His poetry is rather too erotic and passionate, you know, for some tastes; and he has just come in for a terrible slating from the —— *Review* that was published yesterday; he saw a copy of it at the station by accident. Perhaps you've read it?'

'No.'

'So much the better. O, it is not worth thinking of; just one of those articles written to order, to please the narrow-minded set of subscribers upon whom the circulation depends. But he's upset by it. He says it is the misrepresentation that hurts him so; that, though he can stand a fair attack, he can't stand lies that he's powerless to refute and stop from spreading. That's just Trewe's weak point. He lives so much by himself that these things affect him much more than they would if he were in the bustle of fashionable or commercial life. So he wouldn't come here, making the excuse that it all looked so new and monied – if you'll pardon –'

'But – he must have known – there was sympathy here! Has he never said anything about getting letters from this address?'

'Yes, yes, he has, from John Ivy – perhaps a relative of yours, he thought, visiting here at the time?'

'Did he – like Ivy, did he say?'

'Well, I don't know that he took any great interest in Ivy.'

'Or in his poems?'

'Or in his poems – so far as I know, that is.'

Robert Trewe took no interest in her house, in her poems, or in their writer. As soon as she could get away she went into the nursery and tried to let off her emotion by unnecessarily kissing the children, till she had a sudden sense of disgust at being reminded how plain-looking they were, like their father.

The obtuse and single-minded landscape-painter never once perceived from her conversation that it was only Trewe she wanted, and not himself. He made the best of his visit, seeming to enjoy the society of Ella's husband, who also took a great fancy to him, and showed him everywhere about the neighbourhood, neither of them noticing Ella's mood.

The painter had been gone only a day or two when, while sitting upstairs alone one morning, she glanced over the London paper just arrived, and read the following paragraph: –

'SUICIDE OF A POET

'Mr Robert Trewe, who has been favourably known for some years as one of our rising lyrists, committed suicide at his lodgings at Solentsea on Saturday evening last by shooting himself in the right temple with a revolver. Readers hardly need to be reminded that Mr Trewe has recently attracted the attention of a much wider public than had hitherto known him, by his new volume of verse, mostly of an impassioned kind, entitled "Lyrics to a Woman Unknown", which has been already favourably noticed in these pages for the extraordinary gamut of feeling it traverses, and which has been made the subject of a severe, if not ferocious, criticism in the —— *Review*. It is supposed, though not certainly known, that the article may have partially conduced to the sad act, as a copy of the review in question was found on his writing-table; and he has been observed to be in a somewhat depressed state of mind since the critique appeared.'

Then came the report of the inquest, at which the following letter was read, it having been addressed to a friend at a distance: –

'DEAR ——, – Before these lines reach your hands I shall be delivered from the inconveniences of seeing, hearing, and knowing more of the things around me. I will not trouble you by giving my reasons for the step I have taken, though I can assure you they were sound and logical. Perhaps had I been blessed with a mother, or a sister, or a female friend of another sort tenderly devoted to me, I might have thought it worth while to continue my present existence. I have long dreamt of such an unattainable creature, as you know; and she, this undiscoverable, elusive one, inspired my last volume; the imaginary woman alone, for, in spite of what has been said in some quarters, there is no real woman behind the title. She has continued to the last unrevealed, unmet, unwon. I think it desirable to mention this in order that no blame may attach to any real woman as having been the cause of my decease by cruel or cavalier treatment of me. Tell my landlady that I am sorry to have caused her this unpleasantness; but my occupancy of the rooms will soon be forgotten. There are ample funds in my name at the bank to pay all expenses.

R. TREWE'

Ella sat for a while as if stunned, then rushed into the adjoining chamber and flung herself upon her face on the bed.

Her grief and distraction shook her to pieces; and she lay in this frenzy of sorrow for more than an hour. Broken words came every now and then from her quivering lips: 'O, if he had only known of me – known of me – me! . . . O, if I had only once met him – only once; and put my hand upon his hot forehead – kissed him – let him know how I loved him – that I would have suffered shame and scorn, would have lived and died, for him! Perhaps it would have saved his dear life! . . . But no – it was not allowed! God is a jealous God; and that happiness was not for him and me!'

All possibilities were over; the meeting was stultified. Yet it was almost visible to her in her fantasy even now, though it could never be substantiated –

> The hour which might have been, yet might not be,
> Which man's and woman's heart conceived and bore,
> Yet whereof life was barren.

She wrote to the landlady at Solentsea in the third person, in as subdued a style as she could command, enclosing a postal order for a sovereign, and informing Mrs Hooper that Mrs Marchmill had seen in the papers the sad account of the poet's death, and having been, as Mrs Hooper was aware, much interested in Mr Trewe during her stay at Coburg House, she would be obliged if Mrs Hooper could obtain a small portion of his hair before his coffin was closed down, and send it her as a memorial of him, as also the photograph that was in the frame.

By the return-post a letter arrived containing what had been requested. Ella wept over the portrait and secured it in her private drawer; the lock of hair she tied with white ribbon and put in her bosom, whence she drew it and kissed it every now and then in some unobserved nook.

'What's the matter?' said her husband, looking up from his newspaper on one of these occasions. 'Crying over something? A lock of hair? Whose is it?'

'He's dead!' she murmured.

'Who?'

'I don't want to tell you, Will, just now, unless you insist!' she said, a sob hanging heavy in her voice.

'O, all right.'

'Do you mind my refusing? I will tell you some day.'

'It doesn't matter in the least, of course.'

He walked away whistling a few bars of no tune in particular; and when he had got down to his factory in the city the subject came into Marchmill's head again.

He, too, was aware that a suicide had taken place recently at the house they had occupied at Solentsea. Having seen the volume of poems in his wife's hand of late, and heard fragments of the landlady's conversation about Trewe when they were her tenants, he all at once said to himself, 'Why of course it's he! . . . How the devil did she get to know him? What sly animals women are!'

Then he placidly dismissed the matter, and went on with his daily affairs. By this time Ella at home had come to a determination. Mrs Hooper, in sending the hair and photograph, had informed her of the day of the funeral; and as the morning and noon wore on an overpowering wish to know where they were laying him took possession of the sympathetic woman.

Caring very little now what her husband or anyone else might think of her eccentricities, she wrote Marchmill a brief note, stating that she was called away for the afternoon and evening, but would return on the following morning. This she left on his desk, and having given the same information to the servants, went out of the house on foot.

When Mr Marchmill reached home early in the afternoon the servants looked anxious. The nurse took him privately aside, and hinted that her mistress's sadness during the past few days had been such that she feared she had gone out to drown herself. Marchmill reflected. Upon the whole he thought that she had not done that. Without saying whither he was bound he also started off, telling them not to sit up for him. He drove to the railway-station, and took a ticket for Solentsea.

It was dark when he reached the place, though he had come by a fast train, and he knew that if his wife had preceded him thither it could only have been by a slower train, arriving not a great while before his own. The season at Solentsea was now past: the parade was gloomy, and the flys were few and cheap. He asked the way to the Cemetery, and soon reached it. The gate was locked, but the keeper let him in, declaring, however, that there was nobody within the precincts. Although it was not late, the autumnal darkness had now become intense; and he found some difficulty in keeping to the serpentine path which led to the quarter where, as the man had told him, the one or two interments for the day had taken place. He stepped upon the grass, and, stumbling over some pegs, stooped now and then to discern if possible a figure against the sky. He could see none; but lighting on a spot where the soil was trodden, beheld a crouching object beside a newly-made grave. She heard him, and sprang up.

'Ell, how silly this is!' he said indignantly. 'Running away from home – I never heard such a thing! Of course I am not jealous of this unfortunate man; but it is too ridiculous that you, a married woman with three children and a fourth coming, should go losing your head like this over a dead lover! . . . Do you know you were locked in? You might not have been able to get out all night.'

She did not answer.

'I hope it didn't go far between you and him, for your own sake.'

'Don't insult me, Will.'

'Mind, I won't have any more of this sort of thing; do you hear?'

'Very well,' she said.

He drew her arm within his own, and conducted her out of the Cemetery. It was impossible to get back that night; and not wishing to be recognized in their present sorry condition he took her to a miserable little coffee-house close to the station, whence they departed early in the morning, travelling almost without speaking, under the sense that it was one of those dreary situations occurring in married life which words could not mend, and reaching their own door at noon.

The months passed, and neither of the twain ever ventured to start a conversation upon this episode. Ella seemed to be only too frequently in a sad and listless mood, which might almost have been called pining. The time was approaching when she would have to undergo the stress of childbirth for a fourth time, and that apparently did not tend to raise her spirits.

'I don't think I shall get over it this time!' she said one day.

'Pooh! what childish foreboding! Why shouldn't it be as well now as ever?'

She shook her head. 'I feel almost sure I am going to die; and I should be glad, if it were not for Nelly, and Frank, and Tiny.'

'And me!'

'You'll soon find somebody to fill my place,' she murmured, with a sad smile. 'And you'll have a perfect right to; I assure you of that.'

'Ell, you are not thinking still about that – poetical friend of yours?'

She neither admitted nor denied the charge. 'I am not going to get over my illness this time,' she reiterated. 'Something tells me I shan't.'

This view of things was rather a bad beginning, as it usually is; and, in fact, six weeks later, in the month of May, she was lying in her room, pulseless and bloodless, with hardly strength enough left to follow up one feeble breath with another, the infant for whose unnecessary life she was slowly parting with her own being fat and well. Just before her death she spoke to Marchmill softly: –

'Will, I want to confess to you the entire circumstances of that – about you know what – that time we visited Solentsea. I can't tell what possessed me – how I could forget you so, my husband! But I had got into a morbid state: I thought you had been unkind; that you had neglected me; that you weren't up to my intellectual level, while he was, and far above it. I wanted a fuller appreciator, perhaps, rather than another lover –'

She could get no further then for very exhaustion; and she went off in sudden collapse a few hours later, without having said anything more to her husband on the subject of her love for her poet. William Marchmill, in truth, like most husbands of several years' standing, was little disturbed by retrospective jealousies, and had not shown the least anxiety to press her for confessions concerning a man dead and gone beyond any power of inconveniencing him more.

But when she had been buried a couple of years it chanced one day that, in turning over some forgotten papers that he wished to destroy before his second wife entered the house, he lighted on a lock of hair in an envelope, with the photograph of the deceased poet, a date being written on the back in his late wife's hand. It was that of the time they spent at Solentsea.

Marchmill looked long and musingly at the hair and portrait, for something struck him. Fetching the little boy who had been the death of his mother, now a noisy toddler, he took him on his knee, held the lock of hair against the child's head, and set up the photograph on the table behind, so that he could closely compare the features each countenance presented. By a known but inexplicable trick of Nature there were undoubtedly strong traces of resemblance to the man Ella had never seen; the dreamy and peculiar expression of the poet's face sat, as the transmitted idea, upon the child's, and the hair was of the same hue.

'I'm damned if I didn't think so!' murmured Marchmill. 'Then she *did* play me false with that fellow at the lodgings! Let me see: the dates – the second week in August ... the third week in May.... Yes ... Yes.... Get away, you poor little brat! You are nothing to me!'

1893

POEMS

Home and Family

Domicilium

IT faces west, and round the back and sides
High beeches, bending, hang a veil of boughs,
And sweep against the roof. Wild honeysucks
Climb on the walls, and seem to sprout a wish
(If we may fancy wish of trees and plants)
To overtop the apple-trees hard by.

Red roses, lilacs, variegated box
Are there in plenty, and such hardy flowers
As flourish best untrained. Adjoining these
Are herbs and esculents; and farther still
A field; then cottages with trees; and last
The distant hills and sky.

Behind, the scene is wilder. Heath and furze
Are everything that seems to grow and thrive
Upon the uneven ground. A stunted thorn
Stands here and there, indeed; and from a pit
An oak uprises, springing from a seed
Dropped by some bird a hundred years ago.

                              In days bygone –
Long gone – my father's mother, who is now
Blest with the blest, would take me out to walk.
At such a time I once inquired of her
How looked the spot when first she settled here.
The answer I remember. 'Fifty years
Have passed since then, my child, and change has marked
The face of all things. Yonder garden-plots
And orchards were uncultivated slopes

O'ergrown with bramble bushes, furze and thorn:
That road a narrow path shut in by ferns,
Which, almost trees, obscured the passer-by.

'Our house stood quite alone, and those tall firs
And beeches were not planted. Snakes and efts
Swarmed in the summer days, and nightly bats
Would fly about our bedrooms. Heathcroppers
Lived on the hills, and were our only friends;
So wild it was when first we settled here.'

A Church Romance

(Mellstock: circa 1835)

SHE turned in the high pew, until her sight
Swept the west gallery, and caught its row
Of music-men with viol, book, and bow
Against the sinking sad tower-window light.

She turned again; and in her pride's despite
One strenuous viol's inspirer seemed to throw
A message from his string to her below,
Which said: 'I claim thee as my own forthright!'

Thus their hearts' bond began, in due time signed.
And long years thence, when Age had scared romance,
At some old attitude of his or glance
That gallery-scene would break upon her mind,
With him as minstrel, ardent, young, and trim,
Bowing 'New Sabbath' or 'Mount Ephraim'.

Afternoon Service at Mellstock

(Circa 1850)

ON afternoons of drowsy calm
    We stood in the panelled pew,
Singing one-voiced a Tate-and-Brady psalm
    To the tune of 'Cambridge New'.

We watched the elms, we watched the rooks,
    The clouds upon the breeze,
Between the whiles of glancing at our books,
    And swaying like the trees.

So mindless were those outpourings! –
    Though I am not aware
That I have gained by subtle thought on things
    Since we stood psalming there.

One We Knew

(M.H. 1772–1857)

SHE told how they used to form for the country dances –
    'The Triumph', 'The New-rigged Ship' –
To the light of the guttering wax in the panelled manses,
    And in cots to the blink of a dip.

She spoke of the wild 'poussetting' and 'allemanding'
    On carpet, on oak, and on sod;
And the two long rows of ladies and gentlemen standing,
    And the figures the couples trod.

She showed us the spot where the maypole was yearly
                      planted,
    And where the bandsmen stood
While breeched and kerchiefed partners whirled, and panted
    To choose each other for good.

She told of that far-back day when they learnt astounded
    Of the death of the King of France:
Of the Terror; and then of Bonaparte's unbounded
    Ambition and arrogance.

Of how his threats woke warlike preparations
    Along the southern strand,
And how each night brought tremors and trepidations
    Lest morning should see him land.

She said she had often heard the gibbet creaking
  As it swayed in the lightning flash,
Had caught from the neighbouring town a small child's
                                    shrieking
  At the cart-tail under the lash. . . .

With cap-framed face and long gaze into the embers –
  We seated around her knees –
She would dwell on such dead themes, not as one who
                                    remembers,
  But rather as one who sees.

She seemed one left behind of a band gone distant
  So far that no tongue could hail:
Past things retold were to her as things existent,
  Things present but as a tale.

20 May 1902

The Self-Unseeing

HERE is the ancient floor,
Footworn and hollowed and thin,
Here was the former door
Where the dead feet walked in.

She sat here in her chair,
Smiling into the fire;
He who played stood there,
Bowing it higher and higher.

Childlike, I danced in a dream;
Blessings emblazoned that day;
Everything glowed with a gleam;
Yet we were looking away!

On One Who Lived and Died Where
He Was Born

WHEN a night in November
   Blew forth its bleared airs
An infant descended
   His birth-chamber stairs
   For the very first time,
   At the still, midnight chime;
All unapprehended
   His mission, his aim. –
Thus, first, one November,
An infant descended
     The stairs.

On a night in November
   Of weariful cares,
A frail aged figure
   Ascended those stairs
   For the very last time:
   All gone his life's prime,
All vanished his vigour,
   And fine, forceful frame:
Thus, last, one November
Ascended that figure
     Upstairs.

On those nights in November –
   Apart eighty years –
The babe and the bent one
   Who traversed those stairs
   From the early first time
   To the last feeble climb –
That fresh and that spent one –
   Were even the same:
Yea, who passed in November
As infant, as bent one,
     Those stairs.

Wise child of November!
　From birth to blanched hairs
Descending, ascending,
　Wealth-wantless, those stairs;
　Who saw quick in time
　As a vain pantomime
Life's tending, its ending,
　The worth of its fame.
Wise child of November,
Descending, ascending
　　Those stairs!

Love

When I Set Out for Lyonnesse

(1870)

WHEN I set out for Lyonnesse,
 A hundred miles away,
 The rime was on the spray,
And starlight lit my lonesomeness
When I set out for Lyonnesse
 A hundred miles away.

What would bechance at Lyonnesse
 While I should sojourn there
 No prophet durst declare,
Nor did the wisest wizard guess
What would bechance at Lyonnesse
 While I should sojourn there.

When I came back from Lyonnesse
 With magic in my eyes,
 All marked with mute surmise
My radiance rare and fathomless,
When I came back from Lyonnesse
 With magic in my eyes!

The Going

WHY did you give no hint that night
That quickly after the morrow's dawn,
And calmly, as if indifferent quite,

You would close your term here, up and be gone
    Where I could not follow
    With wing of swallow
To gain one glimpse of you ever anon!

    Never to bid goodbye,
    Or lip me the softest call,
Or utter a wish for a word, while I
Saw morning harden upon the wall,
    Unmoved, unknowing
    That your great going
Had place that moment, and altered all.

Why do you make me leave the house
And think for a breath it is you I see
At the end of the alley of bending boughs
Where so often at dusk you used to be;
    Till in darkening dankness
    The yawning blankness
Of the perspective sickens me!

    You were she who abode
    By those red-veined rocks far West,
You were the swan-necked one who rode
Along the beetling Beeny Crest,
    And, reining nigh me,
    Would muse and eye me,
While Life unrolled us its very best.

Why, then, latterly did we not speak,
Did we not think of those days long dead,
And ere your vanishing strive to seek
That time's renewal? We might have said,
    'In this bright spring weather
    We'll visit together
Those places that once we visited.'

    Well, well! All's past amend,
    Unchangeable. It must go.
I seem but a dead man held on end
To sink down soon. . . . O you could not know

That such swift fleeing
　　No soul foreseeing –
Not even I – would undo me so!

　　　　　　　　　　　　December 1912

The Haunter

HE does not think that I haunt here nightly:
　　How shall I let him know
That whither his fancy sets him wandering
　　I, too, alertly go? –
Hover and hover a few feet from him
　　Just as I used to do,
But cannot answer the words he lifts me –
　　Only listen thereto!

When I could answer he did not say them:
　　When I could let him know
How I would like to join in his journeys
　　Seldom he wished to go.
Now that he goes and wants me with him
　　More than he used to do,
Never he sees my faithful phantom
　　Though he speaks thereto.

Yes, I companion him to places
　　Only dreamers know,
Where the shy hares print long paces,
　　Where the night rooks go;
Into old aisles where the past is all to him,
　　Close as his shade can do,
Always lacking the power to call to him,
　　Near as I reach thereto!

What a good haunter I am, O tell him!
　　Quickly make him know
If he but sigh since my loss befell him
　　Straight to his side I go.

> Tell him a faithful one is doing
>> All that love can do
> Still that his path may be worth pursuing,
>> And to bring peace thereto.

The Voice

WOMAN much missed, how you call to me, call to me,
Saying that now you are not as you were
When you had changed from the one who was all to me,
But as at first, when our day was fair.

Can it be you that I hear? Let me view you, then,
Standing as when I drew near to the town
Where you would wait for me: yes, as I knew you then,
Even to the original air-blue gown!

Or is it only the breeze, in its listlessness
Travelling across the wet mead to me here,
You being ever dissolved to wan wistlessness,
Heard no more again far or near?

> Thus I; faltering forward,
> Leaves around me falling,
Wind oozing thin through the thorn from norward,
> And the woman calling.

December 1912

After a Journey

HERETO I come to view a voiceless ghost;
    Whither, O whither will its whim now draw me?
Up the cliff, down, till I'm lonely, lost,
    And the unseen waters' ejaculations awe me.
Where you will next be there's no knowing,
    Facing round about me everywhere,

With your nut-coloured hair,
And grey eyes, and rose-flush coming and going.

Yes: I have re-entered your olden haunts at last;
   Through the years, through the dead scenes I have tracked
                                    you;
What have you now found to say of our past –
   Scanned across the dark space wherein I have lacked you?
Summer gave us sweets, but autumn wrought division?
   Things were not lastly as firstly well
      With us twain, you tell?
But all's closed now, despite Time's derision.

I see what you are doing: you are leading me on
   To the spots we knew when we haunted here together,
The waterfall, above which the mist-bow shone
   At the then fair hour in the then fair weather,
And the cave just under, with a voice still so hollow
   That it seems to call out to me from forty years ago,
      When you were all aglow,
And not the thin ghost that I now frailly follow!

Ignorant of what there is flitting here to see,
   The waked birds preen and the seals flop lazily;
Soon you will have, Dear, to vanish from me,
   For the stars close their shutters and the dawn whitens
                         hazily.
Trust me, I mind not, though Life lours,
   The bringing me here; nay, bring me here again!
      I am just the same as when
Our days were a joy, and our paths through flowers.

Pentargan Bay

Beeny Cliff

(March 1870–March 1913)

I

O THE opal and the sapphire of that wandering western sea,
And the woman riding high above with bright hair flapping
free –
The woman whom I loved so, and who loyally loved me.

II

The pale mews plained below us, and the waves seemed far
away
In a nether sky, engrossed in saying their ceaseless babbling
say,
As we laughed light-heartedly aloft on that clear-sunned
March day.

III

A little cloud then cloaked us, and there flew an irised rain,
And the Atlantic dyed its levels with a dull misfeatured stain,
And then the sun burst out again, and purples prinked the
main.

IV

– Still in all its chasmal beauty bulks old Beeny to the sky,
And shall she and I not go there once again now March is
nigh,
And the sweet things said in that March say anew there by
and by?

V

What if still in chasmal beauty looms that wild weird
western shore,
The woman now is – elsewhere – whom the ambling pony
bore,
And nor know nor cares for Beeny, and will laugh there
nevermore.

At Castle Boterel

As I drive to the junction of lane and highway,
  And the drizzle bedrenches the waggonette,
I look behind at the fading byway,
  And see on its slope, now glistening wet,
    Distinctly yet

Myself and a girlish form benighted
  In dry March weather. We climb the road
Beside a chaise. We had just alighted
  To ease the sturdy pony's load
    When he sighed and slowed.

What we did as we climbed, and what we talked of
  Matters not much, nor to what it led, –
Something that life will not be balked of
  Without rude reason till hope is dead,
    And feeling fled.

It filled but a minute. But was there ever
  A time of such quality, since or before,
In that hill's story? To one mind never,
  Though it has been climbed, foot-swift, foot-sore,
    By thousands more.

Primaeval rocks form the road's steep border,
  And much have they faced there, first and last,
Of the transitory in Earth's long order;
  But what they record in colour and cast
    Is – that we two passed.

And to me, though Time's unflinching rigour,
  In mindless rote, has ruled from sight
The substance now, one phantom figure
  Remains on the slope, as when that night
    Saw us alight.

I look and see it there, shrinking, shrinking,
  I look back at it amid the rain

For the very last time; for my sand is sinking,
 And I shall traverse old love's domain
  Never again.

March 1913

During Wind and Rain

THEY sing their dearest songs –
He, she, all of them – yea,
Treble and tenor and bass,
 And one to play;
With the candles mooning each face. . . .
 Ah, no; the years O!
How the sick leaves reel down in throngs!

They clear the creeping moss –
Elders and juniors – aye,
Making the pathways neat
 And the garden gay;
And they build a shady seat. . . .
 Ah, no; the years, the years;
See, the white storm-birds wing across!

They are blithely breakfasting all –
Men and maidens – yea,
Under the summer tree,
 With a glimpse of the bay,
While pet fowl come to the knee. . . .
 Ah, no; the years O!
And the rotten rose is ript from the wall.

They change to a high new house,
He, she, all of them – aye,
Clocks and carpets and chairs
 On the lawn all day,
And brightest things that are theirs. . . .
 Ah, no; the years, the years;
Down their carved names the rain-drop ploughs.

To Meet, or Otherwise

WHETHER to sally and see thee, girl of my dreams,
    Or whether to stay
And see thee not! How vast the difference seems
    Of Yea from Nay
Just now. Yet this same sun will slant its beams
    At no far day
On our two mounds, and then what will the difference
    weigh!

Yet I will see thee, maiden dear, and make
    The most I can
Of what remains to us amid this brake
    Cimmerian
Through which we grope, and from whose thorns we
                                        ache
    While still we scan
Round our frail faltering progress for some path or plan.

By briefest meeting something sure is won;
    It will have been:
Nor God nor Demon can undo the done,
    Unsight the seen,
Make muted music be as unbegun,
    Though things terrene
Groan in their bondage till oblivion supervene.

So, to the one long-sweeping symphony
    From times remote
Till now, of human tenderness, shall we
    Supply one note,
Small and untraced, yet that will ever be
    Somewhere afloat
Amid the spheres, as part of sick Life's antidote.

A Broken Appointment

YOU did not come,
And marching Time drew on, and wore me numb. –
Yet less for loss of your dear presence there
Than that I thus found lacking in your make
That high compassion which can overbear
Reluctance for pure lovingkindness' sake
Grieved I, when, as the hope-hour stroked its sum,
    You did not come.

You love not me,
And love alone can lend you loyalty;
– I know and knew it. But, unto the store
Of human deeds divine in all but name,
Was it not worth a little hour or more
To add yet this: Once you, a woman, came
To soothe a time-torn man; even though it be
    You love not me?

Neutral Tones

WE stood by a pond that winter day,
And the sun was white, as though chidden of God,
And a few leaves lay on the starving sod;
    —They had fallen from an ash, and were grey.

Your eyes on me were as eyes that rove
Over tedious riddles of years ago;
And some words played between us to and fro
    On which lost the more by our love.

The smile on your mouth was the deadest thing
Alive enough to have strength to die;
And a grin of bitterness swept thereby
    Like an ominous bird a-wing. . . .

Since then, keen lessons that love deceives,
And wrings with wrong, have shaped to me

Your face, and the God-curst sun, and a tree,
        And a pond edged with greyish leaves.

1867

Beyond the Last Lamp

(Near Tooting Common)

I

WHILE rain, with eve in partnership,
Descended darkly, drip, drip, drip,
Beyond the last lone lamp I passed
        Walking slowly, whispering sadly,
        Two linked loiterers, wan, downcast:
Some heavy thought constrained each face,
And blinded them to time and place.

II

The pair seemed lovers, yet absorbed
In mental scenes no longer orbed
By love's young rays. Each countenance
        As it slowly, as it sadly
        Caught the lamplight's yellow glance,
Held in suspense a misery
At things which had been or might be.

III

When I retrod that watery way
Some hours beyond the droop of day,
Still I found pacing there the twain
        Just as slowly, just as sadly,
        Heedless of the night and rain.
One could but wonder who they were
And what wild woe detained them there.

IV

Though thirty years of blur and blot
Have slid since I beheld that spot,

And saw in curious converse there
  Moving slowly, moving sadly
  That mysterious tragic pair,
Its olden look may linger on –
All but the couple; they have gone.

V

Whither? Who knows, indeed. . . . And yet
To me, when nights are weird and wet,
Without those comrades there at tryst
  Creeping slowly, creeping sadly,
  That lone lane does not exist.
There they seem brooding on their pain,
And will, while such a lane remain.

To Lizbie Browne

I

  DEAR Lizbie Browne,
  Where are you now?
  In sun, in rain? –
  Or is your brow
  Past joy, past pain,
  Dear Lizbie Browne?

II

  Sweet Lizbie Browne,
  How you could smile,
  How you could sing! –
  How archly wile
  In glance-giving,
  Sweet Lizbie Browne!

III

  And, Lizbie Browne,
  Who else had hair
  Bay-red as yours,
  Or flesh so fair
  Bred out of doors,
  Sweet Lizbie Browne?

IV

When, Lizbie Browne,
You had just begun
To be endeared
By stealth to one,
You disappeared
My Lizbie Browne!

V

Ay, Lizbie Browne,
So swift your life,
And mine so slow,
You were a wife
Ere I could show
Love, Lizbie Browne.

VI

Still, Lizbie Browne,
You won, they said,
The best of men
When you were wed. . . .
Where went you then,
O Lizbie Browne?

VII

Dear Lizbie Browne,
I should have thought,
'Girls ripen fast,'
And coaxed and caught
You ere you passed,
Dear Lizbie Browne!

VIII

But, Lizbie Browne,
I let you slip;
Shaped not a sign;
Touched never your lip
With lip of mine,
Lost Lizbie Browne!

IX
So, Lizbie Browne,
When on a day
Men speak of me
As not, you'll say,
'And who was he?' –
Yes, Lizbie Browne!

The Ruined Maid

'O 'MELIA, my dear, this does everything crown!
Who could have supposed I should meet you in Town?
And whence such fair garments, such prosperi-ty?' –
'O didn't you know I'd been ruined?' said she.

– 'You left us in tatters, without shoes or socks,
Tired of digging potatoes, and spudding up docks;
And now you've gay bracelets and bright feathers three!' –
'Yes: that's how we dress when we're ruined,' said she.

– 'At home in the barton you said "thee" and "thou",
And "thik oon", and "theäs oon", and "t'other"; but now
Your talking quite fits 'ee for high compa-ny!' –
'Some polish is gained with one's ruin,' said she.

– 'Your hands were like paws then, your face blue and bleak
But now I'm bewitched by your delicate cheek,
And your little gloves fit as on any la-dy!' –
'We never do work when we're ruined,' said she.

– 'You used to call home-life a hag-ridden dream,
And you'd sigh, and you'd sock; but at present you seem
To know not of megrims or melancho-ly!' –
'True. One's pretty lively when ruined,' said she.

– 'I wish I had feathers, a fine sweeping gown,
And a delicate face, and could strut about Town!' –
'My dear – a raw country girl, such as you be,
Cannot quite expect that. You ain't ruined,' said she.

Westbourne Park Villas 1866

One Ralph Blossom Soliloquizes

('*It being deposed that vij women who were mayds before he knew them have been brought upon the towne [rates?] by the fornicacions of one Ralph Blossom, Mr Maior inquired why he should not contribute xiv pence weekly toward their mayntenance. But it being shewn that the sayd R.B. was dying of a purple feaver, no order was made.*'
— Budmouth Borough Minutes: 16—)

WHEN I am in hell or some such place,
A-groaning over my sorry case,
What will those seven women say to me
Who, when I coaxed them, answered 'Aye' to me?

'I did not understand your sign!'
Will be the words of Caroline;
While Jane will cry, 'If I'd had proof of you,
I should have learnt to hold aloof of you!'

'I won't reproach: it was to be!'
Will dryly murmur Cicely;
And Rosa: 'I feel no hostility,
For I must own I lent facility.'

Lizzy says: 'Sharp was my regret,
And sometimes it is now! But yet
I joy that, though it brought notoriousness,
I knew Love once and all its gloriousness!'

Says Patience: 'Why are we apart?
Small harm did you, my poor Sweet Heart!
A manchild born, now tall and beautiful,
Was worth the ache of days undutiful.'

And Anne cries: 'O the time was fair,
So wherefore should you burn down there?
There is a deed under the sun, my Love,
And that was ours. What's done is done, my Love.
These trumpets here in Heaven are dumb to me
With you away. Dear, come, O come to me!'

Faith and Doubt

The Impercipient

(At a Cathedral Service)

THAT with this bright believing band
    I have no claim to be,
That faiths by which my comrades stand
    Seem fantasies to me,
And mirage-mists their Shining Land,
    Is a strange destiny.

Why thus my soul should be consigned
    To infelicity,
Why always I must feel as blind
    To sights my brethren see,
Why joys they've found I cannot find,
    Abides a mystery.

Since heart of mine knows not that ease
    Which they know; since it be
That He who breathes All's Well to these
    Breathes no All's-Well to me,
My lack might move their sympathies
    And Christian charity!

I am like a gazer who should mark
    An inland company
Standing upfingered, with, 'Hark! hark!
    The glorious distant sea!'
And feel, 'Alas, 'tis but yon dark
    And wind-swept pine to me!'

Yet I would bear my shortcomings
    With meet tranquillity,
But for the charge that blessed things
    I'd liefer not have be.
O, doth a bird deprived of wings
    Go earth-bound wilfully!

Enough. As yet disquiet clings
    About us. Rest shall we.

The Darkling Thrush

I LEANT upon a coppice gate
    When Frost was spectre-grey,
And Winter's dregs made desolate
    The weakening eye of day.
The tangled bine-stems scored the sky
    Like strings of broken lyres,
And all mankind that haunted nigh
    Had sought their household fires.

The land's sharp features seemed to be
    The Century's corpse outleant,
His crypt the cloudy canopy,
    The wind his death-lament.
The ancient pulse of germ and birth
    Was shrunken hard and dry,
And every spirit upon earth
    Seemed fervourless as I.

At once a voice arose among
    The bleak twigs overhead
In a full-hearted evensong
    Of joy illimited;
An aged thrush, frail, gaunt, and small,
    In blast-beruffled plume,
Had chosen thus to fling his soul
    Upon the growing gloom.

So little cause for carolings
    Of such ecstatic sound
Was written on terrestrial things
    Afar or nigh around,
That I could think there trembled through
    His happy good-night air
Some blessed Hope, whereof he knew
    And I was unaware.

31 December 1900

The Oxen

CHRISTMAS Eve, and twelve of the clock.
    'Now they are all on their knees,'
An elder said as we sat in a flock
    By the embers in hearthside ease.

We pictured the meek mild creatures where
    They dwelt in their strawy pen,
Nor did it occur to one of us there
    To doubt they were kneeling then.

So fair a fancy few would weave
    In these years! Yet, I feel,
If someone said on Christmas Eve,
    'Come; see the oxen kneel

'In the lonely barton by yonder coomb
    Our childhood used to know,'
I should go with him in the gloom,
    Hoping it might be so.

1915

In the Servants' Quarters

'MAN, you too, aren't you, one of these rough followers of
          the criminal?
All hanging hereabout to gather how he's going to bear
Examination in the hall.' She flung disdainful glances on
The shabby figure standing at the fire with others there,
    Who warmed them by its flare.

'No indeed, my skipping maiden: I know nothing of the trial
          here,
Or criminal, if so he be. – I chanced to come this way,
And the fire shone out into the dawn, and morning airs are
          cold now;
I, too, was drawn in part by charms I see before me play,
    That I see not every day.

'Ha, ha!' then laughed the constables who also stood to
        warm themselves,
The while another maiden scrutinized his features hard,
As the blaze threw into contrast every line and knot that
        wrinkled them,
Exclaiming, 'Why, last night when he was brought in by the
        guard,
    You were with him in the yard!'

'Nay, nay, you teasing wench, I say! You know you speak
        mistakenly.
Cannot a tired pedestrian who has legged it long and far
Here on his way from northern parts, engrossed in humble
        marketings,
Come in and rest awhile, although judicial doings are
    Afoot by morning star?'

'O, come, come!' laughed the constables. 'Why, man, you
        speak the dialect
He uses in his answers; you can hear him up the stairs.
So own it. We sha'n't hurt ye. There he's speaking now! His
        syllables

Are those you sound yourself when you are talking
                                        unawares,
    As this pretty girl declares.'

'And you shudder when his chain clinks!' she rejoined. 'O
                                        yes, I noticed it.
And you winced, too, when those cuffs they gave him
    echoed to us here.
They'll soon be coming down, and you may then have to
    defend yourself
Unless you hold your tongue, or go away and keep you clear
    When he's led to judgment near!'

'No! I'll be damned in hell if I know anything about the
    man!
No single thing about him more than everybody knows!
Must not I even warm my hands but I am charged with
    blasphemies?' . . .
– His face convulses as the morning cock that moment
    crows,
    And he droops, and turns, and goes.

Lyrics and Meditations

Great Things

SWEET cyder is a great thing,
  A great thing to me,
Spinning down to Weymouth town
  By Ridgway thirstily,
And maid and mistress summoning
  Who tend the hostelry:
O cyder is a great thing,
  A great thing to me!

The dance it is a great thing,
  A great thing to me,
With candles lit and partners fit
  For night-long revelry;
And going home when day-dawning
  Peeps pale upon the lea:
O dancing is a great thing,
  A great thing to me!

Love is, yea, a great thing,
  A great thing to me,
When, having drawn across the lawn
  In darkness silently,
A figure flits like one a-wing
  Out from the nearest tree:
O love is, yes, a great thing,
  A great thing to me!

Will these be always great things,
    Great things to me? . . .
Let it befall that One will call,
    'Soul, I have need of thee:'
What then? Joy-jaunts, impassioned flings,
    Love, and its ecstasy,
Will always have been great things,
    Great things to me!

Going and Staying

I

THE moving sun-shapes on the spray,
The sparkles where the brook was flowing,
Pink faces, plightings, moonlit May,
These were the things we wished would stay;
    But they were going.

II

Seasons of blankness as of snow,
The silent bleed of a world decaying,
The moan of multitudes in woe,
These were the things we wished would go;
    But they were staying.

III

Then we looked closelier at Time,
And saw his ghostly arms revolving
To sweep off woeful things with prime,
Things sinister with things sublime
    Alike dissolving.

Shut Out That Moon

CLOSE up the casement, draw the blind,
    Shut out that stealing moon,
She wears too much the guise she wore

Before our lutes were strewn
    With years-deep dust, and names we read
        On a white stone were hewn.

Step not forth on the dew-dashed lawn
        To view the Lady's Chair,
Immense Orion's glittering form,
        The Less and Greater Bear:
Stay in; to such sights we were drawn
        When faded ones were fair.

Brush not the bough for midnight scents
        That come forth lingeringly,
And wake the same sweet sentiments
        They breathed to you and me
When living seemed a laugh, and love
        All it was said to be.

Within the common lamp-lit room
        Prison my eyes and thought;
Let dingy details crudely loom,
        Mechanic speech be wrought:
Too fragrant was Life's early bloom,
        Too tart the fruit it brought!

1904

The Pine Planters

(*Marty South's Reverie*)

I

WE work here together
        In blast and breeze;
He fills the earth in,
        I hold the trees.

He does not notice
        That what I do
Keeps me from moving
        And chills me through.

He has seen one fairer
    I feel by his eye,
Which skims me as though
    I were not by.

And since she passed here
    He scarce has known
But that the woodland
    Holds him alone.

I have worked here with him
    Since morning shine,
He busy with his thoughts
    And I with mine.

I have helped him so many,
    So many days,
But never win any
    Small word of praise!

Shall I not sigh to him
    That I work on
Glad to be nigh to him
    Though hope is gone?

Nay, though he never
    Knew love like mine,
I'll bear it ever
    And make no sign!

II

From the bundle at hand here
    I take each tree,
And set it to stand, here
    Always to be;
When, in a second,
    As if from fear
Of Life unreckoned
    Beginning here,
It starts a sighing
    Through day and night,

Though while there lying
    'Twas voiceless quite.

It will sigh in the morning,
    Will sigh at noon,
At the winter's warning,
    In wafts of June;
Grieving that never
    Kind Fate decreed
It should for ever
    Remain a seed,
And shun the welter
    Of things without,
Unneeding shelter
    From storm and drought.

Thus, all unknowing
    For whom or what
We set it growing
    In this bleak spot,
It still will grieve here
    Throughout its time,
Unable to leave here,
    Or change its clime;
Or tell the story
    Of us today
When, halt and hoary,
    We pass away.

On the Esplanade

(Midsummer: 10 p.m.)

THE broad bald moon edged up where the sea was wide,
    Mild, mellow-faced;
Beneath, a tumbling twinkle of shines, like dyed,
    A trackway traced
To the shore, as of petals fallen from a rose to waste,
    In its overblow,

And fluttering afloat on inward heaves of the tide: –
All this, so plain; yet the rest I did not know.

The horizon gets lost in a mist new-wrought by the night:
        The lamps of the Bay
That reach from behind me round to the left and right
        On the sea-wall way
For a constant mile of curve, make a long display
        As a pearl-strung row,
Under which in the waves they bore their gimlets of light: –
All this was plain; but there was a thing not so.

Inside a window, open, with undrawn blind,
        There plays and sings
A lady unseen a melody undefined:
        And where the moon flings
Its shimmer a vessel crosses, whereon to the strings
        Plucked sweetly and low
Of a harp, they dance. Yea, such did I mark. That, behind,
My Fate's masked face crept near me I did not know!

After a Romantic Day

        THE railway bore him through
An earthen cutting out from a city:
        There was no scope for view,
Though the frail light shed by a slim young moon
        Fell like a friendly tune.

        Fell like a liquid ditty,
And the blank lack of any charm
        Of landscape did no harm.
The bald steep cutting, rigid, rough,
        And moon-lit, was enough
For poetry of place: its weathered face
Formed a convenient sheet whereon
The visions of his mind were drawn.

The Five Students

THE sparrow dips in his wheel-rut bath,
　　The sun grows passionate-eyed,
And boils the dew to smoke by the paddock-path;
　　As strenuously we stride, –
Five of us; dark He, fair He, dark She, fair She, I,
　　All beating by.

The air is shaken, the high-road hot,
　　Shadowless swoons the day,
The greens are sobered and cattle at rest; but not
　　We on our urgent way, –
Four of us; fair She, dark She, fair He, I, are there,
　　But one – elsewhere.

Autumn moulds the hard fruit mellow,
　　And forward still we press
Through moors, briar-meshed plantations, clay-pits yellow,
　　As in the spring hours – yes,
Three of us; fair He, fair She, I, as heretofore,
　　But – fallen one more.

The leaf drops: earthworms draw it in
　　At night-time noiselessly,
The fingers of birch and beech are skeleton-thin,
　　And yet on the beat are we, –
Two of us; fair She, I. But no more left to go
　　The track we know.

Icicles tag the church-aisle leads,
　　The flag-rope gibbers hoarse,
The home-bound foot-folk wrap their snow-flaked heads,
　　Yet I still stalk the course –
One of us. . . . Dark and fair He, dark and fair She, gone:
　　The rest – anon.

Heredity

I AM the family face;
Flesh perishes, I live on,
Projecting trait and trace
Through time to times anon,
And leaping from place to place
Over oblivion.

The years-heired feature that can
In curve and voice and eye
Despise the human span
Of durance – that is I;
The eternal thing in man,
That heeds no call to die.

The Superseded

I

As newer comers crowd the fore,
    We drop behind.
– We who have laboured long and sore
    Times out of mind,
And keen are yet, must not regret
    To drop behind.

II

Yet there are some of us who grieve
    To go behind;
Staunch, strenuous souls who scarce believe
    Their fires declined,
And know none spares, remembers, cares
    Who go behind.

III

'Tis not that we have unforetold
    The drop behind;
We feel the new must oust the old
    In every kind;
But yet we think, must we, must *we*,
    Too, drop behind?

I Look Into My Glass

I LOOK into my glass,
And view my wasting skin,
And say, 'Would God it came to pass
My heart had shrunk as thin!'

For then, I, undistrest
By hearts grown cold to me,
Could lonely wait my endless rest
With equanimity.

But Time, to make me grieve,
Part steals, lets part abide;
And shakes this fragile frame at eve
With throbbings of noontide.

Afterwards

WHEN the Present has latched its postern behind my
                          tremulous stay,
  And the May month flaps its glad green leaves like wings,
Delicate-filmed as new-spun silk, will the neighbours say,
  'He was a man who used to notice such things'?

If it be in the dusk when, like an eyelid's soundless blink,
  The dewfall-hawk comes crossing the shades to alight
Upon the wind-warped upland thorn, a gazer may think,
  'To him this must have been a familiar sight.'

If I pass during some nocturnal blackness, mothy and warm,
  When the hedgehog travels furtively over the lawn,
One may say, 'He strove that such innocent creatures should
                                come to no harm,
  But he could do little for them; and now he is gone.'

If, when hearing that I have been stilled at last, they stand at
                                the door,
  Watching the full-starred heavens that winter sees,
Will this thought rise on those who will meet my face no
                                more,
  'He was one who had an eye for such mysteries'?

And will any say when my bell of quittance is heard in the
                                gloom,
  And a crossing breeze cuts a pause in its outrollings,
Till they rise again, as they were a new bell's boom,
  'He hears it not now, but used to notice such things'?

Nature: Flowers, Birds and Animals

Weathers

I

THIS is the weather the cuckoo likes,
    And so do I;
When showers betumble the chestnut spikes,
    And nestlings fly:
And the little brown nightingale bills his best,
And they sit outside at 'The Travellers' Rest',
And maids come forth sprig-muslin drest,
And citizens dream of the south and west,
    And so do I.

II

This is the weather the shepherd shuns,
    And so do I;
When beeches drip in browns and duns,
    And thresh, and ply;
And hill-hid tides throb, throe on throe,
And meadow rivulets overflow,
And drops on gate-bars hang in a row,
And rooks in families homeward go,
    And so do I.

The Yellow-Hammer

WHEN, towards the summer's close,
    Lanes are dry,
And unclipt the hedgethorn rows,
    There we fly!

While the harvest waggons pass
    With their load,
Shedding corn upon the grass
    By the road.

In a flock we follow them,
    On and on,
Seize a wheat-ear by the stem,
    And are gone. . . .

With our funny little song,
    Thus you may
Often see us flit along,
    Day by day.

Before and After Summer

I

LOOKING forward to the spring
One puts up with anything.
On this February day
Though the winds leap down the street,
Wintry scourgings seem but play,
And these later shafts of sleet
– Sharper pointed than the first –
And these later snows – the worst –
Are as a half-transparent blind
Riddled by rays from sun behind.

II

Shadows of the October pine
Reach into this room of mine:
On the pine there swings a bird;
He is shadowed with the tree.
Mutely perched he bills no word;
Blank as I am even is he.
For those happy suns are past,

Fore-discerned in winter last.
When went by their pleasure, then?
I, alas, perceived not when.

Last Week in October

THE trees are undressing, and fling in many places –
On the grey road, the roof, the window-sill –
Their radiant robes and ribbons and yellow laces;
A leaf each second so is flung at will,
Here, there, another and another, still and still.

A spider's web has caught one while downcoming,
That stays there dangling when the rest pass on;
Like a suspended criminal hangs he, mumming
In golden garb, while one yet green, high yon,
Trembles, as fearing such a fate for himself anon.

The Blinded Bird

So zestfully canst thou sing?
And all this indignity,
With God's consent, on thee!
Blinded ere yet a-wing
By the red-hot needle thou,
I stand and wonder how
So zestfully thou canst sing!

Resenting not such wrong,
Thy grievous pain forgot,
Eternal dark thy lot,
Groping thy whole life long,
After that stab of fire;
Enjailed in pitiless wire;
Resenting not such wrong!

Who hath charity? This bird.
Who suffereth long and is kind,
Is not provoked, though blind
And alive ensepulchred?
Who hopeth, endureth all things?
Who thinketh no evil, but sings?
Who is divine? This bird.

Birds at Winter Nightfall

(*Triolet*)

AROUND the house the flakes fly faster,
And all the berries now are gone
From holly and cotonea-aster
Around the house. The flakes fly! – faster
Shutting indoors that crumb-outcaster
We used to see upon the lawn
Around the house. The flakes fly faster,
And all the berries now are gone!

Max Gate

The Selfsame Song

A BIRD sings the selfsame song,
With never a fault in its flow,
That we listened to here those long
     Long years ago.

A pleasing marvel is how
A strain of such rapturous rote
Should have gone on thus till now
     Unchanged in a note!

– But it's not the selfsame bird. –
No: perished to dust is he. . . .
As also are those who heard
     That song with me.

The Robin

WHEN up aloft
I fly and fly,
I see in pools
The shining sky,
And a happy bird
Am I, am I!

When I descend
Towards their brink
I stand, and look,
And stoop, and drink,
And bathe my wings,
And chink and prink.

When winter frost
Makes earth as steel
I search and search
But find no meal,
And most unhappy
Then I feel.

But when it lasts,
And snows still fall,
I get to feel
No grief at all,
For I turn to a cold stiff
Feathery ball!

The Last Chrysanthemum

WHY should this flower delay so long
    To show its tremulous plumes?
Now is the time of plaintive robin-song,
    When flowers are in their tombs.

Through the slow summer, when the sun
    Called to each frond and whorl

That all he could for flowers was being done,
    Why did it not uncurl?

It must have felt that fervid call
    Although it took no heed,
Waking but now, when leaves like corpses fall,
    And saps all retrocede.

Too late its beauty, lonely thing,
    The season's shine is spent,
Nothing remains for it but shivering
    In tempests turbulent.

Had it a reason for delay,
    Dreaming in witlessness
That for a bloom so delicately gay
    Winter would stay its stress?

– I talk as if the thing were born
    With sense to work its mind;
Yet it is but one mask of many worn
    By the Great Face behind.

To Flowers from Italy in Winter

SUNNED in the South, and here today;
    – If all organic things
Be sentient, Flowers, as some men say,
    What are your ponderings?

How can you stay, nor vanish quite
    From this bleak spot of thorn,
And birch, and fir, and frozen white
    Expanse of the forlorn?

Frail luckless exiles hither brought!
    Your dust will not regain
Old sunny haunts of Classic thought
    When you shall waste and wane;

But mix with alien earth, be lit
With frigid Boreal flame,
And not a sign remain in it
To tell man whence you came.

A Sheep Fair

THE day arrives of the autumn fair,
And torrents fall,
Though sheep in throngs are gathered there,
Ten thousand all,
Sodden, with hurdles round them reared:
And, lot by lot, the pens are cleared,
And the auctioneer wrings out his beard,
And wipes his book, bedrenched and smeared,
And rakes the rain from his face with the edge of his hand,
As torrents fall.

The wool of the ewes is like a sponge
With the daylong rain:
Jammed tight, to turn, or lie, or lunge,
They strive in vain.
Their horns are soft as finger-nails,
Their shepherds reek against the rails,
The tied dogs soak with tucked-in tails,
The buyers' hat-brims fill like pails,
Which spill small cascades when they shift their stand
In the daylong rain.

POSTSCRIPT

Time has trailed lengthily since met
At Pummery Fair
Those panting thousands in their wet
And woolly wear:
And every flock long since has bled,
And all the dripping buyers have sped,
And the hoarse auctioneer is dead,

Who 'Going-going!' so often said,
As he consigned to doom each meek, mewed band
At Pummery Fair.

Last Words to a Dumb Friend

PET was never mourned as you,
Purrer of the spotless hue,
Plumy tail, and wistful gaze
While you humoured our queer ways,
Or outshrilled your morning call
Up the stairs and through the hall –
Foot suspended in its fall –
While, expectant, you would stand
Arched, to meet the stroking hand;
Till your way you chose to wend
Yonder, to your tragic end.

Never another pet for me!
Let your place all vacant be;
Better blankness day by day
Than companion torn away.
Better bid his memory fade,
Better blot each mark he made,
Selfishly escape distress
By contrived forgetfulness,
Than preserve his prints to make
Every morn and eve an ache.

From the chair whereon he sat
Sweep his fur, nor wince thereat;
Rake his little pathways out
Mid the bushes roundabout;
Smooth away his talons' mark
From the claw-worn pine-tree bark,
Where he climbed as dusk embrowned,
Waiting us who loitered round.

Strange it is this speechless thing,
Subject to our mastering,
Subject for his life and food
To our gift, and time, and mood;
Timid pensioner of us Powers,
His existence ruled by ours,
Should – by crossing at a breath
Into safe and shielded death,
By the merely taking hence
Of his insignificance –
Loom as largened to the sense,
Shape as part, above man's will,
Of the Imperturbable.

As a prisoner, flight debarred,
Exercising in a yard,
Still retain I, troubled, shaken,
Mean estate, by him forsaken;
And this home, which scarcely took
Impress from his little look,
By his faring to the Dim
Grows all eloquent of him.

Housemate, I can think you still
Bounding to the window-sill,
Over which I vaguely see
Your small mound beneath the tree,
Showing in the autumn shade
That you moulder where you played.

2 October 1904

Shortening Days at the Homestead

THE first fire since the summer is lit, and is smoking into the
room:
The sun-rays thread it through, like woof-lines in a loom.
Sparrows spurt from the hedge, whom misgivings appal
That winter did not leave last year for ever, after all.

Like shock-headed urchins, spiny-haired,
Stand pollard willows, their twigs just bared.

Who is this coming with pondering pace,
Black and ruddy, with white embossed,
His eyes being black, and ruddy his face,
And the marge of his hair like morning frost?
    It's the cider-maker,
     And appletree-shaker,
And behind him on wheels, in readiness,
His mill, and tubs, and vat, and press.

Snow in the Suburbs

EVERY branch big with it,
  Bent every twig with it;
Every fork like a white web-foot;
Every street and pavement mute:
Some flakes have lost their way, and grope back upward, when
Meeting those meandering down they turn and descend again.
  The palings are glued together like a wall,
  And there is no waft of wind with the fleecy fall.

  A sparrow enters the tree,
  Whereon immediately
A snow-lump thrice his own slight size
Descends on him and showers his head and eyes,
    And overturns him,
    And near inurns him,
And lights on a nether twig, when its brush
Starts off a volley of other lodging lumps with a rush.

  The steps are a blanched slope,
  Up which, with feeble hope,
A black cat comes, wide-eyed and thin;
    And we take him in.

War

The Eve of Waterloo
(Chorus of Phantoms)

THE eyelids of eve fall together at last,
And the forms so foreign to field and tree
Lie down as though native, and slumber fast!

Sore are the thrills of misgiving we see
In the artless champaign at this harlequinade,
Distracting a vigil where calm should be!

The green seems opprest, and the Plain afraid
Of a Something to come, whereof these are the
                                        proofs, –
Neither earthquake, nor storm, nor eclipse's shade!

Yea, the coneys are scared by the thud of hoofs,
And their white scuts flash at their vanishing heels,
And swallows abandon the hamlet-roofs.

The mole's tunnelled chambers are crushed by wheels,
The lark's eggs scattered, their owners fled;
And the hedgehog's household the sapper unseals.

The snails draws in at the terrible tread,
But in vain; he is crushed by the felloe-rim;
The worm asks what can be overhead,

And wriggles deep from a scene so grim,
And guesses him safe; for he does not know
What a foul red flood will be soaking him!

Beaten about by the heel and toe
Are butterflies, sick of the day's long rheum
To die of a worse than the weather-foe.

Trodden and bruised to a miry tomb
Are ears that have greened but will never be gold,
And flowers in the bud that will never bloom.

So the season's intent, ere its fruit unfold,
Is frustrate, and mangled, and made succumb,
Like a youth of promise struck stark and cold! . . .

And what of these who to-night have come?
The young sleep sound; but the weather awakes
In the veterans, pains from the past that numb;

Old stabs of Ind, old Peninsular aches,
Old Friedland chills, haunt their moist mud bed,
Cramps from Austerlitz; till their slumber breaks.

And each soul shivers as sinks his head
On the loam he's to lease with the other dead
From tomorrow's mist-fall till Time be sped!

From 'The Dynasts'

Drummer Hodge

I

THEY throw in Drummer Hodge, to rest
    Uncoffined – just as found:
His landmark is a kopje-crest
    That breaks the veldt around;
And foreign constellations west
    Each night above his mound.

II

Young Hodge the Drummer never knew –
    Fresh from his Wessex home –
The meaning of the broad Karoo,
    The Bush, the dusty loam,

And why uprose to nightly view
    Strange stars amid the gloom.

III

Yet portion of that unknown plain
    Will Hodge for ever be;
His homely Northern breast and brain
    Grow to some Southern tree,
And strange-eyed constellations reign
    His stars eternally.

The Man He Killed

'HAD he and I but met
    By some old ancient inn,
We should have sat us down to wet
    Right many a nipperkin!

'But ranged as infantry,
    And staring face to face,
I shot at him as he at me,
    And killed him in his place.

'I shot him dead because –
    Because he was my foe,
Just so: my foe of course he was;
    That's clear enough; although

'He thought he'd 'list, perhaps,
    Off-hand like – just as I –
Was out of work – had sold his traps –
    No other reason why.

'Yes; quaint and curious war is!
    You shoot a fellow down
You'd treat if met where any bar is,
    Or help to half-a-crown.'

1902

Channel Firing

THAT night your great guns, unawares,
Shook all our coffins as we lay,
And broke the chancel window-squares,
We thought it was the Judgment-day

And sat upright. While drearisome
Arose the howl of wakened hounds:
The mouse let fall the altar-crumb,
The worms drew back into the mounds,

The glebe cow drooled. Till God called, 'No;
It's gunnery practice out at sea
Just as before you went below;
Th· world is as it used to be:

'All nations striving strong to make
Red war yet redder. Mad as hatters
They do no more for Christés sake
Than you who are helpless in such matters.

'That this is not the judgment-hour
For some of them's a blessed thing,
For if it were they'd have to scour
Hell's floor for so much threatening . . .

'Ha, ha. It will be warmer when
I blow the trumpet (if indeed
I ever do; for you are men,
And rest eternal sorely need).'

So down we lay again. 'I wonder,
Will the world ever saner be,'
Said one, 'than when He sent us under
In our indifferent century!'

And many a skeleton shook his head.
'Instead of preaching forty year,'
My neighbour Parson Thirdly said,
'I wish I had stuck to pipes and beer.'

Again the guns disturbed the hour,
Roaring their readiness to avenge,
As far inland as Stourton Tower,
And Camelot, and starlit Stonehenge.

April 191.·

A Jingle on the Times

1

'I AM a painter
   Of Earth's pied hue;
What can my pencil
   Do for you?'
'– You can do nothing,
   Nothing, nothing.
Nations want nothing
   That you can do.'

2

'I am a sculptor,
   A worker who
Preserves dear features
   The tombs enmew.' –
'– Sculpture, sculpture!
   More than sculpture
For dear remembrance
   Have we to do.'

3

'I am a poet,
   And set in view
Life and its secrets
   Old and new.' –
'– Poets we read not,
   Heed not, feed not,
Men now need not
   What they do.'

4

'I'm a musician,
    And balm I strew
On the passions people
    Are prone unto.' –
'– Music? Passions
    Calmed by music?
Nothing but passions
    Today will do!'

5

'I am an actor;
    The world's strange crew
In long procession
    My masques review.'
    '– O it's not acting,
    Acting, acting
And glassing nature
    That's now to do!'

6

'I am an architect;
    Once I drew
Glorious buildings,
    And built them too.' –
'– That was in peace-time,
    Peace-time, peace-time,
Nought but demolishing
    Now will do.'

7

'I am a preacher:
    I would ensue
Whatsoever things are
    Lovely, true.' –
'– Preachers are wordy,
    Wordy, wordy;
Prodding's the preaching
    We've now to do.'

8

'How shall we ply, then,
   Our old mysteries?' –
'– Silly ones! Must we
   Show to you
What is the only
   Good, artistic,
Cultured, Christian
   Thing to do?

9

'To manners, amenities,
   Bid we adieu, –
To the old lumber
   Of Right and True!
Fighting, smiting,
   Running through;
That's now the civilized
   Thing to do.'

December 1914

Narrative

The Bride-Night Fire

(A Wessex Tradition)

THEY had long met o' Zundays – her true love and she –
   And at junketings, maypoles, and flings;
But she bode wi' a thirtover[1] uncle, and he
Swore by noon and by night that her goodman should be
Naibour Sweatley – a wight often weak at the knee
From taking o' sommat more cheerful than tea –
   Who tranted,[2] and moved people's things.

She cried, 'O pray pity me!' Nought would he hear;
   Then with wild rainy eyes she obeyed.
She chid when her Love was for clinking off wi' her:
The pa'son was told, as the season drew near,
To throw over pu'pit the names of the pair
   As fitting one flesh to be made.

The wedding-day dawned and the morning drew on;
   The couple stood bridegroom and bride;
The evening was passed, and when midnight had gone
The feasters horned,[3] 'God save the King,' and anon
   The pair took their homealong[4] ride.

[1]*thirtover*, cross   [2]*tranted*, traded as carrier
[3]*horned*, sang loudly   [4]*homealong*, homeward

The lover Tim Tankens mourned heart-sick and leer[1]
   To be thus of his darling deprived:
He roamed in the dark ath'art field, mound, and mere,
And, a'most without knowing it, found himself near
The house of the tranter, and now of his Dear,
   Where the lantern-light showed 'em arrived.

The bride sought her chamber so calm and so pale
   That a Northern had thought her resigned;
But to eyes that had seen her in tidetimes[2] of weal,
Like the white cloud o' smoke, the red battlefield's vail,
   That look spak' of havoc behind.

The bridegroom yet laitered a beaker to drain,
   Then reeled to the linhay[3] for more,
When the candle-snoff kindled some chaff from his grain –
Flames spread, and red vlankers[4] wi' might and wi' main
   Around beams, thatch, and chimley-tun[5] roar.

Young Tim away yond, rafted[6] up by the light,
   Through brimbles and underwood tears,
Till he comes to the orchet, when crooping[7] from sight
In the lewth[8] of a codlin-tree, bivering[9] wi' fright,
Wi' on'y her night-rail to cover her plight,
   His lonesome young Barbree appears.

Her cwold little figure half-naked he views
   Played about by the frolicsome breeze,
Her light-tripping totties,[10] her ten little tooes,
All bare and besprinkled wi' Fall's[11] chilly dews,
While her great gallied[12] eyes through her hair hanging loose
   Shone as stars through a tardle[13] o' trees.

---

[1]*leer*, empty-stomached   [2]*tidetimes*, holidays
[3]*linhay*, lean-to building   [4]*vlankers*, fire-flakes
[5]*chimley-tun*, chimney-stack   [6]*rafted*, roused
[7]*crooping*, squatting down   [8]*lewth*, shelter
[9]*bivering*, with chattering teeth   [10]*totties*, feet
[11]*Fall*, autumn   [12]*gallied*, frightened
[13]*tardle*, entanglement

She eyed him; and, as when a weir-hatch is drawn,
  Her tears, penned by terror afore,
With a rushing of sobs in a shower were strawn,
Till her power to pour 'em seemed wasted and gone
  From the heft[1] o' misfortune she bore.

'O Tim, my *own* Tim I must call 'ee – I will!
  All the world has turned round on me so!
Can you help her who loved 'ee, though acting so ill?
Can you pity her misery – feel for her still?
When worse than her body so quivering and chill
  Is her heart in its winter o' woe!

'I think I mid[2] almost ha' borne it,' she said,
  'Had my griefs one by one come to hand;
But O, to be slave to thik husbird,[3] for bread,
And then, upon top o' that, driven to wed,
And then, upon top o' that, burnt out o' bed,
  Is more than my nater can stand!'

Like a lion 'ithin en Tim's spirit outsprung –
(Tim had a great soul when his feelings were wrung) –
  'Feel for 'ee, dear Barbree?' he cried;
And his warm working-jacket then straightway he flung
Round about her, and horsed her by jerks, till she clung
Like a chiel on a gipsy, her figure uphung
  By the sleeves that he tightly had tied.

Over piggeries, and mixens,[4] and apples, and hay,
  They lumpered[5] straight into the night;
And finding ere long where a halter-path[6] lay,
Sighted Tim's house by dawn, on'y seen on their way
By a naibour or two who were up wi' the day,
  But who gathered no clue to the sight.

---

[1]*heft*, weight   [2]*mid*, might
[3]*thik husbird*, that rascal   [4]*mixens*, manure-heaps
[5]*lumpered*, stumbled   [6]*halter-path*, bridle-path

Then tender Tim Tankens he searched here and there
   For some garment to clothe her fair skin;
But though he had breeches and waistcoats to spare,
He had nothing quite seemly for Barbree to wear,
Who, half shrammed[1] to death, stood and cried on a chair
   At the caddle[2] she found herself in.

There was one thing to do, and that one thing he did,
   He lent her some clothes of his own,
And she took 'em perforce; and while swiftly she slid
Them upon her Tim turned to the winder, as bid,
Thinking, 'O that the picter my duty keeps hid
   To the sight o' my eyes mid[3] be shown!'

In the tallet[4] he stowed her; there huddied[5] she lay,
   Shortening sleeves, legs, and tails to her limbs;
But most o' the time in a mortal bad way,
Well knowing that there'd be the divel to pay
If 'twere found that, instead o' the elements' prey,
   She was living in lodgings at Tim's.

'Where's the tranter?' said men and boys; 'where can he be?'
   'Where's the tranter?' said Barbree alone.
'Where on e'th is the tranter?' said everybod-y:
They sifted the dust of his perished roof-tree,
   And all they could find was a bone.

Then the uncle cried, 'Lord, pray have mercy on me!'
   And in terror began to repent.
But before 'twas complete, and till sure she was free,
Barbree drew up her loft-ladder, tight turned her key –
Tim bringing up breakfast and dinner and tea –
   Till the news of her hiding got vent.

Then followed the custom-kept rout, shout, and flare
Of a skimmity-ride[6] through the naibourhood, ere
   Folk had proof o' wold[7] Sweatley's decay.

---

[1]*shrammed*, numbed   [2]*caddle*, quandary   [3]*mid*, might   [4]*tallet*, loft
[5]*huddied*, hidden   [6]*skimmity-ride*, satirical procession with effigies   [7]*wold*, old

Whereupon decent people all stood in a stare,
Saying Tim and his lodger should risk it, and pair:
So he took her to church. An' some laughing lads there
Cried to Tim, 'After Sweatley!' She said, 'I declare
    I stand as a maiden to-day!'

Written 1866; printed 1875

A Trampwoman's Tragedy

(182–)

I

FROM Wynyard's Gap the livelong day,
    The livelong day,
We beat afoot the northward way
    We had travelled times before.
The sun-blaze burning on our backs,
Our shoulders sticking to our packs,
By fosseway, fields, and turnpike tracks
    We skirted sad Sedge-Moor.

II

Full twenty miles we jaunted on,
        We jaunted on, –
My fancy-man, and jeering John,
        And Mother Lee, and I.
And, as the sun drew down to west,
We climbed the toilsome Poldon crest,
And saw, of landskip sights the best,
        The inn that beamed thereby.

III

For months we had padded side by side,
        Ay, side by side
Through the Great Forest, Blackmoor wide,
        And where the Parret ran.
We'd faced the gusts on Mendip ridge,

Had crossed the Yeo unhelped by bridge,
Been stung by every Marshwood midge,
    I and my fancy-man.

IV

Lone inns we loved, my man and I,
    My man and I;
'King's Stag', 'Windwhistle' high and dry,
    'The Horse' on Hintock Green,
The cosy house at Wynyard's Gap,
'The Hut' renowned on Bredy Knap,
And many another wayside tap
    Where folk might sit unseen.

V

Now as we trudged – O deadly day,
    O deadly day! –
I teased my fancy-man in play
    And wanton idleness.
I walked alongside jeering John,
I laid his hand my waist upon;
I would not bend my glances on
    My lover's dark distress.

VI

Thus Poldon top at last we won,
    At last we won,
And gained the inn at sink of sun
    Far-famed as 'Marshal's Elm'.
Beneath us figured tor and lea,
From Mendip to the western sea –
I doubt if finer sight there be
    Within this royal realm.

VII

Inside the settle all a-row –
    All four a-row
We sat, I next to John, to show
    That he had wooed and won.
And then he took me on his knee,
And swore it was his turn to be

My favoured mate, and Mother Lee
    Passed to my former one.

VIII

Then in a voice I had never heard,
    I had never heard,
My only Love to me: 'One word,
    My lady, if you please!
Whose is the child you are like to bear? –
His? After all my months o' care?'
God knows 'twas not! But, O despair!
    I nodded – still to tease.

IX

Then up he sprung, and with his knife –
    And with his knife
He let out jeering Johnny's life,
    Yes; there, at set of sun.
The slant ray through the window nigh
Gilded John's blood and glazing eye,
Ere scarcely Mother Lee and I
    Knew that the deed was done.

X

The taverns tell the gloomy tale,
    The gloomy tale,
How that at Ivel-chester jail
    My Love, my sweetheart swung;
Though stained till now by no misdeed
Save one horse ta'en in time o' need;
(Blue Jimmy stole right many a steed
    Ere his last fling he flung.)

XI

Thereaft I walked the world alone,
    Alone, alone!
On his death-day I gave my groan
    And dropt his dead-born child.
'Twas nigh the jail, beneath a tree,
None tending me; for Mother Lee

Had died at Glaston, leaving me
    Unfriended on the wild.

XII

And in the night as I lay weak,
    As I lay weak,
The leaves a-falling on my cheek,
    The red moon low declined —
The ghost of him I'd die to kiss
Rose up and said: 'Ah, tell me this!
Was the child mine, or was it his?
    Speak, that I rest may find!'

XIII

O doubt not but I told him then,
    I told him then,
That I had kept me from all men
    Since we joined lips and swore.
Whereat he smiled, and thinned away
As the wind stirred to call up day . . .
— 'Tis past! And here alone I stray
    Haunting the Western Moor.

NOTES. – 'Windwhistle' (Stanza IV). The highness and dryness of Windwhistle Inn was impressed upon the writer two or three years ago, when, after climbing on a hot afternoon to the beautiful spot near which it stands and entering the inn for tea, he was informed by the landlady that none could be had, unless he would fetch water from a valley half a mile off, the house containing not a drop, owing to its situation. However, a tantalizing row of full barrels behind her back testified to a wetness of a certain sort, which was not at that time desired.

'Marshal's Elm' (Stanza VI), so picturesquely situated, is no longer an inn, though the house, or part of it, still remains. It used to exhibit a fine old swinging sign.

'Blue Jimmy' (Stanza X) was a notorious horse-stealer of Wessex in those days, who appropriated more than a hundred horses before he was caught, among others one belonging to a neighbour of the writer's grandfather. He was hanged at the now demolished Ivel-chester or Ilchester jail above mentioned – that building formerly of so many sinister associations in the minds of the local peasantry, and the continual haunt of fever, which at last led to its condemnation.

Its site is now an innocent-looking green meadow.

April 1902

The Sacrilege

A Ballad-Tragedy

(*Circa 182–*)

PART I

'I HAVE a Love I love too well
Where Dunkery frowns on Exon Moor;
I have a Love I love too well,
  To whom, ere she was mine,
"Such is my love for you," I said,
"That you shall have to hood your head
A silken kerchief crimson-red,
  Wove finest of the fine."

'And since this Love, for one mad moon,
On Exon Wild by Dunkery Tor,
Since this my Love for one mad moon
  Did clasp me as her king,
I snatched a silk-piece red and rare
From off a stall at Priddy Fair,
For handkerchief to hood her hair
  When we went gallanting.

'Full soon the four weeks neared their end
Where Dunkery frowns on Exon Moor;
And when the four weeks neared their end,
  And their swift sweets outwore,
I said, "What shall I do to own
Those beauties bright as tulips blown,
And keep you here with me alone
  As mine for evermore?"

'And as she drowsed within my van
On Exon Wild by Dunkery Tor –
And as she drowsed within my van,
  And dawning turned to day,
She heavily raised her sloe-black eyes

And murmured back in softest wise,
"One more thing, and the charms you prize
    Are yours henceforth for aye.

' "And swear I will I'll never go
While Dunkery frowns on Exon Moor
To meet the Cornish Wrestler Joe
    For dance and dallyings,
If you'll to yon cathedral shrine,
And finger from the chest divine
Treasure to buy me ear-drops fine,
    And richly jewelled rings."

'I said: "I am one who has gathered gear
From Marlbury Downs to Dunkery Tor,
Who has gathered gear for many a year
    From mansion, mart and fair;
But at God's house I've stayed my hand,
Hearing within me some command –
Curbed by a law not of the land
    From doing damage there!"

'Whereat she pouts, this Love of mine,
As Dunkery pouts to Exon Moor,
And still she pouts, this Love of mine,
    So cityward I go.
But ere I start to do the thing,
And speed my soul's imperilling
For one who is my ravishing
    And all the joy I know,

'I come to lay this charge on thee –
On Exon Wild by Dunkery Tor –
I come to lay this charge on thee
    With solemn speech and sign:
Should thing go ill, and my life pay
For botchery in this rash assay,
You are to take hers likewise – yea,
    The month the law takes mine.

'For should my rival, Wrestler Joe,
Where Dunkery frowns on Exon Moor—
My reckless rival, Wrestler Joe,
          My Love's bedwinner be,
My rafted spirit would not rest,
But wander weary and distrest
Throughout the world in wild protest:
          The thought nigh maddens me!'

PART II

Thus did he speak – this brother of mine –
On Exon Wild by Dunkery Tor,
Born at my birth of mother of mine,
          And forthwith went his way
To dare the deed some coming night. . . .
I kept the watch with shaking sight,
The moon at moments breaking bright,
          At others glooming grey.

For three full days I heard no sound
Where Dunkery frowns on Exon Moor,
I heard no sound at all around
          Whether his fay prevailed,
Or one more foul the master were,
Till some afoot did tidings bear
   How that, for all his practised care,
          He had been caught and jailed.

They had heard a crash when twelve had chimed
By Mendip east of Dunkery Tor,
When twelve had chimed and moonlight climbed;
          They watched, and he was tracked
By arch and aisle and saint and knight
Of sculptured stonework sheeted white
In the cathedral's ghostly light,
          And captured in the act.

Yes; for this Love he loved too well
Where Dunkery sights the Severn shore,
All for this Love he loved too well
      He burst the holy bars,
Seized golden vessels from the chest
To buy her ornaments of the best,
At her ill-witchery's request
      And lure of eyes like stars. . . .

When blustering March confused the sky
In Toneborough Town by Exon Moor,
When blustering March confused the sky
      They stretched him; and he died.
Down in the crowd where I, to see
The end of him, stood silently,
With a set face he lipped to me –
      'Remember.' 'Ay!' I cried.

By night and day I shadowed her
From Toneborough Deane to Dunkery Tor,
I shadowed her asleep, astir,
      And yet I could not bear –
Till Wrestler Joe anon began
To figure as her chosen man,
And took her to his shining van –
      To doom a form so fair!

He made it handsome for her sake –
And Dunkery smiled to Exon Moor –
He made it handsome for her sake,
      Painting it out and in;
And on the door of apple-green
A bright brass knocker soon was seen,
And window-curtains white and clean
      For her to sit within.

And all could see she clave to him
As cleaves a cloud to Dunkery Tor,
Yea, all could see she clave to him,
        And every day I said,
'A pity it seems to part those two
That hourly grow to love more true:
Yet she's the wanton woman who
        Sent one to swing till dead!'

That blew to blazing all my hate,
While Dunkery frowned on Exon Moor,
And when the river swelled, her fate
        Came to her pitilessly. . . .
I dogged her, crying: 'Across that plank
They use as bridge to reach yon bank
A coat and hat lie limp and dank;
        Your goodman's, can they be?'

She paled, and went, I close behind –
And Exon frowned to Dunkery Tor,
She went, and I came up behind
        And tipped the plank that bore
Her, fleetly flitting across to eye
What such might abode. She slid awry;
And from the current came a cry,
        A gurgle; and no more.

How that befell no mortal knew
From Marlbury Downs to Exon Moor;
No mortal knew that deed undue
        But he who schemed the crime,
Which night still covers. . . . But in dream
Those ropes of hair upon the stream
He sees, and he will hear that scream
        Until his judgment-time.

Occasional Poems

The Last Signal

(11 Oct. 1886)

A Memory of William Barnes

SILENTLY I footed by an uphill road
That led from my abode to a spot yew-boughed;
Yellowly the sun sloped low down to westward,
    And dark was the east with cloud.

Then, amid the shadow of that livid sad east,
    Where the light was least, and a gate stood wide,
Something flashed the fire of the sun that was facing it,
    Like a brief blaze on that side.

Looking hard and harder I knew what it meant –
    The sudden shine sent from the livid east scene;
It meant the west mirrored by the coffin of my friend there,
    Turning to the road from his green,

To take his last journey forth – he who in his prime
    Trudged so many a time from that gate athwart the
                          land!
Thus a farewell to me he signalled on his grave-way,
    As with a wave of his hand.

Winterborne-Came Path

The Convergence of the Twain

(Lines on the loss of the 'Titanic')

I

In a solitude of the sea
Deep from human vanity,
And the Pride of Life that planned her, stilly couches she.

II

Steel chambers, late the pyres
Of her salamandrine fires,
Cold currents thrid, and turn to rhythmic tidal lyres.

III

Over the mirrors meant
To glass the opulent
The sea-worm crawls – grotesque, slimed, dumb, indifferent.

IV

Jewels in joy designed
To ravish the sensuous mind
Lie lightless, all their sparkles bleared and black and blind.

V

Dim moon-eyed fishes near
Gaze at the gilded gear
And query: 'What does this vaingloriousness down here?' . . .

VI

Well: while was fashioning
This creature of cleaving wing,
The Immanent Will that stirs and urges everything

VII

Prepared a sinister mate
For her – so gaily great –
A Shape of Ice, for the time far and dissociate.

VIII

And as the smart ship grew
In stature, grace, and hue,
In shadowy silent distance grew the Iceberg too.

IX

Alien they seemed to be:
No mortal eye could see
The intimate welding of their later history,

X

Or sign that they were bent
By paths coincident
On being anon twin halves of one august event,

XI

Till the Spinner of the Years
Said 'Now!' And each one hears,
And consummation comes, and jars two hemispheres.

To Shakespeare

After Three Hundred Years

BRIGHT baffling Soul, least capturable of themes,
Thou, who display'dst a life of commonplace,
Leaving no intimate word or personal trace
Of high design outside the artistry
    Of thy penned dreams,
Still shalt remain at heart unread eternally.

Through human orbits thy discourse to-day,
Despite thy formal pilgrimage, throbs on
In harmonies that cow Oblivion,
And, like the wind, with all-uncared effect
    Maintain a sway
Not fore-desired, in tracks unchosen and unchecked.

And yet, at thy last breath, with mindless note
The borough clocks but samely tongued the hour,

The Avon just as always glassed the tower,
Thy age was published on thy passing-bell
        But in due rote
With other dwellers' deaths accorded a like knell.

And at the strokes some townsman (met, maybe,
And thereon queried by some squire's good dame
Driving in shopward) may have given thy name,
With, 'Yes, a worthy man and well-to-do;
        Though, as for me,
I knew him but by just a neighbour's nod, 'tis true.

'I' faith, few knew him much here, save by word,
He having elsewhere led his busier life;
Though to be sure he left with us his wife.'
– 'Ah, one of the tradesmen's sons, I now recall. . . .
        Witty, I've heard. . . .
We did not know him. . . . Well, good-day. Death comes
                                    to all.'

So, like a strange bright bird we sometimes find
To mingle with the barn-door brood awhile,
Then vanish from their homely domicile –
Into man's poesy, we wot not whence,
        Flew thy strange mind,
Lodged there a radiant guest, and sped for ever thence.

1916

At Lulworth Cove a Century Back

HAD I but lived a hundred years ago
I might have gone, as I have gone this year,
By Warmwell Cross on to a Cove I know,
And Time have placed his finger on me there:

'*You see that man?*' – I might have looked, and said,
'O yes: I see him. One that boat has brought
Which dropped down Channel round Saint Alban's Head.
So commonplace a youth calls not my thought.'

'*You see that man?*' – 'Why yes; I told you; yes:
Of an idling town-sort; thin; hair brown in hue;
And as the evening light scants less and less
He looks up at a star, as many do.'

'*You see that man?*' – 'Nay, leave me!' then I plead,
'I have fifteen miles to vamp across the lea,
And it grows dark, and I am weary-kneed:
I have said the third time; yes, that man I see!'

'Good. That man goes to Rome – to death, despair;
And no one notes him now but you and I:
A hundred years, and the world will follow him there,
And bend with reverence where his ashes lie.'

September 1920

NOTE. – In September 1820 Keats, on his way to Rome, landed one day on the
Dorset coast, and composed the sonnet, 'Bright Star! would I were steadfast as
thou art.' The spot of his landing is judged to have been Lulworth Cove.

SHORT STORY COLLECTIONS
IN EVERYMAN

A SELECTION

The Secret Self
Short Stories by Women
'A superb collection' *Guardian* **£4.99**

Selected Short Stories
and Poems
THOMAS HARDY
The best of Hardy's Wessex in a
unique selection **£4.99**

The Best of
Sherlock Holmes
ARTHUR CONAN DOYLE
All the favourite adventures in one
volume **£4.99**

Great Tales of Detection
Nineteen Stories
Chosen by Dorothy L. Sayers **£3.99**

Short Stories
KATHERINE MANSFIELD
A selection displaying the
remarkable range of Mansfield's
writing **£3.99**

Selected Stories
RUDYARD KIPLING
Includes stories chosen to reveal the
'other' Kipling **£4.50**

The Strange Case of
Dr Jekyll and Mr Hyde
and Other Stories
R. L. STEVENSON
An exciting selection of gripping
tales from a master of suspense **£3.99**

Modern Short Stories 2:
1940-1980
Thirty-one stories from the greatest
modern writers **£3.50**

The Day of Silence and
Other Stories
GEORGE GISSING
Gissing's finest stories, available for
the first time in one volume **£4.99**

Selected Tales
HENRY JAMES
Stories portraying the tensions
between private life and the outside
world **£5.99**

£4.99

£6.99

AVAILABILITY
All books are available from your local bookshop or direct from
**Littlehampton Book Services Cash Sales, 14 Eldon Way, LinesideEstate,
Littlehampton, West Sussex BN17 7HE.** PRICES ARE SUBJECT TO CHANGE.

To order any of the books, please enclose a cheque (in £ sterling) made payable to
Littlehampton Book Services, or phone your order through with credit card details (Access,
Visa or Mastercard) on 0903 721596 (24 hour answering service) stating card number and
expiry date. Please add £1.25 for package and postage to the total value of your order.